THE BODY

IN THE

CHURCHYARD

The Twelfth Hawkridge Book

The characters in this book are fictitious.
Any resemblance to any person, living or dead, is coincidental.

Copyright R.J.Daniel 2006

This book is sold subject to the condition that it shall not, by way of trade or otherwise, be lent, resold, hired out or otherwise circulated or used without the author's prior consent.

British Library Cataloguing In Publication Data
A Record of this Publication is available from the British Library

ISBN 1846853222
978-1-84685-322-7

First Published 2006 by
Exposure Publishing, an imprint of Diggory Press,
Three Rivers, Minions, Liskeard, Cornwall, PL14 5LE, UK
WWW.DIGGORYPRESS.COM

BY THE SAME AUTHOR

The End of an Era

In the Hawkridge Series

Murder in the Park
Murder in Providence
It couldn't happen in Dorset
The Qatar Affair
Diamonds in Dorset
Bedsits in Bath
Problems at Portland
Nuclear. No! How?
Submarines and Swindlers
Requiem for a Sapper

SUFFOLK COUNTY LIBRARIES & HERITAGE	
30127 07341257 4	
HJ	21-Oct-2009
AF CRI	£7.99

ABOUT THE AUTHOR

Jack Daniel lives in Bath, England with his wife, Elizabeth and two small long haired dachshunds. He has two sons. He is a naval constructor, now retired.

He saw sea service with the British Navy in World War 11 and was assigned to the US Manhattan Project for the Bikini atomic tests.

He subsequently designed several classes of warships for the Royal Navy, notably frigates and nuclear attack and ballistic missile submarines, reflecting his lifetime association with submarines that began in the war.

He was Head of the Royal Corps of Naval Constructors when he resigned and joined the Board of British Shipbuilders.

His memoirs, the End of an Era, were published in 2003.

The Body in the Churchyard is the twelfth of twenty books featuring the Hawkridge family and their friends in pursuit of the ungodly.

For Liz and the two boys

Who make everything enjoyable.

Chapter One

IT'S the long, hot, summer of the year 2003 and groups from US Universities are making continuation studies visits to Europe.

Two such groups are spending a short time in the county of Dorset; that from Yale gathering background material for their theses on Thomas Hardy and that from Harvard undertaking research on the Anglo-Saxon Chronicles.

The Yale group of seven, four girls and three young men, is led by Associate Professor Stephen Hamsworth, in his mid-thirties, a graduate from Harvard, already recognized as a coming man in US academic literary circles. That his reputation was helped by the fact that he had captained the Harvard football side and beat the old enemy, Yale, in that time, he made no apology, he was young, fit and handsome in an ex-football player's craggy way, and he enjoyed everything that he did.

The Harvard group of four girls and two young men was led by Associate Professor Kathryn Hawkins Glover, brunette, slender and attractive and herself a Harvard graduate. She was three years younger than Stephen and as an undergraduate had observed him from afar and thought him an over-muscled, conceited, example of the male sex. At the time she'd assumed that he was at Harvard on a scholarship crafted to conceal the real purpose, which was to make him eligible to play football for the university. It had been a small shock when he'd been awarded a first in English and continued at the university working towards a doctorate.

He'd been awarded his doctorate the same summer that she'd graduated. At social events he'd never been short of company, indeed he was usually at the center of an admiring group of female students. For the daughter of one of the oldest New England families, that was enough, he was not the sort of young man her parents would expect her to bring home to Beacon Hill. He'd danced with her at the graduation ball and asked her in a cheeky sort of way why he hadn't seen more of her and she'd walked away from him the moment the music stopped. Her mother was a member of that fast disappearing breed, a Daughter of the American Revolution and she knew that's what Mama would expect her to do. But in her innermost self she had to admit that she'd enjoyed the dance.

Having gained his doctorate there had been speculation that Stephen might become a professional football player and join one of the major league clubs that were known to have made tempting offers but no, he accepted a teaching post in the English Department of Yale.

After a short visit to London to visit the British Museum and Poets' Corner of Westminster Abbey, where Hardy is buried, but really to let the boys and girls see the sights, the Yale group had established themselves in Dorchester. As Stephen said, where else but a few miles from where Hardy was born, in a cottage on the edge of the bleak moor at Higher Bockhampton? This was where the young Hardy had walked to school each day, this was where he had studied architecture and this was where he had returned in middle age to live in Max Gate. What more could anyone ask for? But he was already aware of an undercurrent of discontent. The young people had looked along Dorchester's main street the first night and asked if they might move to Bournemouth where, they understood, people actually came out at night.

The Harvard group were housed in an hotel close to the sea front and the town center in Bournemouth and seemed content with their lot. Mornings were spent with Kathryn, studying, discussing and analyzing the material they had collected and the afternoons were assigned for recreation and private study. And if the emphasis was more on the former than the latter, who would complain? They, too, had visited London and had spent a useful week having, by prior arrangement, been given a sight of copies of major manuscripts held by the British Library, the most important of which was the Beowulf manuscript, followed by a visit to the Bodleian Library at Oxford to see the Junius manuscript, two of the three late tenth century manuscripts of poetry held in Britain. When they left Dorset the plan was to visit Exeter to see the third tenth century manuscript, the Exeter Book, held by Exeter Cathedral. All of this had taken a great deal of arranging and they must be sure appear at the date and time arranged.

The reason for visiting Dorset was that it was at the core of Wessex where the early Anglo-Saxon kings had resisted the invasion of the Danes, none more famously than Alfred the Great. At one of their morning discussion periods she reminded her students that Alfred had not expected to become the leader of the West Saxons. He was a younger son and a scholar. He had visited Rome, learnt Latin and translated religious works into English to encourage literacy. He inspired others to collect manuscripts from monasteries and translate them into English so that people could learn from them. These became known as the Anglo-Saxon Chronicles, the first continuous history of a European people written in their own language. But first there was the matter of getting rid of the Danes who sought to extend their already large territorial gains in England.

She reminded her students of this during one of the morning discussions, remarking that after visiting Exeter they would drive north across the part of Somerset that for thousands of years was a vast lake and marsh before modern drainage systems had been introduced and in which was the island of Athelney between the rivers Tone and Parrett where, in the year 878, Alfred took refuge and from whence he emerged, raised an army and defeated the Danish invaders at a place south-east of Bath called Edington which they might visit on the way to Heathrow.

Another reason for coming to Dorset, which Kathryn had kept strictly to herself until this time, was that she believed that this was where her mother's kinsfolk, the Hawkins, had lived before emigrating to the New World in 1693, the same year that an ornament inscribed with the Anglo-Saxon King Alfred's name and known as The Alfred Jewel, had been found at Athelney. Her father's ancestors were well researched. The Glovers had arrived in the United States from Yorkshire in the 1830's and had made their fortune building railways.

Once more in her hotel room she studied the well-thumbed papers that she had brought with her. Pastor Francis Hawkins accompanied by his wife and child had sailed from Southampton and on arrival in Boston in 1693 had been given land in the New Towne area where, in 1636, the early settlers had established a school, called the Harvard School, in recognition of a substantial endowment from the estate of a Pastor Harvard who was born in London and came to the colony a year before his early death in 1638.

Life was hard and all hands were required to clear the trees and scrub from their land to wrest a living from the soil but despite the need for their labour, Pastor Hawkins insisted that his children, boys and girls, take time to learn to read and write and do simple sums. By sheer hard work they prospered and in due course two of the sons went and worked for merchants in Boston proper on the Shawmut peninsular. Next the sons put their savings in a ship, trading between Boston and Bristol, England, then another ship and some property ashore for warehouses. They married the daughters of fellow merchants and set up homes in Boston or across the River Charles in Cambridge, as New Towne was now called, Their children in turn worked for the firm ashore and afloat during the years of Boston's hey-day as the most important and prosperous port in the North American colonies.

Notwithstanding their loyalty to the British throne, the Hawkins had been prominent among the councilmen petitioning the governor for fair treatment for the colonists as the government in London tried to impose taxes on them. Things had come to a head following the passing of the Stamp Act in 1765. Continued unrest led to the Boston Massacre in 1770 in which British troops fired on the settlers and the Boston Tea Party in 1773 in which the cargos of three ships were dumped into the harbour. One of those ships was a Hawkins ship.

When the governor and soldiers sailed away in the face of George Washington's forces, several loyalist merchants went too, but the Hawkins' fought on the side of the colonists and subsequently made their voices heard in the discussions that led eventually to the Articles of Confederation that were agreed at the Constitutional Convention in May 1787 from which the present-day US Constitution evolved.

This was all recorded in a small booklet that her mother had written. She had painstakingly established the family history between the Hawkins of the early 1700's and the present time, drawing a discreet veil over ancestors who had gone west in more than one sense. Kathryn's interest was in the family before 1720 and particularly before 1693, in England. She believed that they had come from Dorset and intended to systematically visit the country parishes in search of a lead. Today she was going to do the Winterbornes, starting with the most remote village, Winterborne Houghton and working her way back towards Poole and Bournemouth.

She took the Winterborne road and the first village that she came to looked like the villages one conjures up in ones mind when reading Dickens, mellow and clean with flowers and trees everywhere. There

The Body in the Churchyard

was a green with a duck-pond, a tearoom, and an inn and in the distance she could see a church spire. Where better to start than here? She'd have a cup of tea and ask the proprietor some questions. She parked her rental-car outside and opened the door of the Cosy Tea Room.

A small bell delicately tinkled as she opened the door. The tearoom was the front room of a village house and held four tables, each with four chairs. Kathryn thought that it must be a bit of a squeeze when sixteen people are there. The room had two windows, one facing the village street and one at the side. She chose the table facing the street and had barely settled when she was conscious of an elderly woman standing beside her.

"Good afternoon, madam," said the woman in cultured tones.

"Good afternoon," said Kathryn.

"Can I get you something?"

"Yes, please, a cup of tea, without cream or sugar."

"We serve tea by the pot."

"Very well," said Kathryn, thinking you wouldn't last long in Cambridge. Mass.

"A pot of tea with no milk or sugar, Mary."

"Yes," said Kathryn and only then realized that the remark wasn't intended for her but for a second woman, seemingly as old as the first, who had materialized on her other side.

"You're from the United States, aren't you?" said the first woman as the one called Mary turned on her heel.

"Yes," said Kathryn, who prided herself on her neutral accent. "How did you know?"

"We visited New York with our parents, we enjoyed it very much and then we had all your soldiers over here during the war to help us defeat those awful Nazi's."

"My name's Kathryn Glover from Harvard University and I plan to do some research while I'm here." This was meant as a gentle lead-in to the search for her ancestors.

"I'm Daisy Roberts," said the elderly woman. "My sister Mary and I used to be the village schoolteachers."

Sister Mary returned on cue with a tray on which was a teapot, milk jug, sugar basin, cup and saucer, tea plate, knife and spoon and a plate with four small cakes on it.

Kathryn arranged these items on the table and said,
"Have you lived hereabouts all your lives?"

"Yes, except when our parents took us abroad on educational trips to broaden our minds," said the one called Daisy.

"It was ever so nice," said Mary. "I would have liked to live in Paris."

"Shh Mary, we don't speak of that," said her elder sister.

Kathryn would have liked to ask what had happened to the young Mary in Paris but instead she said,

"I believe that my ancestors came from round here, do you happen to know of anyone called Hawkins?"

The sisters thought for a moment.

"I'm not aware of anyone called Hawkins," said Daisy. "Many generations of the local population passed through our hands at the school but never a Hawkins."

"The only family with a name like that is the squire, his family has lived at the Manor House since before Oliver Cromwell's time," said Mary.

Daisy picked up the theme,

"The squire is Sir David Hawkridge. He's, or rather he was, a General in the army. He's retired now and his elder son is keeping up the family tradition in the army."

Mary interrupted to say, "He's married to an American girl called Sally-Ann."

Daisy ploughed on, regardless. "The General owns the Manor House and its estates which include this village, the school and the church. I would suggest that you might start your search by consulting the Reverend Ford and looking through the parish records. How far back are you interested in?"

"We know that Pastor Francis Hawkins and his wife and baby son arrived in Boston in 1693. We think that they sailed from Southampton."

"If anyone can help you, it'll be Mr Ford," said Mary, "but 1693 may be before they started keeping proper parish records."

"I don't think that's so," said Kathryn, "churches were required to keep records of baptisms and deaths from the middle of the sixteenth century."

"Fancy that," said Mary.

Kathryn poured herself a second cup of tea and decided that having a pot wasn't a bad idea, except that the designer of her pot had clearly allowed sufficient volume for two cups of tea with milk, and that volume didn't give two full cups for people who didn't take milk. It also took longer to drink because it lacked the cooling effect of the milk. All this passed through her mind while she listened to Daisy's recital of what a blessing it was that someone called Timmy had married a lovely half-French girl and they had lots and lots of money.

"And two small children," chipped in Mary.

Kathryn rather took to Mary. She dragged her mind away from imagining half a French girl having two children. This wouldn't do. Wool gathering was for peasants.

Eventually the sisters left her to drink her second three quarters of a cup of tea and nibble at a second cake.

She settled the bill and they both came out to point the way to the church. Kathryn left the car where it was and walked through the village, past the Tolbrite Arms to the church. She was impressed. The churchyard was neatly kept, the church was open and nearby was what was obviously the vicarage with shining windows and a garden full of flowers. Kathryn entered the churchyard through the wicket gate, relieved to find a place where she might search but nevertheless feeling that she was behaving somewhat like the drunk who searches under a street light for the penny he dropped up the street in the dark.

She made two complete circuits of the churchyard and went into the church. The brass shone, the altar cloth was spotless and there were flowers wherever there was a place for them. This was exactly what her reading on old English churches had led her to expect and she said a small prayer of thankfulness that all that was good had not yet been swept away by today's uncaring world. She had half expected someone to appear and when no one came, was torn between going to the vicarage and asking for help and going away and coming back tomorrow.

She decided to follow her original plan and start at the most distant Winterborne.

She hit a snag at the first village that in a roadside sign, mostly covered by tall grass, proclaimed itself to be Winterborne Houghton. There was a church but it was shut and seemed to be neglected. She ploughed her way through long grass, nettles and elderberry trees in the churchyard, stumbling over the tombstones of the long departed. She scrubbed at some with handfuls of grass in an effort to read the inscriptions. There was no one about and seemingly no one awake in the few nearby houses so she climbed into her hire-car and backed out of the lane, turned and drove to Winterborne Stickland. This appeared to be a bigger place except that the church was locked and had the same neglected look, set in a mass of long, untended grass and the ever-present elders. A notice in a small glass fronted box set inside the church porch announced that the young mothers meeting would be held at 2.30p.m. on Tuesday. Four years ago.

    She told herself that if she was to have any success in what she regarded as field work, she mustn't give up as easily as she had at the last place, so she decided that she'd walk right round the outside of the church and look for tombstones. The church entrance was at the western end of the Nave and she guessed that there would be entrances at the transept, in the case of a small church like this, probably giving on to the vestry that the clergy and choir would use. She corrected that to 'or had once used'. She turned the corner to walk down the overgrown path towards the transept and saw that there was another building in the churchyard. When she came closer she read Church Hall in faded black paint over the entrance. This building had the same, sad, neglected look with young trees growing around it and partly obscuring the windows.

    The shadows were beginning to lengthen and she rather wished that she hadn't spent so long at the Cosy Tea Room talking with the sisters' Roberts. Doubtless the day was still bright and cheerful outside where she had left the car but the churchyard was surrounded by trees that, together with the more immediate vegetation, added to the gloom.

    Opposite to the vestry door there was a path to the Church Hall and Kathryn took it, the better to see the graves which, for the most part were overgrown and with stonework decayed and broken. The path continued past the door to the hall and along the side. She turned the corner and there she saw the girl. She thought that she was asleep and instinctively said, "Oh, I'm sorry, I didn't mean to startle you."

    The figure, sitting on the ground with her back to the hall, made no movement but continued to stare at the nearby trees.

"Are you alright?" asked Kathryn, sensing something wrong.

She bent down close to the girl and realized that she had been speaking to the dead.

There's nothing in 'Europe on twenty dollars a day' that deals with this sort of situation, so Kathryn ran back to her car, where she'd foolishly left her phone, and dialed 911. Then she wondered if she should have dialed 999 and was about to do that when a voice asked her which service she required. Kathryn said,

"I don't know, I've just found the dead body of a girl in the churchyard."

"Where would that be, Miss?" said a calm voice.

"Round the side of the church hall."

"No, I mean which town and which church?"

"A place called Winterborne."

"Which Winterborne, Miss?"

"Oh, I see what you mean, Winterborne Stickland. You see, I was looking at the tombstones."

"You're sure that the girl is dead?" in the same calm voice.

"Yes, I felt for her pulse and she's also, well, stiff." Kathryn had baulked at the last word, countless movie gangsters had talked of stiffs and she hadn't really thought why, until now.

"Please wait there until someone comes."

"How long will that be?" asked Kathryn.

"They should be with you in half an hour, please wait there."

"No I won't," said Kathryn in a loud voice. "It's getting dark and I'm not going to stay in an overgrown churchyard with a dead body. If anybody wants me I'll be at the Cosy Tea Room." And she rang off, backed her car out of Church Lane and drove southwards to Tolbrite.

Chapter Two

SHE stopped outside a dark and deserted looking tearoom. The windows in the nearby cottages were bright and inviting and in her rear-view mirror Kathryn could see the lights of the Tolbrite Arms. She felt in need of the comforting presence of other people; live ones. She turned the car round and followed the signs to park at the rear of the pub.

She liked English inns and this one took her fancy from the start. The entrance porch led to a small foyer with an opening to the left into the main bar and a glass door to the right into a dining room. Wide stairs led to the upstairs rooms, and beside them the foyer narrowed to a passage leading to the kitchens and what the English call the usual offices. The bar room had windows on to the road, beneath which were upholstered benches facing tables with chairs on the other side, then more tables and chairs and in the far wall a huge open fireplace in which glowed some logs. On the inner side of the room was a bar extending nearly the length of the room with some bar stools for lonely, yet sociable, drinkers. The lighting was the sort of lighting in which a plain woman, with a little effort, might look attractive.

Kathryn perched on a bar stool and the barmaid came along the bar, smiled at her and asked her if she'd like to order. "Yes please, I need a large scotch with some ice, I've just found a girl's body."

"Where?" said the barmaid. "Have you told anyone?" She turned and went to an opening at the rear and called "Will."

An open faced young man appeared. She judged that he was about her age and the barmaid was younger than Kathryn.

"This lady says that she's just found a dead girls body."

"Where?" said Will.

"In the churchyard at a place called Winterborne Stickland, I was looking at tombstones."

"Did you tell the police?"

"I phoned 911 and told someone. They said that I should stay there till they came but it was spooky so I said that I'd come here. Well, not here exactly, I said the first thing that came into my head which was the Tea Room because I'd been in there this afternoon."

An older woman appeared behind the bar.

"This lady's just found a girl's body in the churchyard at Winterborne Stickland, Ma." said the fair-headed barmaid who, Kathryn gathered, was called Gloria.

"What on earth was she doing there?" said Mrs Trowbridge.

"I was looking at the tombstones," said Kathryn indignantly. "Some of us are more interested in your history than you seem to be."

"Do you think that I should go up there and tell the police that this lady is here?" said Will to his wife and mother-in-law. He turned to Kathryn, "you'll have to make a statement at some time; can you wait here until someone comes to take it?"

"Yes but if they don't come soon I'll have to go back to my hotel in Bournemouth where I've got a group of students for whom I'm responsible."

"You go and explain things, love," said Gloria. "Trade won't pick up until later." Thinking 'and I'll have a nice piece of news to tell them when they do.' Will disappeared and shortly afterward they heard him drive off.

Gloria said, "My Will's ever so good, he was a Commando, you know."

"Was he?" replied Kathryn absently, wondering what a Commando was; then she remembered, the same as the US Army's Rangers, tough, highly trained, shock troops.

"He's the Maintenance Manager for the estate. He's the General's right hand man and we're great friends of his son and his wife, you've probably heard of him, Timmy Hawkridge who owns all those radio stations?"

"I can't say that I do, you see, I'm from the United States."

"I knew that there was something different," said Gloria, "but I didn't like to say. Timmy's got some radio stations in America, too."

"There are thousands of radio stations in the States," said Kathryn.

"If I'd known you better when you came in," said Gloria, "I'd have suggested that you didn't have whisky and offered you wine instead. You see, Timmy Hawkridge's wife Helene and her mother, Claire-Marie, own a lot of vineyards in France and produce gorgeous wine and we sell a lot of it."

To Kathryn's relief Gloria was called to attend upon some other customers who had just come in.

Will arrived in Winterborne Stickland and drove along Church Lane. He had already decided that the girl had been murdered. Girls don't go round the back of church halls to die. They might go there with boys for other things but they don't go there to die. He decided not to get too close to the church in case the murderer's car had left tyre tracks which the police would want to examine; so he parked and stood in the lane. He could understand why the American girl hadn't wanted to wait there. It was spooky. It must be much more than half an hour since she had phoned.

Eventually a police car arrived with siren sounding and blue lights flashing. Will stepped out in front of it and stopped its approach to the church. Two policemen got out and put on their caps.

A constabulary voice asked, "Are you the person who reported the incident? We were told it was a lady, an American lady."

"She's down at our pub in Tolbrite. She was too scared to stay here alone until you got here."

"She could have gone to one of the houses in the village," said the constable.

"She probably thought that they were all full of murderers," said Will.

"What makes you think this dead girl, if there is one, that is, was murdered, Sir. Have you examined her?"

"I've not gone one step beyond where I'm standing," said Will. "I was just thinking that no girl would willingly go round the far side of the Church Hall."

"How do you know that the supposed body is on the far side of the hall, Sir?"

"Because the American lady who arrived in our pub in a distressed state said so, that's why," said Will, beginning to wish that he hadn't come. "I came here to tell you that she's at our pub."

"What's this lady's name, Sir?"

"How the hell should I know. Look, I've told you where she is and now I'm going, I've got a pub to look after."

"Not so fast, Sir, if you please," said the second constable, "we'd like you to come with us to check that there really is a body."

The first policeman led the way with his companion bringing up the rear. Their torches lit the way and strange shadows beckoned at them. They reached the transept door and turned to the right towards

The Body in the Churchyard

the Church Hall. Their lights took them past the door and round the corner and there was the girl's body, sitting against the wall of the hall.

The first policeman said, "We must be careful not to disturb anything." He shone his torch fully on the girl's face and said, "You're from these parts Sir, do you have any idea who she is?"

Will bent to get a better view and said, "No, I don't recognise her. It's difficult to tell in this light."

"We'd better leave the poor kid until the morning; if we bring in the ambulance people and the heavy squad in the dark you can say goodbye to any clues there may be. If you'd lead the way, Sir, we'll come to the pub and take the lady's statement."

Will regained his car and drove off. The policemen were reporting-in by phone when he left. He'd almost blurted out her name, Mary Barton, whose grandmother lived in Tolbrite. Judging by the tone of their questions when they'd arrived, they'd have practically had him in handcuffs if he'd admitted that he knew the murdered girl. He hadn't forgotten the antique furniture scam that Inspector Clouseau had arrested him for. Admittedly for only one day before Tim had got him released but one day was long enough as far as he was concerned. The Dorset police didn't deserve to be helped.

Poor Mary, she'd called herself Marylyn. She'd grown to be a beauty. Her Gran had scrimped and saved to bring her up and suddenly it had seemed the scrawny brat was a curvaceous beauty. He'd watched the same thing happen with Gloria, she was the kid who lived in the village pub and was always hanging around the old forge garage until one day he had suddenly realized that she was both beautiful and desirable.

He hadn't known where Marylyn had gone until they had got involved in that lark with the Northern Irish crook who was running call-girl, blackmail and extortion rackets in Bournemouth. The end for Mr Big had come when he, Will, had been shot at by the big man's minder in the car park of the Connaught Towers. Luckily, he'd missed. It was at this time that he'd learned from a tearful Gran that Marylyn had told her that she hadn't been born with anything other than good looks and a beautiful body that men found desirable and she intended to make her living by making them pay for it.

Will arrived back at the pub and explained that the police were coming to interview Kathryn. The police car arrived less than five minutes later and Mrs Trowbridge invited them to use a corner of the dining room.

The policeman asked Kathryn,

"Could we have your name and address please, Miss."

"Kathryn Hawkins Glover, Union House, Beacon Hill, Boston, Mass., presently staying at the West Esplanade Hotel, Bournemouth."

"Are you on holiday, Miss?"

"No, I'm in charge of a group of Harvard students doing research in England."

"Thank you. What were you doing in the churchyard?"

"Looking at the tombstones."

From the look on their faces she could see that they thought this to be at the best, a curious way for an attractive young woman to spend her time. She added,

"I'm looking for my ancestors, you see."

"Much better look in the church records, Miss," said the first policeman.

"My problem this afternoon was finding a church that's actually still in use. There appear to be few Christians left in England."

"Oh, I wouldn't say that, Miss, it's simply that they no longer go to church," said the second policeman. "At about what time did you get to the church at Stickland?"

"I don't know the time but it wasn't more than twenty minutes before I found the girl's body and went back to my car to phone you."

"Say not more than half an hour before the time that your call was logged?"

"That'll do."

"Please take us through your movements if you will."

"The church was shut and neglected. I decided to walk round the outside and look for old tombstones. I went to the right, that's probably south, then turned the corner and walked along the side of the church, probably east, until I came to the Transept."

"How do you spell that, Miss?" asked the first policeman, "With a c or an s?"

Kathryn put him right and went on. "I could see that there was another building and as I got closer I saw the words Church Hall painted over the door. At the transept, with an s, I saw that there was an overgrown path to the Church Hall and so, there being no tombstones between the buildings, I took that path, walked past the door and turned left to walk down the side of the hall and found the girl sitting there."

"Did you touch her?"

"No. Sorry, that's not true, I put my fingers on her neck to feel for her pulse."

"And that's all?"

"Yes. When I first saw her I said something like Hello and when she made no reply and no movement I went close and looked into her face and felt her pulse. Then I realized that she was dead and ran to call you."

"You're sure you don't know the deceased?" asked the first policeman.

"I am sure that I have never seen the poor young thing before, I have only been in Britain for ten days."

Kathryn realized that this was a silly thing to have said, she'd been in Britain lots of times before but she decided not to explain this to the police lest it confuse the issue.

"That'll be all for now, Miss, the inspector may want to have a word with you. When are you planning to leave the area?"

"In nine days time. Then we go to Exeter for a day or so. What's the name of your Inspector?"

"He's not ours, Miss," said the policeman with a grin, "He's Detective Inspector Stevens."

"Thanks, I must remember that," said Kathryn.

The two policemen evidently found this faintly amusing.

"Thank you for your help, Miss, Goodnight."

Kathryn went back into the saloon where Gloria poured her a Bouchier red wine and asked her how she had got on. Will reappeared in time to hear that she might expect a call or visit from a Detective Inspector Stevens. Will and Gloria fell about laughing.

"Old Clouseau. You'll have to watch out for him, he'll try to arrest you. With a few friends we help Timmy and Helene pursue the ungodly, the crooks who it seems the law can't or won't touch. One set of cases started when a body was found one Saturday morning in the Manor House Park when Tim had some VIP Arabs there and Clouseau wanted to arrest Tim. The next time he actually arrested me because a car used in a hit-and-run accident was left outside our garage."

Gloria said, "At the time Will was in bed with me. We weren't married then and Will didn't want my parents to know." She blushed.

"And good old Ma's evidence got me off," said Will. "She'd known for some while that Gloria was sneaking me up into her room and had kept quiet about it."

"So I have to be careful with Inspector Clouseau?"

"Yes," said Will. "Remember, the name he goes by in the Bournemouth police station is Detective Inspector Stevens."

He and Gloria again dissolved in laughter.

Kathryn departed shortly afterwards with a story to tell to her students.

The scene-of-crime team was at the churchyard early the next day. There had been heavy dew, the trees and grass were dripping wet, as were the victims clothes. They took photographs and carefully searched near to the body and the area beyond. They found cigarette ends and other items and put each in a separate bag, marked with the position where it was found. The police surgeon who arrived at the same time as the team said that the indications were that the victim had been dead not more than thirty six hours, he'd know better after the post-mortem. It looked as if she had been stifled by something placed over her nose and mouth, he'd know more about that, too, after the post mortem.

Detective Inspector Stevens arrived at eight-thirty accompanied by Detective Constable Clare Thornton. The doctor was just leaving. He told Stevens his initial views and promised more when the p.m. was done. Stevens expressed his extreme displeasure that the doctor couldn't be more precise and was told in as many words to do his own job and leave others to do theirs. Stevens was left with his own people who had learnt to ignore him. He had gone through practically the entire plain-clothes staff in Bournemouth in an effort to find an officer to serve as his assistant. They had all proved unsuitable. In plain language they had all asked for a shift after a week or so of service with Stevens except for WDC Thornton who stoically pressed on despite the Inspector's rudeness, bullying and stupidity.

Detective Superintendent Harding knew all about Stevens and had tried to have him sent back to the uniform branch. Unfortunately the uniform branch knew all about Inspector Stevens and wouldn't have him at any price. Appointment to another Dorset station was equally out because they too knew him. At a small drinks party held recently to celebrate someone's retirement, Mrs Harding had quietly asked Clare Thornton how she got on with Inspector Stevens and she'd replied that she had no problem, the inspector reminded her of her father. He too was a stupid, bullying, git without a friend in the world who was now in a care-home at a place called Paulton, near Bristol.

Inspector Stevens asked what progress had been made and why the body was still there.

"We thought that you'd want to see it. It's unusual, we've not had one sitting up before. The doc thinks that perhaps something was put over her face while she was standing with her back to the hall and she then sort of slipped down."

"If someone did that to me I don't think my legs would look like that," said WDC Thornton.

"You don't know how your legs would go," snapped Stevens.

"Common sense says that they wouldn't go like that," said Thornton.

"Anyway, what does it matter how her legs are, she's dead, isn't she?"

"How it matters, Inspector," persisted the WDC, "is to suggest that she wasn't killed here and that her body was brought here and put down to sit like a rag doll."

"I don't see that it means that at all."

Clare Thornton turned away and shrugged to the other members of the team who had been listening to the exchange. One of the younger officers opened his mouth to speak and shut it when his sergeant shook his head. The sergeant said,

"We can move the body, then, Inspector?"

"Yes, then we won't have any more silly ideas about legs, will we?" Stevens laughed. No one else did. He turned to the sergeant,

"What about the American woman who found the body. Why isn't she here? Why didn't uniform hold her over-night?"

"They were satisfied with her explanation that she came upon the body by accident."

"A likely story; half the Americans are under the control of the mafia. Are we checking up on her?"

"That's your job, Inspector, we're scene-of-crime," said the sergeant.

Stevens turned to Clare Thornton and said, "Make a note of that."

"Yes, Inspector, check up on any mafia connections."

"And bring her into the station for questioning."

"We can't do that, Inspector, especially to a foreign national, we have to go to her."

"You go and question her then, I'm too busy. Come on, we've wasted enough time here, I've got other cases to attend to."

WDC Thornton managed to contact Kathryn at the hotel and arranged to see her at two that afternoon. She found a young and attractive woman waiting for her who suggested that they should talk in the lounge.

"I've already prepared a statement," said Kathryn. "I've put everything in that I can remember."

"Fine," smiled Clare Thornton. "I'll read it and ask questions to which you've already provided answers."

And that is precisely what she did. At the end Kathryn said, "There's one thing bothering me."

"And what's that?"

"Remember that it wasn't very light round the side of the hall where the body was and I didn't take everything in but I can't see how her legs could have been out like that if she'd fallen or slipped down."

"That's exactly what I said to the Inspector."

"Inspector Clouseau?" said Kathryn.

Clare Thornton burst out laughing. "Who calls him that?"

"As far as I know the entire population of Tolbrite."

"Wait till I tell the boys." On which happy note she left.

Chapter Three

THE wheels of justice began to turn. There was no trace of the girl's identity. Notwithstanding a meticulous search of the churchyard and the surrounding properties, no handbag or purse had been found. The post-mortem confirmed that she had been smothered and traces of wool from whatever had been used were recovered from her mouth and nostrils. It also revealed that she was in the early stages of pregnancy.

Her photograph was shown to the various sections within police headquarters and later in the day, when they got round to looking at it, the Vice section informed Inspector Stevens that they thought that the murdered girl was a prostitute called Marylyn Barton who was known to have an apartment in Boscome Heights, close to the sea front in one of the better parts of town.

Inspector Stevens and WDC Thornton went to Boscome Heights and required the porter to give them access to Miss Barton's apartment. With a certain amount of grumbling and muttered references to search warrants, the porter let them in and hovered inside the door while Clare Thornton went quickly into all the rooms and pronounced them empty.

The rooms were not over-furnished and were finished in the sort of pastel shades that Clare herself would have chosen. There was one jarring feature, the books on the bookshelves seemed to be in disarray, some open, some on the floor and several cupboards and drawers were open.

Someone had hurriedly searched the room. Clare wondered if the Inspector had noticed and decided to keep silent while the porter was there.

Stevens said, "When did you last see Miss Barton?"

"Haven't seen her for a couple of days," said the porter.

"Was that unusual?"

"No, not really although she usually told me if she was going to be away. She sometimes went away for a week or more on one of those big charter yachts."

"And she didn't tell you this time?"

"No, she went out the other evening as happy as a lark and I was off duty when she came back."

"She did come back then?" asked Clare Thornton.

"Well, her spare key is missing from the office. Why are you asking all these questions, there's no real harm in what she does and she's a lot nicer to the likes of me than some of the starched old biddies who live here, I can tell you."

"So you know how she earned the money to pay her rent?" asked Clare.

"Well, I used to see men going up to her apartment, if that's what you mean but I didn't pry."

"I suppose she tipped you well to keep quiet," said Stevens dismissively.

"It's none of my business who a resident has to visit them as long as it doesn't disturb the other residents," said the porter a trifle piously, "and what if she did slip me a pound or two, God knows that I earn it, working all hours."

"Do the residents have to provide references giving the name of who to call in an emergency?"

"A sort of next-of-kin?"

"Yes. Do you have one for Miss Barton?"

"If there is one it'll be down in the office."

They exited the girl's apartment with Inspector Stevens instructing Clare Thornton to seal the apartment pending further examination.

In the foyer the porter led the way to the cubicle behind his desk. He leafed through some files in a cabinet and took one out.

"Here it is, Marylyn Barton." He turned over and read out "Contact Address Mrs Mary Barton, Spring Cottage, Tolbrite." He turned to Stevens and said,

"That's a village out Dorchester way...."

"We know where it is, you fool, we're the police."

"There's no need to be rude," said the porter. "I was only trying to be helpful. You still haven't told me why you're here?"

"We think that she may have had an accident," said Clare.

"Oh I see," said the porter, "nothing serious I trust?"

The Inspector gave a grunt. Clare said,

"Has anyone been in her apartment in the past two days?"

"There were two men looking for her the night before last," said the porter. "Not together but separate like and there was one last night."

"What time would that be?" asked Clare.

"The other night one was about eight, I'd seen him here before and the other was sometime before ten. I didn't know him. Then last night it was one I didn't know."

Clare picked up the nuance in the words "But you knew the one who came at eight o'clock on the first night?"

"Yes, Mr Jackson, the newsagent."

"And what about the ten o'clock man?"

"He seemed to be angry when he found that she wasn't in. I heard the way he drove off."

"And last night's man?" persisted Clare.

"Just hurried past my desk, ran up the stairs instead of waiting for the lift and came down about ten minutes later and hurried out, keeping his face turned away from me."

"You must have got some impression of the man even though you didn't see his face," persisted Clare despite the Inspector's show of impatience. "Was he tall, did he have a limp, was he a white man?"

"He was taller than he is," pointing at back of the 5 foot 10 inch Inspector who had turned away. "He didn't have a limp and, now that you remind me, the hand that he held up to cover his face was sort of sun-burnt. And he had a large signet ring."

Clare thanked the man for his help.

Inspector Stevens told her to stop this nonsense and told the porter that more police would be along to take the girl's room apart. The porter said that he'd inform his owners.

In the car Clare said, "That was interesting, Inspector."

"Waste of time if you ask me, there's nothing to be learnt there."

"But what about the state of her room, all those drawers and cupboards open?"

"All girl's rooms are like that. They have no concept of tidiness these days."

"But we'll ask the forensic team to finger-print all the likely places, won't we?" asked Clare.

"I suppose so, give them something to do, dressed up in their fancy white suits."

Clare Thornton decided to change the subject,

"This is the bit that I don't like."

"What's that?" growled Stevens.

"Well, I suppose that we've now got to go and bring this Mrs Mary Barton of Spring Cottage, Tolbrite in to view the body to see if the victim is her granddaughter."

"What's wrong with that?" said Stevens.

"There's nothing *wrong* with it but it's tragic and painful, this girl may be her only relative, perhaps she helps support her gran, there's no end to the grief it might cause."

"If she was supporting her grandmother it serves the old woman right for taking money earned immorally," said Stevens, "and in any case, *we're* not going to bring her in to view the body, *you* are."

Talk about mixed blessings, thought Clare Thornton; on the good side she'd be away from the Inspector for a few hours. She'd call first at the village pub and have a word with Gloria and her husband Will who, according to the case notes, had attended the scene of the crime on the day the body was discovered.

She phoned the mortuary and was assured that it would be all right to bring someone to view the girl's body the next day.

Inspector Stevens invited the vice squad to ask around the clubs for anyone who had seen Marylyn Barton in the last few days and reported to Detective Superintendent Harding that satisfactory progress was being made.

The following morning WDC Clare Thornton drove to Tolbrite. The sun was shining with white clouds hurrying across a blue sky and doubtless preventing rain from falling, the gardens of the cottages were overflowing with flowers, the cottages themselves were newly painted and all seemed to be at peace in the world. And she was probably going to shatter an old lady's world. She parked outside the Tolbrite Arms as Gloria emerged to see who this early arrival might be.

"Hello, Gloria, remember me?"

"Yes, you're Clare. We last met when there was that spy business at Portland."

"That's right and the red headed army captain was shot at when they arrested the spies," said Clare. " She seems to make a habit of being attacked. Have you seen her since?"

"Yes, she comes down quite often to meet Tim and Helene and the rest of us and we hear something of what she's up to," said Gloria, "Can I offer you a coffee?"

"That would be nice, I've got a rotten job to do and anything that puts it off is welcome."

By this time Clare was sitting at a table in the bar and Gloria was getting the coffee. Mrs Trowbridge put her head in to say Hello.

"What's the rotten job then?" asked Gloria, half knowing but resolved to keep quiet, she didn't want her Will to be questioned about why he hadn't identified the body two nights ago.

"We think that the girl who's body was found in the churchyard in Winterborne Stickland is Marylyn Barton and I've come to ask her grandmother to come and identify the body."

"Oh dear," said Gloria. "Poor Mary, she's all her grandmother's got in the world. Somebody will have to go with her. I'll have a word with Will. When do you want her to come?"

"It's up to her but it has to be today."

Gloria phoned Will who was at one of the estate's farms with Lady Hawkridge. She told him what Clare had said.

She heard him repeating what she'd said to Lady Hawkridge then,

"Gloria, Lady Hawkridge will go with old Mrs Barton. Please ask your police friend to wait until we get there?"

Gloria raised her eyebrows at Clare who had heard the conversation and she nodded.

"Yes Will, she'll wait."

In what seemed to be only a few minutes the estate car pulled up outside and the squire of Tolbrite's wife and Will came in.

The situation was rehearsed again and Margaret, Lady Hawkridge, said, "There's no point in putting it off, let's go and see old Mrs Barton." She turned to Clare and said, "I suppose one of us couldn't take the old lady's place? We've known Mary Barton all her life, saw her grow up."

"I'm not sure what the rules are but if the old lady is too ill or upset it might be alright for someone else to identify her."

"Let's go then," said Margaret.

They trooped off along the village street, Lady Hawkridge, Clare and Gloria, followed by Will in the car.

Their progress was observed and noted by the Roberts sisters at the Cosy Tea Room.

Margaret knocked on the door of Spring Cottage. She thought how lovely and smart the cottage and it's garden was and, not for the first time, said a prayer for her son and daughter-in-law for pouring all that money into the Manor House Trust to maintain the estate. What a relief from the grinding penury of yesteryear that had taken all of her and David's money and still hadn't been enough.

There was movement inside the cottage and an elderly woman who still had a countrywoman's rosy cheeks opened the door.

"Oh, your ladyship, what a surprise, I'm afraid that I'm all in a mess...."

"It's alright Mrs Barton, We've got some bad news, I'm afraid that the police think that Mary's had a bad accident and they'd like you to come with us and see her."

It took a moment for this to sink in and the old woman's face went white, "But she can't have, she was here on Sunday, not our Mary, she calls herself Marylyn these days, what hospital's she in, in Bournemouth I suppose?"

She ran out of things to say. Margaret took hold of her arm and said,

"Get your coat, my dear. Will we see to your cottage, is there anything cooking?"

"No, your ladyship it's too early for dinner."

The old lady got her coat, insisted on locking her own door and got into the back of the estate car with Margaret. With a word to Gloria, Will drove off, followed by Clare Thornton in her police car. Gloria went back to the pub, happy not to be going on the sad mission, having assured Margaret that she would see that the General was told where his wife had gone.

The Manor House butler, known to one and all as the Sergeant, took the message. He found the General, Sir David Hawkridge, GCB, DSO, MC, Bart, in his study overlooking the entrance of the Manor House where he spent most mornings, except Sunday, reading The Times. From the window he could see across the park to the spire of the church and the village beyond. On his left, to the north, the main drive finished at a bridge wide enough to take a hay wagon over the River Winterborne that flowed lazily through the park with meadows and the Long Wood beyond. Dragons and demons had lurked in that wood when he was a small boy and he understood from his elder son's children that they were still there. It was unchanging; from this window he'd watched his two son's and daughter climb the same trees that he'd climbed as a boy and now he was watching his grandchildren make the same discoveries.

The main drive, beneath his window led to the Winterborne road, half a mile to the south as did the service drive behind the house and stables. The 'proper' way to the village was down the drive and along the Winterborne road. It was not only a long way round but dangerous with the number of vehicles that now used the road to the villages. The family always walked the shorter way across the park, past the church and vicarage. Or went the long way round by car when it rained.

The General mused on how their lives had changed in the last few years. It was all due to Helene, Tim's wife. He'd been disappointed when young Tim had refused to go to Sandhurst when he left Winchester, preferring to go to Oxford instead. The elder son, David (known in the family as David two) had followed the family tradition and was now a major, serving in the MoD, married to an American girl called Sally-Ann and with two children. Timmy had got a first and then instead of accepting the post the college at Oxford had offered had gone into the entertainment business where people have long hair and beards. He'd had a flair for picking future stars and made recordings on the Hawkridge Media label, then he'd started to build and own radio stations which didn't play endless, mindless, pop music and that had also been a success. He now owned close on thirty radio stations in the UK, the USA and Canada and managed a station in Qatar.

He'd been invited to build and run a station in Qatar by the Emir's son who had been the Hawkridge boys' friend at Winchester. When it had first been mooted he'd asked his bank for someone who could speak Arabic and they had sent blonde, blue eyed, curvaceous Helene who had spent the first seven years of her life in Amman where her father was an RAF Wing Commander attached to the Jordanian Air Force and her mother the daughter of the French Ambassador. Timmy had been lost from the moment she had walked into his office. After a few adventures with the ungodly, they had married. They too now had two children who would, in time, inherit not only the Hawkridge Media empire but also a good part of Burgundy and it's vineyards.

The General brought his thoughts back to where he'd started. It was all due to Helene. For security reasons the first meeting with the

Sheikh had been held at the Manor House. Timmy had brought his financial adviser, Helene, a murdered man's body had been found in the park, and that stupid policeman had all-but arrested Timmy. Helene seemed to get on with everyone and workaholic Timmy, who had hitherto only found time to visit his parents about six times a year, brought her down every weekend thereafter. It had been some time before they had discovered that she and her mother, Claire-Marie, were numbered among the really rich people in France. The effect on Margaret had been electric, she looked ten years younger – she said that it was because she could now look a villager who said that his roof was leaking, in the eye and say truthfully that she'd get it fixed. The General admitted in his heart that Margaret, the Sergeant and young Will now ran the estate using Timmy and Helene's money.

Getting roofs fixed made him think of young Will. Village boy Will, Old Will the blacksmith's son, had been the friend and playmate of his children and the friendship had lasted into adulthood. Will had done a spell in the Royal Marines and had returned to work for his father in the village garage as the forge had now become. Will and Gloria had become an item but the garage didn't make enough to support Old Will, Young Will and a bride. Again, it had been Helene who produced the answer, they'd closed the garage and converted it to the estate maintenance depot with Old Will as caretaker with a little flat on the premises and young Will as the salaried Estate Maintenance Manager with a house for him and his bride. Timmy had also insisted that Will run a chat-show on Radio Bournemouth and this hour, on Monday nights, now had one of the station's highest audience ratings.

He thought about Margaret and old Mrs Barton. What a rotten thing for an old woman to have to do, to go and look at the body of her granddaughter. He hoped that Margaret wouldn't be upset. He wondered what she'd do with the old lady afterwards? Perhaps she'd bring her back to the Manor House and ask the Sergeant and his wife, Mrs Hodges, to look after her. He felt guilty, the Sergeant had been his batman driver for donkeys years and had retired when he had, to come and look after him. In all those years his wife was always referred to as Mrs Hodges and the General thought that perhaps he should have asked the Sergeant what his wife's Christian name was. He expected that Margaret would know.

The Sergeant found him sleeping peacefully in his chair and decided not to waken him for luncheon but to await her Ladyship's return.

Will parked beside the mortuary and Clare pulled in beside him. During the journey Margaret had done her best to prepare the old woman for the worst, telling her that Marylyn was dead. She still didn't know if she had got through to her. Clare asked them to wait in the car while she went in to make sure that everything was ready.

She returned and asked Mrs Barton to come with her. The old woman climbed out of the car and took Clare's arm and allowed herself to be led into the grim building. Margaret and Will walked behind, not wishing to see the body but feeling they should be there should Clare need help.

It was all over quite quickly. Mrs Barton and Clare stood behind a glass screen on the other side of which was a slight form completely covered by a sheet. At a nod from Clare an attendant uncovered the head and shoulders of the body. Mrs Barton put her hand to her mouth and said, "Mary, oh my little Mary, what have they done to you?"

Clare said, "Is that your granddaughter, Mary Barton?"

"Yes," said the old woman. "That's my little Mary, she's a good girl, really."

Clare nodded to the attendant who replaced the cover and wheeled the body away. She then turned a weeping Mrs Barton and they left the building. Margaret fell into place beside the old lady and said, "Come on dear, we'll take you home now."

"Yes," said Will, "and have a nice cup of tea."

Clare who was nearly in tears herself, said, "Can I leave her in your hands?"

"Yes, dear, we'll look after her."

They helped the old woman into the estate car and followed Clare out of the car park where she turned left and Will turned right.

Margaret sat with her arm round Mrs Barton letting her cry into the tissues that Will produced from the car front-door pocket. When they were almost at Tolbrite she said,

"Would you like to come up to the Manor and have a nice cup of tea with Mrs Hodges?"

"No thank you, your Ladyship, I'll just go home. I'm better left alone."

"You're sure you'll be alright?"

"Yes. She was all I had you know, ever since a tiny tot, such a sweet child and she never changed, no matter what people said."

"Yes she was a lovely girl and that's how we'll all remember her, won't we Will?"

"Yes," said Will. "Gloria and I'll look in early this evening to see that you're alright."

He stopped the car outside Spring Cottage and helped Mrs Barton get out. He took her key and opened the front door and Margaret saw her safely in, saying, "perhaps you'd put the kettle on, Will, there's something that I must do, I'll only be a minute."

Margaret turned and walked along the road to the Cosy Tea Room and said to a surprised Daisy. "Mrs Barton has just identified the dead body of her granddaughter. She wants to be left alone, I want you to keep an eye on her and see that she has something to eat. Put it on my account, understand?"

"Yes your ladyship, give her what she wants. I always said that that girl would come to a bad end, didn't I Mary?"

Margaret turned on her with her eyes blazing. "Now listen to me, both of you. I let you live here rent-free. If I hear one whisper that you've said something bad about the dead girl or upset old Mrs Barton in any way, I'll give you a bill for last year's rent and have you out of this house quicker than you can say Jack Robinson. Do I make myself clear?"

"Yes, your ladyship," said an astounded Daisy who'd never heard Margaret raise her voice before, "we won't say a word."

"You'd better not. That girl's transgressions, if they were transgressions, died with her. She's now one of Gods children going home to a merciful father. She never had a chance in this world, let's pray that she has a better one in the next."

"I'll pray for her," said Mary.

With which an indignant Margaret turned on her heel and marched back to Spring Cottage where Will was pouring boiling water into a teapot.

They settled the old woman with a cup of tea, checked that the gas was off and reminded her that Gloria would be along and left. Will drove Margaret home to where the General was asking the Sergeant what had happened to lunch?

Chapter Four

THE police asked around the club circuit if anyone had seen Marylyn Barton on the night of May 23rd.

Chalky White, the doorman at the Half Moon club and an army friend of Will, said that he thought that she had been at the club that night. The barman and waitresses confirmed this and thought that she had danced a couple of times with an American who had come with a group of young Americans. One waitress said that she thought that Marylyn had left with the American; he hadn't been there when the group left because she'd heard them laughing about it when they paid the bill. She liked Americans, they were friendly and good tippers.

Detective Inspector Stevens took over. It was his case. He visited the club and had to come back in the early evening when the members of the staff were again on duty. WDC Thornton took their statements. They repeated substantially what they had told the detective constable from the vice squad.

Pressed on the point by Clare Thornton, Chalky thought that Marylyn had left a few minutes before the American. He'd heard a car door slam and a car drive away before the American came back into the foyer. He hadn't seen him go outside the club but he'd been busy signing some people in, it was only just after ten and clients were just starting to arrive in numbers. At the time he'd probably assumed that the American had gone back in and rejoined his party in which the girls outnumbered the boys. He remembered that because it was usually the other way round in club-land.

The American party had left just before midnight. He couldn't swear if the American who had danced with Marylyn was with them.

It came to Clare that Inspector Stevens would say that one didn't need a deerstalker hat, a cloak and a meerschaum pipe to solve this crime. American goes to nightclub with a group of friends. He is attracted to a girl he dances with and leaves the club with her. A female member of the group is insanely jealous and follows them and eventually smothers the girl. She then takes her to a remote churchyard and dumps her. Next day, unable to resist and frightened that she may have left a clue, she returns to the scene, has a good look round and pretends to find the body, thus explaining any footprints and tyre marks she may have made the previous night. The Inspector would doubtless add that she, Clare Thornton, had actually taken the woman's written statement and hadn't seen what was plain to be seen.

WDC Thornton's job would be to visit the hotels and ask if they had a group of young Americans staying there on the night of 23rd May. Her experience was that asking over the phone seldom produced reliable answers. Unless she stood in front of the receptionist and asked for the information, little was forthcoming. And in any case it got her away from the Inspector. She'd have to watch it, she was now thinking of him as Inspector Clouseau.

She knew that a group of American students was staying at the West Esplanade Hotel, that's where she'd interviewed the lady professor who'd found the body. So she started there. The receptionist confirmed that they had a group of young Americans in residence. Enquiry showed that they were out but Clare was assured that they always came back for lunch and had the afternoons free. Clare said that she'd come back at two o'clock and was reminded by the receptionist that Americans take an early lunch, just after one o'clock might be better. They usually sat in a corner of the foyer after lunch and talked about their work for half an hour or so before breaking up. They were due to leave in about eight days time.

She decided that she wouldn't report anything to Inspector Clouseau until she'd been back to the hotel and questioned the group, The rest of the morning dragged somewhat and she was back at the hotel at a quarter to one. Sure enough, a group of six young people came out of the dining room and sat in the foyer. They were casually, yet expensively dressed and were smiling, obviously enjoying their visit. They had left a spare seat and this was take by the girl who had found the body, with an armful of files and papers that she proceeded to distribute. Everyone was smiling.

Clare approached the group, Kathryn recognized her and smiled a "Hello."

"I'm sorry to interrupt you but pleased to have caught you all together. I'm Detective Constable Clare Thornton and I'm looking into the death of the girl who's body one of you found."

"Told you so, Kathryn," grinned one of the boys, "nothing but harm can come from raking up old bones."

The Body in the Churchyard

They all enjoyed the joke and Clare couldn't imagine either of these fresh faced young men in the role she had cast. Never mind, she went on,

"We have reason to believe that the murdered girl was at the Half Moon night club the night that she died."

If she'd expected looks of consternation she was disappointed. The seven of them sat and looked at her until one of the boys said,

"I said we should do a bit of clubbing, that's where the action is."

"You go on your own buster," said one of the girls.

Kathryn said, "Why are you telling us?"

"Because we have been told that a party of young Americans were in the club that night."

"Well it wasn't us, worse luck," said the boy. "If you'd like someone to go undercover at the night club, I'm available."

"Don't you believe him, officer," said the second boy, "his folk gave me strict orders to see that he's in bed by eleven every night."

"You can see what we girls have to put up with," said Kathryn, "sorry that we couldn't help you."

"I'm sorry to have bothered you," said Clare, turning away.

"There is another set," said one of the girls, "from Yale." Clare turned back. "We're from Harvard."

"Oh," said Clare, "do you happen to know where they're staying?"

"No," said the girl. "I met one of the girls in the bookshop yesterday and she said that they're here studying Thomas Hardy and their leader booked them in at a place called Dorchester because it has the right ambience and after the first night the crew mutinied and moved themselves to the brighter lights of Bournemouth."

"We're doing the Anglo-Saxon Chronicles," said a girl, "not many people round here seem to have heard of them."

"I have to confess that includes me," said Clare. "What exactly are they?"

Kathryn looked at the girl who had spoken and gave a little nod. The girl needed little encouragement,

"You have to appreciate that although the Romans brought writing to England, no one had a written language for the Germanic languages that the natives spoke and that stories were handed down from generation to generation. The missionaries who brought

Christianity from Rome spoke Latin and brought Latin manuscripts. In various monasteries the scholars copied the texts and added their thoughts and contemporary references. We are indebted to the Venerable Bede's Historia Ecclesiastica gentis Anglorum." She formed these words carefully, then hurried on, "for much of this."

"Get to it, babe" said the pro-clubbing boy with a wide grin.

"The monks included stories that they heard from travellers concerning happenings elsewhere and often these were inaccurate but nevertheless tell historians that something happened, if you see what I mean. Are you sure that you want to hear this?"

"Yes," said Clare, "It's interesting."

"From about 700 AD onwards, most manuscripts were being written in old English, the various dialects of Saxon or Anglian and rich people who weren't priests were able to read and write. Anyway, in King Alfred's time some of these manuscripts were circulated between the monasteries and more copies were made available. Some continued to be added to, and seven versions and fragments survive to the present time and are known as the Anglo-Saxon Chronicles."

"They cover the period from 1AD until about 1200AD," said the boy, "and all the really good university libraries have got copies."

"Thank you" said Clare, "I envy you your studies."

"You wouldn't if you had to pass exams in it," said one of the girls.

Clare thanked them again and regained her car to continue her search of the hotels. She reasoned that a group wouldn't be staying at a place like the Grand but, being Americans, would expect a reasonable standard, so she would start on the four star hotels. What a boon it was to be able to leave the car on double yellow lines. It was late in the afternoon and further from the sea front that she found them, a group of American students were staying there, two of whom, according to the hotel receptionist, had Yale emblazoned on their sweater.

She asked if any of them were in and after inspecting the keyboard the receptionist said that it looked as if the professor was in. Clare asked if she might speak with him on the phone and was directed to a phone round the corner from, but visible to, reception. She dialed the room number she'd been given.

A voice said, "Professor Hamsworth."

Clare said, "Professor Hamsworth, this is the Bournemouth police, could I have a word with you, please?"

"Has anything happened to one of the students?" with genuine concern.

"No, nothing like that. I'd just like a word if I may."

"Where are you?"

"Down in the foyer of your hotel."

"OK, give me five minutes and I'll be down."

Clare had visions of bearded professors escaping down fire escapes but within five minutes a clean shaven, handsome, craggy looking, youngish man emerged from the lift and looked around for a policewoman in uniform. Plain clothed Clare introduced herself and he suggested that they sit in the lounge.

"And to what do I owe this unexpected pleasure?" asked the professor.

"We're making enquiries into the death of a young woman on the night of the 23rd."

Stephen Harmsworth showed polite interest.

"I believe that you knew her," said Clare.

"I hardly know anyone in England," smiled Stephen. "What gave you that idea?"

"You are reported to have been with her that evening."

"Now see here," he was serious now, "I haven't been out with any English girl this trip."

"Where were you on the night of the 23rd May?"

"Two or three nights ago?" He thought for a moment and said, "that was the night we went to the night club, Blue Moon or Half Moon, something like that, just along the road."

"And what did you do when you left the club, professor?"

"It's coming back to me now, I left the kids to it and walked back to the hotel."

"What time would that have been?"

"Let me see. I was dancing with this rather attractive English girl and suddenly she asked me the time and said, 'much as I'd prefer to stay with you, I'm afraid that I've got an appointment and I've got to go' and she turned away and walked out of the door. That must have been about five minutes before ten o'clock."

"And what did you do?"

He looked at Clare, raised his eyebrows and grinned and said, "I'm not used to girls walking away when I've had them in my arms and I've never been deserted in the middle of a dance floor before, so it took me some moments to recover. Then I followed her, thinking that she'd have to go to the cloakroom so I went out of the entrance meaning to catch her when she came out but I was just in time to see her legs as she got into a green Jaguar car and she'd gone in a roar of exhaust and tyre rubber. At the time I thought that she'd got into the driver's seat but then I remembered that you have them the other way round over here and that there was a man in the other seat, driving the Jag."

"Did you see the man?"

"No, I only realized that he was there at the last moment. If you press me I'd say that he was on the swarthy side, had close cropped hair and was about my size."

"Over six feet?"

"Yes, he sat tall in the car."

"Did you see anyone on your walk back to the hotel?"

"Of course. I saw lots of people, Bournemouth isn't like Dorchester, but no one who I know, no one who can vouch for me as the saying goes, except the hotel porter to whom I said goodnight as I walked past his desk."

"Didn't you have to ask him for your room key?"

"No, I took it with me. It's an old habit from my student days when I used to sneak girls into my room at Harvard."

"I thought that you were from Yale?"

"We are. I teach at Yale but I was educated at Harvard. You haven't told me, do you mean to say that rather lovely young girl who I danced with is dead?"

"Yes, I'm afraid so."

"Why are the police interested, how did she die?"

"She was murdered that night. You may have read about it in the papers."

"My God, how awful. It might have been the swarthy car driver, mightn't it?"

"It might have been anyone," said Clare.

"But not me, I assure you."

The Body in the Churchyard

"This is quite an American affair, the girl who found the body is from Boston, from Harvard, in fact."

"A student?"

"No, an associate professor called Glover."

"Not the fair Kathryn?"

"I think that's her name, Kathryn Hawkins Glover."

"The very same. Another one of my non-successes. She was three of four years behind me and I used to see her on the campus. I was the college football captain and the co-eds seemed to like me but Kathryn kept her distance. Her mother *is* Boston society and they own half of Boston. They're disgustingly rich and over the centuries seem to have endowed a good part of Harvard so I suppose that weighed on her."

He stopped, thought a bit, grinned and said, "Come to think of it, the murdered girl wasn't the only girl who left me on a dance floor. At a graduation ball I finally got to dance with Kathryn and when the music stopped she'd gone without a word. What's she doing here or aren't you allowed to say?"

"She's got a group of young people from Harvard at the West Esplanade Hotel. One of her students has already met one of yours."

"My, my, an all American reunion. I'll have to toddle along there and see if she remembers me."

"Because you must be one of the last people to see Marylyn Barton alive I'm afraid that I'll have to ask you for a signed statement. If you like I'll type up the relevant part of what you have said in reply to my questions today and bring it back for you to agree and sign."

"And if I don't like?"

She smiled at him. "Then I'll have to ask you to come to the police station to give a formal statement, Sir."

"I like it your way. Perhaps we'll have a coffee next time."

Clare drove back to the police station thinking that Professor Stephen Hamsworth had probably broken a few sophomore hearts in his time. Probably still was. She realized that she'd have to question the Yale students to check his story and she should have stayed at the hotel and done it that afternoon so she turned round and re-appeared at the reception desk. She showed her warrant card,

"I was here before. I'd like to speak with one of the students from Yale, preferably a girl, are any of them in?"

The receptionist studied her computer screen and touched some keys and said, "One of them's on that phone," nodding towards the phone that Clare had used earlier.

Clare picked up the phone and said, "This is the Bournemouth police, who am I talking with?"

"Charlotte Bergen."

"Miss Bergen, an incident happened that has a remote connection with the people who were in the Half Moon night club on the 23rd May, that's the night that you were there. I just want to check up on your impressions. I'm in the foyer, can we meet?"

"I'm not dressed to come down so you'd better come up."

Charlotte Bergen proved to be a girl with big brown eyes and black hair and was wrapped in a bath towel.

"You can see why I couldn't come down. What is it that you want to ask me?"

"You went to the night club. Talk me through the evening, please."

"It was better than we'd expected. We had a meal and some drinks and as the evening wore on the prof and the three boys danced with each of us. Then about ten the prof disappeared. He didn't tell us and we had a look for him before we came back at gone eleven."

"He just disappeared?" said Clare.

"Yes. After he'd danced with us he asked an English girl to dance with him. Perhaps she was a hostess, anyway she was sitting on a stool at the bar and the prof asked her to dance. Then he asked her again and stood at the bar with her. She was a very attractive girl and didn't have that hard look that bar hostesses sometimes have," said world-wise Charlotte. She went on,

"Well, about ten o'clock they were dancing together when she stopped, said something to the prof and walked off the tiny dance floor and out of the door. I was looking at them at the time and he looked kind of dumb, he started to walk back towards our tables, then seemed to make his mind up and turned and went out of the door. That's the last we saw of him until breakfast the next day."

"Did the girl he had been dancing with come back?"

"No, that's when I for one decided that they'd gone off together, you know...." Her voice trailed away.

"But you still thought that you should look for the professor?"

"Yes, because although it looked like, well, you know, a pick-up, I couldn't believe that the prof would do it, if you know what I mean, he's not that sort."

"When you looked for the professor what did the doorman say?"

"He said that the last he saw of the prof he was going out of the club at about ten o'clock. We asked him if the prof was with the girl and he said that he thought that he wasn't."

"Had any of you seen the English girl before?"

"No, only that once at the club. Why are you asking these questions?"

"Because the English girl was found murdered the next day."

Charlotte's eyes widened and she almost dropped the towel.

"Oh and you think that the prof may have done it?"

"We think no such thing," said Clare sharply, "we're simply trying to find out all that we can about what she was doing during her last few hours and you and the professor are filling in some gaps."

"But he could have, couldn't he?"

"So could a hundred other people. Does your prof have a car?"

"No but we've got the mini-bus."

"Where's it kept and who has the keys?" said Clare, thinking that's another thing for forensic to check.

"It's in the hotel car-park and the prof has the reserve set of keys and Sandy Trimble, one of the boys, has the other set."

"Has the mini-bus been moved since you arrived here?"

"Only to take us to the churchyard at Stinsford but the prof didn't come with us."

Clare showed polite interest. This wasn't what she'd come for. Charlotte went on,

"The hotel receptionist in Dorchester said that Thomas Hardy was buried in the churchyard at this church and we knew that she was wrong because we'd visited the place where he's buried in the Poets' corner in Westminster Abbey. So we took the mini-bus and went to this church and sure enough, there's a gravestone for Thomas Hardy. When we got back we asked the prof and he said that that was where Hardy wanted to be buried, alongside his wife and parents, so when the London lot insisted that his ashes be buried in Poets' corner, his wife had his heart cut out and buried where he wanted it to be."

Charlotte was now in full flight. "I like his poetry. The prof said that he was married to his first wife, Emma, for forty years and was mean to her and seldom spoke to her, yet when she died he started writing this lovely poetry that reads as if he's talking to her. The prof says that he was a very complex character and that's why we're studying him."

Clare said, "Thank you Charlotte, that's been most useful." She moved to the door and grinned at her, "You can get dressed now."

Stephen Hamsworth decided that there was time before dinner to walk along to the West Esplanade Hotel. He wondered if Kathryn had changed in the years since graduation. He'd seen in a learned publication that she'd been awarded an associate professorship and had wondered if the family wealth had anything to do with it. He was a Democrat with a capital D and he'd read that the Glover's had made substantial contributions to the Republican Party. Wealth and privilege went hand in hand. When he was being honest with himself he admitted that he was just plain envious.

He walked past the hotel and walked back again. What was he doing? If he bumped into her in the street or somewhere that would be OK. If he sat in the foyer of her hotel it would look funny, funny peculiar as the English say. If he went in and asked for her it would look downright silly. Then there was the question of what would he say? He could hardly say 'you know that body of a girl that you found. Well I was dancing with her that evening and the police think that I may have killed her.'

At about that time, Clare Thornton, in the shower, was thinking, he never asked me how she was killed or where the body was found. Inspector Clouseau would consider that to be proof positive that he already knew.

Chapter Five

THERE had been an outbreak of credit card theft in Bournemouth. Fred Smart, private investigator and proprietor of the Southern Enquiries detective agency, thought about it. It wasn't exactly an outbreak, because credit cards were being stolen in Bournemouth ever since they had been invented but recently it had more than doubled and he was sure that it was no longer random thievery to finance someone's craving for drugs but was now part of an organized operation. Two months ago there had been a rash of thefts using credit cards in Brighton. And two months before that it had been Oxford.

The usual modus-operandi of the earlier credit card thieves was to use the card to purchase something that they could sell-on for ready cash, which usually resulted in their being caught. Today's operation was much more sophisticated, the credit cards were invariably used to extract as much money as possible from cash machines.

To do this, the thief would not only have to steal the card but would have to know the card-holders personal identification number, their PIN number. The police and the banks had issued urgent notices reminding users not to let anyone look over their shoulder when using cash machines but still it was happening. One of the big banks had commissioned Southern Enquiries to investigate – could private enterprise succeed where, so far, the police had failed?

That Southern Enquiries existed at all was due to a girl called Angela, the harbour master's assistant at Poole. Fred had a degree in economics and had worked for a firm in the City of London that undertook confidential enquiries into firm and people's financial affairs. The City firm undertook such enquiries for Hawkridge Media and, because his was a valuable account, undertook other detective work for Timmy Hawkridge. It's staff enjoyed these diversions that usually led to the capture of crooks.

Fred had been engaged in one such 'lark' as Will called them, at Poole, when he'd met and fallen in love with Angela. The crime under investigation was the importation and reproduction of stolen antique French furniture, brought in through Poole in a luxury motor cruiser. The capture of the crooks had involved Helene's mother, Claire-Marie, in France and the Timmy Hawkridge Irregulars on this side of the channel. Fred had asked to be allowed to work from Bournemouth so that he could be with Angela and when this was refused had resigned and Timmy had helped him set up Southern Enquiries, operating from an office in the Hawkridge Radio Bournemouth complex. The venture had prospered and he'd since been joined by Paula Simms, another of his former colleagues.

When they were not overseas on business, Timmy and Helene and the children spent one weekend a month at the Bouchier Chateau in France and three at the Manor House, on one of which Claire-Marie would be with them, thus she saw her only child and her grandchildren at least twice a month.

After dinner on Saturday evenings Timmy and Helene walked across the park to the village pub where Fred, Angela and Paula joined them; the other members of the irregulars, Will and Gloria, being the other side of the bar. On the Claire-Marie weekends she would come too and perch on a bar stool and talk about the old squadron days when she accompanied her husband on his RAF postings and this years grape harvest, on which she was an acknowledged expert, all in high good humour.

The other feature of these Saturday night gatherings was that Angela would play a medley of old and new tunes, classics and pop, on the piano. In the adventure in which they had recovered the abducted baby of Tanya, one of Timmy's current recording stars, they had discovered that Angela was a gifted pianist who nowadays played only for her own amusement. Timmy had persuaded her to make a trial recording and as a result she had since made three albums for Hawkridge Media plus some spots in Tanya's albums. She and Fred now owned a nice house but she had refused all offers to go on the road in the entertainment world, preferring her job at the harbour.

When Timmy and Helene arrived on the Saturday following the discovery of Marylyn Barton's body in the churchyard, the others had all arrived.

As Gloria poured out their glasses of wine, Will described Kathryn Glover's arrival at the pub the night she'd found the body, what he'd done and what he knew of subsequent events, up to bringing old Mrs Barton back from the mortuary.

"When we were collecting old Mrs Barton, Clare told me that Marylyn had spent her last evening at the Half Moon Club," said Gloria.

The Body in the Churchyard

"Perhaps Chalky White knew her," said Will.

"That American girl who found the body was ever so nice," said Gloria. "Her students are studying what King Alfred did."

"Who's in charge of the case?" asked Timmy.

"Can't you guess?" grinned Will, "It's Inspector Clouseau."

"Then God help the Americans," said Helene.

"If you find that they need help, Fred, do all that you can and charge it to us."

"I can't see how we can come into it," said Fred, "but I'll help if they ask."

"What have you and Paula been doing?"

"I told you that the bank had asked us to investigate the theft of credit cards, didn't I?"

"Yes, have you got any leads?"

"Not yet, we're still thinking about how the latest variation is done?"

"What is the latest variation?" asked Helene.

"It started off with people stealing credit cards and using them to buy things," said Fred. "Then they moved on to using a stolen card to extract money from cash machines, for which the crook needed to know the PIN number. Now, it seems, money's being taken from people's accounts by means of cash machines even though they haven't lost their credit cards. Four months ago it was Oxford, two months ago it was Brighton and now it's Bournemouth's turn."

"They're certain that the money's being taken from cash machines and it's not an internet swindle?" asked Timmy.

"The bank assures us that the cash machine is central to the theft, the machine's record of transactions executed during a day and the balance of cash in the machine at the end of the day, confirm it."

"OK, so unless the crooks have got a private line into whoever makes and issues credit cards, the crooks have to have access to the credit card and the PIN number," said Timmy. "You should concentrate on working out how they get the PIN number."

"That is the problem," said Fred.

"The usual explanation is that it was seen by someone standing behind them. If I was doing it on a big scale I'd want something more reliable than that."

"Like what?" said his wife.

"Two ideas, Angel. One, the person behind photographs the person tapping in their PIN number or two, someone's found a way of putting in a dummy card that records what was on the magnetic strip of the immediately preceding card."

"That's a bit far fetched, isn't it?" said Helene.

"I would remind you that man has walked on the moon," said Timmy, magisterially.

"Come off it lover but it might suggest an answer to the last scam that Fred mentioned."

"What's that?"

"Where money is drawn from a cash machine even though the card holder hasn't lost the card," said Helene.

"And that is?"

"They get hold of the card and, using some sort of swiping device, copy the magnetic strip onto another card. If you think about it the PIN number is bound to be on the magnetic strip in some form, so bingo, they've got it all in one fell swoop."

"The banks swear blind that the PIN number isn't on the magnetic strip," said Fred.

"They would, wouldn't they? But think about it," said Helene. "Credit cards can be used all over the country and in many countries overseas. Is it likely that when you put in your card and type in your PIN number in a machine in, say, Timbuctoo, a message goes to a land station that transmits it to a satellite that sends it to another satellite that sends it to a land station in..."

"Alright, Angel, I think we get the message," said Timmy. "Assume that the PIN number's encoded on the magnetic tape in some form or other and the cash machine simply checks what you type-in against what's on the card."

"If that's correct it changes our approach, doesn't it?" said Fred.

"Yes, instead of looking for women with tiny TV cameras concealed in high hats you should be thinking of the most likely places where cards could be swiped and copied."

"I think that we should be looking for both," said Paula.

"I don't know what to think," said Gloria who had been listening while polishing the same glass, "you'll make me scared to use my credit card."

"That's the ticket," grinned Will. "Keep talking folk."

The Body in the Churchyard

"Where do you think would be the sort of place where credit cards could be copied?" said Fred, undeterred.

"It has to be a place where credit card transactions take place as a matter of course. I suppose that most people's ideas of the most dishonest professions isn't much help here?" smiled Helene.

"No, I don't think that house agents, lawyers and members of parliament have a big enough daily throughput of credit cards to make them candidates in this case," smiled Timmy. "Pity."

"All very amusing," said Fred, "but it doesn't get us far. What sort of place has a reasonable daily throughput per customer of sufficient value to justify credit card purchases?"

"Petrol stations," said Will.

"You may well be right Will," said Timmy. "In general terms the people with big cars that use a lot of fuel and therefore pay more each time they fill their vehicle up, have more money in the bank. Some don't but we're discussing the average man. Or woman," he hastened to add.

"How many garages are there in the Bournemouth area?" asked Paula who could see that she'd have to do most of the footwork, whatever that might be.

"God alone knows," said Timmy "But there's one other factor." He paused,

"Come on, lover, out with it," said Helene.

"Fred said something about some other places having this problem."

"Yes," said Fred, "the bank told me that four months ago it was Oxford and two months ago it was Brighton."

"Well then, did the mastermind have time to prepare his agent in Bournemouth in two months?" said Timmy, "Or are we dealing with someone who comes to town for a while and then moves on?"

"Like a circus," said Gloria.

"He could put his agents in place earlier than the two months," said Paula. "The two months is the pay-off time and why do they move on?"

"Can you find out how much money is being siphoned off, Fred, If it's tens of thousands a week it might be worth buying a business like a garage."

"It's interesting how we keep coming back to petrol stations, isn't it?" said Helene, "but they do fit the bill, a constant flow of people any of whom pay by credit card but we are ignoring a vital thing, having collected all this cash, how on earth do they get rid of it?"

"Hm," said Timmy, "I'd overlooked the money laundering angle."

"I think that's enough of that for tonight, don't you?" said Gloria. "Are you going to play for us, Angela?"

Fred and Angela and, separately, Paula, drove home thinking over what they had been discussing with Timmy and Helene.

Fred didn't think that the bank would tell him how much money was being stolen. Such information would be highly sensitive. Angela pointed out there would be lots of people who wouldn't realize that someone had milked their account. She developed this theme; she wondered how the crooks judged how much to steal from people's bank accounts. She then remarked that having what to all intents and purposes was a proper credit card and the correct PIN number, they could find out the balance in the target account from the machine and act accordingly. If they cleaned out some accounts early in their time at a given place there would be an outcry and they'd probably find it difficult to operate. Would they wait until the last week and empty all the target accounts? And how would the bank differentiate between genuine losers and account holders who overdrew?

As Fred remarked, the credit card thing seemed to have caught her attention, she was usually fairly silent on the ride home. He, himself, wasn't sure whether cash machines checked PIN numbers with some central giant computer or not. After all, places like big hotels and posh shops did run instant credit checks by passing the card through a machine. Could they make the same check from overseas?

Paula's thoughts were very much on the lines of Angela's with a bit of arithmetic thrown in. There is a limit to how much a customer is allowed to draw out of a cash machine at a time and, she thought, the number of withdrawals permitted per day. How many illegal transactions would have to take place to justify buying a garage? It would have to be a smallish garage because they couldn't risk too many attendants being in the know. She could imagine queues of crooks at every cash machine in Bournemouth frantically drawing money out to pay off the loan. She didn't think that buying a garage featured in the swindle. And so on.

Sundays at the Manor House were always the same. The family walked across the park to church where the General read the lesson, then they chatted with the vicar and his wife and friends and walked home to drinks and lunch. The nanny, Brigitte, usually met them outside the church with the children in the big pram and joined them for the walk home. Timmy was concerned for the children's safety and the Sergeant and Towers, the gamekeeper, were always in sight of them when they were out in the park. These days the Timmy Hawkridge's departed for Chelsea in mid-afternoon so that the children should be in bed at the right time. Before they left Timmy phoned Fred.

"Sorry to bother you on a Sunday, Fred, but it's about what we were speaking of last night. I expect that the bank's experts would point out flaws in a lot of what I said. I keep coming back to the problem of how they get rid of the cash that they steal and that brings me back to one of the questions that I asked you, how much money is being stolen each week?"

"It must be a lot or they wouldn't be employing us."

"Yes, but look at it this way. Say that there are five crooks in the gang. Each could get rid of, say, a thousand pounds a week without attracting attention, putting a few hundred in a bank or building society towards rainy days or to pay into a pension fund and spending the rest. That's five thousand a week and about forty five thousand in two months. That's enough to make a bank sit up, isn't it?"

"I suppose so, what's your point Tim?"

"Perhaps they don't have to find money to buy a business, perhaps it's all down to women with TV cameras in high hats sending pictures to a nearby van and pick-pockets stealing cards, after all."

"And they move on to the next town in case someone starts to wonder about their hats," laughed Fred.

"It could be," replied Timmy. "To cover all the angles I'll get my property people to make some enquiries about businesses like garages that have changed hands recently in the three towns."

"And we'll keep our eyes on the people who use cash machines."

On Monday morning Detective Inspector Stevens went over the evidence in the Barton murder case with WDC Thornton and summarized it as follows,

"So we've got an American professor who spent the evening with her and followed her out of the night club and an American lady professor who conveniently found the body. It sounds fishy to me."

"Why do you say she conveniently found the body? Surely it would have been better for the murderer if the body had never been found?" said Clare.

"Americans don't think like us, let's bring them in for questioning."

"But we have no grounds, Inspector, I've interviewed them and got their statements and there's no reason to suppose that they had anything to do with it. We should be looking for the man in the green Jaguar the professor says he saw her getting into."

"Rubbish. He made that up."

"And what about the man who came to her flat that evening and drove off in a temper, it sounds like the same man to me."

"That's just a red herring, it's these Americans that we've got to break down, I'm sure they're in it together, they both come from Harvard." He managed to make Harvard sound like a place of ill-repute.

"We haven't followed up on what we found in her apartment and I'd also like to see if she left anything with her Gran."

"What on earth for? The old woman identified the body and that's the end of it."

"If I'd been brought up by my Gran that's the place where I'd keep any very private things, where I thought that no-one would look," said Clare.

"You're saying that we should waste time searching the old woman's cottage?"

"Yes Inspector, unless you have any better ideas." Clare could have bitten off her tongue the moment the words came out.

"Yes, Constable, I certainly have got some better ideas. Get uniform to bring in those two professors for questioning in the matter of the murder of Mary Barton. Got that, well, it's an order, do it now. I want them here before twelve."

Thus it was that a police car attended at the West Esplanade Hotel and required Professor Kathryn Glover to come with them to the police station for questioning and another attended at Professor Stephen Hamsworth's hotel with the same request.

Kathryn arrived first and was taken to an interview room. Clare managed to convey by gesture and eyes raised to the ceiling that she had no part in this.

Detective Inspector Stevens took the chair opposite Kathryn.

"Professor Hamsworth's a friend of yours?"

"I know a Professor Hamsworth," said a surprised Kathryn.

"You arranged with this Professor Hamsworth that you'd find the body."

Kathryn was even more startled by this.

"What has Professor Hamsworth to do with this?"

"He was with the deceased that evening."

"You mean that he's here in England, in Bournemouth?" said Kathryn, incredulously.

"As well you know," said Inspector Stevens.

"I assure you that I had not the faintest idea that Professor Hamsworth is in England."

"A likely tale. You could be in it together, he killed her and you got rid of the body. How did you move it to Winterborne Stickland?"

Clare Thornton couldn't believe what she was hearing.

Kathryn decided that this nonsense had gone on long enough, she looked at Clare Thornton and said, "Is this interview being recorded?"

"Yes," said Clare.

"Then I wish to place on official record that I resent both the stupid questions and the aggressive attitude of this idiot of a policeman...."

Stevens started to splutter

".....furthermore, I demand here and now that the United States Embassy be informed that I have been brought here for questioning simply because I happened to find an unfortunate girl's body."

She looked directly at Clare. "I rely on you to do that."

"I'm in charge here. Constable Thornton will do no such thing. I have every right to have you in for questioning."

"I've already been interviewed by your officer and I've given you a statement. I have co-operated fully with the British police and I resent your insinuations that I am implicated in some way in the death of that girl. Now I'm leaving."

With which Kathryn stood up and walked to the door. Clare Thornton stepped to one side and allowed her to open the door and leave.

She was just going to pass through a set of double doors when they were swung open by a policeman and Stephen Hamsworth appeared. He smiled and said,

"Well, well, if it isn't Professor Kathryn Hawkins Glover, so they caught up with you at last. What have you done, robbed a bank? No that's a stupid thing to say, isn't it? Your family own banks, don't they?"

"Hello Stephen, still the life and soul of the party, I see. You won't be so cocky when that idiot police inspector is through with you."

The policemen tried to move him along and he struck their hands away saying,

"Leave me alone, we haven't seen each other in years and now we meet in a police station in Bournemouth England, of all places. How long are you here for? I say you are alone, aren't you?"

"No I've got six students with me and we're in Bournemouth for the rest of the week before moving on to Exeter."

"Let's get together for a drink. I know a nice night club and we can finish that dance you stood me up on at the graduation ball."

"I'd like that. Call me at the West Esplanade Hotel."

Clare had listened to this and was more than ever convinced that they hadn't met before – in Bournemouth, that is - and knew nothing of the murder.

Inspector Stevens appeared in the corridor and demanded to know what was going on, then realized that the man dressed the way Americans dress was probably his prime suspect and shouted,

"Keep them apart, I don't want them comparing notes." Where upon the policeman again grasped Stephen's arm and endeavoured to pull him past Kathryn. Stephen resisted and turned and asked her,

"What on earth's going on?"

"The idiot accused me of collaborating with you in the murder of that English girl."

"He's out of his tiny mind, this is the first time we've met for some years. I say, you're not married, are you?"

Kathryn barely heard the last few words and grinned inwardly; he hadn't changed.

As she walked out of the police station, Stephen was being taken to a seat across the table from Inspector Stevens. Stephen jumped straight in.

"What's this nonsense? Professor Glover has just told me that you accused her of collaborating with me in the murder of that

English girl. Until I came through that door I hadn't seen her in some years. You've got it all wrong."

"I ask the questions here," said Stevens.

"Not very intelligent ones by the sound of it," said Stephen.

"I'm the best judge of that."

"I've got nothing else to say. I was interviewed by this young lady," gesturing towards Clare, "and I told her all that I knew and confirmed it with a statement. She also spoke with one of my students."

"I don't think that your statement is satisfactory," said the Inspector.

"In what way factually or presentationally?"

"You're not telling the truth, you left the club with that girl."

"I didn't and if anyone says to the contrary, they're either mistaken or telling lies. Tell me, what did the doorman say? I spoke with him after the girl had left."

"You didn't say that in your statement," said the Inspector.

"I didn't know that it was important at the time. I told you that I saw her being driven off in a green Jaguar car and assumed that an efficient police force would follow it up. It didn't cross my mind that some idiot policeman would get the wrong end of the stick and as for embroiling Professor Glover in this business, it's beyond belief."

"I'd remind you that you're being questioned in connection with a serious crime."

"And I'd remind you that I know absolutely nothing about it." Stephen decided to stir it up a bit, "I believe that you've accused Professor Glover and myself because we're US citizens. It's a clear case of racial prejudice."

"What are you talking about, you can't have racial prejudice between British and Americans," said Stevens.

"Of course you can, you go to New York and insult a black police inspector the way you've insulted me and watch the roof fall in."

"I mean between white Americans and white Englishmen," said the Inspector, wondering how they had got onto this, "after all we're, er we're the same aren't we?"

"Then why do you keep bothering us, we're visitors to your country?"

Inspector Stevens realized that he was being sidetracked.

"You're being questioned about a capital crime. We take capital crime seriously in this country. I require you to provide me with your fingerprints and a sample of your DNA."

"And I refuse absolutely to provide them," said Stephen. "My only connection with the murdered girl is that I danced with her two, or was it three times, at the night club before she said that she had another appointment and walked out. You know the rest, God knows, I've told it often enough."

"I shall obtain an order requiring you to provide the samples requested and pending that, you will be detained in custody in case you leave the country."

As Clare said afterwards in the police canteen, she didn't know who was the more surprised at Clouseau's stupidity, her or the professor.

"You obnoxious little crumb," said Stephen when he'd recovered from the shock. "You know that I haven't got an attorney here in England and you're taking advantage of it. OK, I claim the right to make one phone call, or is that verboten in the Alice in Wonderland world you seem to live in?"

"Constable Thornton will arrange for you to make one phone call as long as it's within the British Isles." He stood up and said, "This interview is terminated," and walked out of the door.

Clare Thornton checked that the recorder was off and looked at Stephen,

"I'm sorry," she said.

"You can't help it, the guy's nuts. Don't the big-wigs know it? He wouldn't last a week in the States?"

"I'll take you to a phone, professor, if you're ready. Can I get the number for you?"

"Yes please, I want the US Embassy in Grosvenor Square and I want to speak with Charles Howard who's the US Treasury Agent. Got that, Charles Howard, he's a T man." He looked at her and said, "Your grandparents would know all about how the T men sorted out the Chicago gangsters."

"I thought that was G men," said Clare.

She asked someone to get the number and went to leave the room. Stephen said, "You can stay if you like." So she stayed. The phone rang and he picked it up. A voice said,

The Body in the Churchyard

"Is that you, Stephen, they told me that you're calling from Bournemouth police station, is it something to do with one of your students?"

"No Charles, it's me. Some idiot of an Inspector has detained me because a girl who I danced with in a night club was murdered later that night or next morning."

"Good Lord, is the Inspector called Clouseau?"

"No, Detective Inspector Stevens."

"That's the chap, he's mad as a hatter, my friends call him Clouseau."

"That doesn't help me. I'm concerned for my seven students. That reminds me, the girl's body was found in a deserted churchyard by another American professor who was looking for tombstones with her family name and this idiot of an inspector thinks that we're in it together."

"Did you dance with her as well?"

"Eh? Oh, I see what you mean, no she's a girl with a team of six from Harvard, name of Kathryn Hawkins Glover."

"Would that be the Boston Glovers?"

"The very same."

"Is she in the hoosegow with you?"

"I should be so lucky. No they let her go."

"Very wise of them. If they'd arrested her we'd have probably sent in the marines."

"What about me, doesn't Yale rate the marines?"

"No old man, only me and I won't be free until the end of the week. I'll send someone down and I'll also ask Tim Hawkridge to help. You know Timmy, he owns Hawkridge Media, got stations in the mid-west and a gorgeous French wife called Helene."

"I suppose that the least he can do is send in his wife with delicacies for the prisoner."

"Seriously though Stephen, I'll ask for their help, OK?"

"Yes and thanks. It's alright to bluff it out but one feels a bit lonely in these circumstances and hopes that Uncle Sam can help."

Charles Howard phoned Timmy Hawkridge at Canary Wharf and told him the story.

"You say that on the strength of having danced with the murdered girl during the evening Clouseau has detained your friend?"

"That about sums it up."

"I'll ask some questions and I'll also ask a private detective that I know to take a look at things. Leave it with us, Charles."

"Thanks Tim. How are Helene and the children?"

"Blooming, as always. Come down to the Manor House one week end."

"One day I'll take you up on that. How is Elizabeth?"

"Doctor Liz is spoken for and anyone who trespasses risks finishing up as part of the foundations of the next skyscraper her betrothed builds in the City."

"I'm sure that the City of London will survive without my holding it up but thanks for the warning, old boy."

Chapter Six

MIDWAY through the following morning a smartly dressed man presented himself to the desk sergeant at Bournemouth police station and asked to see the officer in charge.

"He's busy, Sir, perhaps I can help you, what's your problem?"

"I haven't got a problem, you have. My names William S. Stratton, I'm from the US Embassy in London and we want to know why a US citizen is being held by you."

The desk sergeant looked down the list that had been turned over to him when he came on duty that morning and, sure enough, there were the letters US against one of the names.

"If you'll wait a moment Sir," The sergeant dialed a number and spoke to someone. A young policewoman appeared and invited the American to follow her. Following her up the stairs Bill Stratton decided that, in the course of his adult years, he'd followed less attractive legs than she had. She tapped on a door, opened it and stood aside as he entered. A tall gray haired man sitting at a desk rose and extended his hand at the same time saying, "Don't go constable." He turned to his American visitor and said,

"Good morning, I'm Detective Superintendent Harding, how can I help you?"

The visitor gave Harding a card and said, "I'm William S Stratton from the US Embassy. I understand that you're holding a US citizen?"

"Holding is hardly the word. I understand that one of my officers invited him to have his finger-prints taken and to provide a DNA sample and he refused."

"Giving such samples is not compulsory under British law, is it?"

"It is in cases of serious crime."

"And Professor Hamsworth is suspected of committing a serious crime, is he. What is he supposed to have done?"

"It's in connection with the murder of a girl."

"And Professor Hamsworth was with the girl?"

Harding looked at Clare Thornton. She said,

"He danced with her a few times at a night club the night she was murdered."

"Did the murdered girl dance with anyone else at the night club?"

Clare felt a little lost. "I suppose so?"

"And did those other men who danced with her spend last night in prison?"

Harding decided that he'd better step in,

"I understand that there is the suspicion that he was acting in collusion with another American professor."

"Another one?" Stratton feigned surprise. "Are there two of them in this jail?"

"No, we let her go."

"Am I allowed to know the name of this second suspect and the part she, you did say she, didn't you, is supposed to have played in the murder?"

Harding mumbled, "She found the body."

"And her name?" Harding looked at Clare, who said,

"Professor Kathryn Glover of Harvard University," and added, "A very nice person."

"It's a good job you didn't put her in jail, you'd have had my ambassador and the US Marines here this morning instead of me. Let's get back to Professor Hamsworth, did he leave the night club with the girl?"

Again Harding looked at Clare,

"No, the evidence is that he didn't. He followed her out of the club and says that he saw her being driven away in a car. He then spoke with the doorman and left. He says that he walked back to his hotel, leaving his group of students in the club."

"It seems to me that Professor Hamsworth is in a position to claim substantial damages against the police for wrongful detention. Now I'd like to see him."

"Thornton, go and get the professor."

"No, I insist that I should see the conditions under which this innocent US citizen has spent the night."

"I can't allow that," said Harding.

Stratton leant across the desk and thrust his face close to Harding's,

"Look, buster, you're in big enough trouble already. My advice to you is, don't make it worse."

Harding said, "Constable, take Mr Stratton down to the cells and have the professor released immediately. He turned to Stratton and said, "I'm sorry about this."

Stratton ignored his outstretched hand and said, "Your apology will be noted in the official protest that we will be making."

Clare escorted the American down to the cells, explaining to those in charge that she was acting under Superintendent Harding's orders and that the American professor was to be released immediately.

The cell door was opened to reveal Stephen Hamsworth prone on the bunk. He raised himself and said to Bill Stratton, grinning, "What took you so long?"

"If you don't watch it I'll tell them to keep you. I'm Bill Stratton from the embassy. You're free to go," They shook hands.

"Who did you see?" asked Stephen.

"A Superintendent Harding."

"Oh, you didn't see the local Inspector Clouseau, the madman who put me in the hoosegow?" He gestured towards Clare, "this poor girl has to work for him."

"No, more's the pity, I'd have enjoyed that," said Stratton.

"You wouldn't, you know, because he's impervious to reason and common sense."

"He's known in Grosvenor Square. Charles Howard tells all his friends about Bournemouth's Clouseau and how he nearly arrested Tim Hawkridge because someone dumped a body in his park."

"Apparently you risk arrest if you tell the police anything in England," said Stephen.

"No, only if you tell Inspector Clouseau," said Bill. "The rest of them aren't bad."

Professor Hamsworth retrieved his modest possessions and they left the police station together. Stratten declined the offer of lunch, pleading urgent business in London and the professor walked back to his hotel with a story to tell his students.

He thought, now I've got an excuse to see Kathryn Glover. When he passed reception he collected his messages, one was from Kathryn Glover asking him to call her.

He called her and said how much easier it would be to talk over lunch and she said why don't you come over here at 12.00. He agreed on condition that he wouldn't be expected to dance with her. She rang off laughing.

Stephen had a hilarious half hour with his students and saw that they had plenty to do and then walked over to the West Esplanade

Hotel. He arrived at Kathryn's hotel with five minutes to spare but she was in the foyer and came forward to greet him. Somehow he had both her hands in his and they stood looking at each other and smiling. Then she suddenly realized what she was doing and took her hands away and said, "Lets go straight in."

Over lunch he told her all that had happened since they had met in the police station and then recapped on all that took place at the Half Moon night club and since. Kathryn told him how she had come upon the body in the churchyard and about her new found friends in the village of Tolbrite who had first told her about the mad Inspector Clouseau. They agreed that it might be fun to go there in Kathryn's rented car that evening.

As the result of certain telephone calls that Timmy had made, the Chief Constable of Dorset required Detective Superintendent Harding to explain why a US citizen, one Professor Stephen Hamsworth, had been detained in custody for the night.

Detective Superintendent Harding who had known nothing of the previous day's interviews until William S Stratton had arrived, was hopping mad but the station was understaffed and so, after a rather unsatisfactory meeting with Inspector Stevens, agreed to leave him on the case, subject to him reporting to Harding every day.

Sheila Dawson the young reporter for the Bournemouth Gazette called at the police station every day to collect news of the previous day and night's happenings. She made her usual morning call at the police station just after the two Americans had left. She was a nice girl with big eyes and best of all she listened, she didn't talk all the time like most modern girls; she let a man speak and so the desk sergeants tended to tell her things. She listened demurely as the desk sergeant lowered his head and voice and half covered his mouth with his hand as he told her how they had held an American professor in the cells all night in connection with the call-girl murder and a man from the US Embassy had leant on the governor and made them let him go. She thought that this was a story that might be picked up by the national dailies with headlines like US Professor held in Bournemouth Call Girl Murder Enquiry. Might make the Channel 4 news.

That afternoon Timmy asked Penny to get Fred on the phone. A minute or so later she buzzed him to say that Sherlock Holmes was on line two.

"Fred, its Tim. Have you had any luck with the bank about how much money is being stolen each week?"

"No, they seem to be very coy about it. Of course there are a lot of banks and I've been commissioned by one of them and they wouldn't wish it to be widely known that they're being ripped-off. There's no reason to suppose that one bank or building society has been singled out and I expect that they are all in the same boat. If one gave way and revealed the true extent of their losses I'm sure that they all would."

"Try again and also ask them if they will tell you the location of the branches or cash machines that have been hit hardest and, or, the people's addresses or districts that have been hardest hit," said Timmy.

"Why so?" asked Fred.

"People tend to use the cash machine or the garage that's most convenient to their homes so if we knew the district or districts that have been most affected you could concentrate on the local garages. Another thing, look for cash machines with a canopy a good few feet above them. The canopy's intended to keep the rain off and it would be a good place to put a tiny TV camera, wouldn't it?"

"I see what you mean. You're right, if the banks want to stop these people they've got to be more forthcoming. They can do the analysis themselves, they don't need to tell us people's names or details of their finances, simply which districts are being hit hardest. I'll get on to them."

"Another thing, Fred, Clouseau detained an American professor in connection with the Marylyn Barton murder. It sounds as if he's really gone over the edge on this one, all the professor did was dance with the girl at the Half Moon club on the night she was killed. Charles Howard got on to me and I said that I'd ask you to see if you can solve the murder mystery."

"Hold on Timmy, we may have a reasonable reputation but we can't compete with the police on a thing like murder. The trail will be ice cold by now."

"See if that rather nice WPC who took mother and old Mrs Barton to the mortuary will give you a run down on the evidence to date. Tell her that the Americans have sought your help, which is the truth except that they've done it through me."

"I'll talk it over with Paula and see what we can do."

He played the recording of Tim's telephone call to Paula and suggested that she try to contact Clare Thornton. Paula said that she'd get Will and Gloria to make the first move.

The fact that their professor was so deeply engaged in talking with the professor from Yale intrigued the young people from Harvard and several of them sought out the Yale undergraduates that afternoon. They had lots to chat about, it's not everyone's prof who gets detained by the police on suspicion of murder and then lunches with one's own prof as if they'd known each other all their lives.

That night's edition of the Bournemouth Gazette had Sheila Dawson's banner headline 'American professor questioned about Marylyn murder.' The fact that he had been released following intervention by the US Embassy was made much of, with the newspaper sitting on the fence between the 'does the US wield too much power' school and the 'did the police make another cock-up' school. Detective Inspector Stevens was mentioned as the arresting officer.

Kathryn had a copy of the paper when she collected Stephen from his hotel that evening. He sat beside her, reading the article as she drove out of town.

She said, "I see that the police declined to comment."

"The few facts that are mentioned are correct, the rest is embroidery. In the circumstances there's little else they could do. I wonder who leaked the story?"

"Do the British have a Freedom of Information Act?" asked Kathryn.

"I don't know but it looks like they don't need one," grinned Stephen. "Let's not let the murder thing spoil the evening."

But of course they couldn't escape it. Gloria recognized her as the professor who had found the body and put two and two together quite quickly that her companion was the professor the evening paper was on about.

Gloria suggested that the professor should introduce her friend to Bouchier red wine and he pronounced it excellent. That settled, with the two of them perched on bar stools awaiting their meal, she recited how Lady Hawkridge – she's ever so nice - had insisted on taking poor old Mrs Barton to the mortuary to identify her granddaughter's body.

Stephen said that he thought it was terrible, he had met the murdered girl and she seemed a very nice person.

"She was. We went to the village school together and I used to play with her when we were small. Her Dad wasn't a very nice man and her mother had a struggle, Lady Hawkridge says that Mary didn't have a chance in life, shame isn't it?"

"Life can be very unfair," said Kathryn, these days only too conscious of the privileges she had taken for granted in her youth.

"That's what Timmy said on Saturday," said Gloria. "Will, my husband, says that Timmy's asked our friend Fred to look into it. Fred's a private detective."

Stephen thought that a private detective wouldn't have much of a chance of solving the crime if the police with all their resources couldn't. Then he remembered Clouseau.

Will came into the bar from the back-room and was introduced and they chatted about Fred's wife, Angela, who made albums of piano music and the cases that they'd helped solve until the professors were told that their meal was awaiting them in the dining room.

Afterwards, Kathryn dropped Stephen back at his hotel. As he got out of the car he let his lips brush her cheek as he thanked her for a lovely, and instructive, evening.

She didn't say "No," when he said, "We must do this again."

The next evening Paula met Clare at the Tolbrite Arms and asked her to tell her what the police knew about the Marylyn Barton murder. Paula laid all the cards out on the table, she was working for Timmy Hawkridge who the US Embassy had asked to help. There was no question of seeking publicity. Anything that Southern Enquiries discovered would be handed to the police and the police would get the credit, if any.

Clare thought about it for some minutes and then said that she had no objection to reciting what she knew of the case.

Paula asked what were the minor objects that had been found near to the body.

"There were two fresh cigarette ends from which we've taken DNA, not the victim's, three matches of the sort that come from those small packs of book-matches they give you in restaurants and clubs with their name on it, and a mottled gray button that could have come from a man's suit."

"Did the paper match ends have any printing on them?" asked Paula, "they sometimes do."

"Yes but it was indistinct and they seemed to be older and unfortunately whoever lit the matches let them burn well down and we got ES CAFE, S CAFE and CAFE."

"As in JAKES CAFE or SADIES CAFÉ," said Paula.

"Yes, we've got experts looking at possible addresses."

"The trouble is," said Paula, "that in my experience these days, book-matches are probably given away more abroad than here and the café could be in many countries."

"True," said Clare, "but book matches are always associated with smoking and most café's discourage smoking."

"Not necessarily on the Continent. I may be doing them an injustice but what about Belgium, the Netherlands and France, perhaps it's JAQUES CAFE?"

"I know but I can't help you on that."

"What else do you have?" asked Paula.

"There's the evidence of Professor Hamsworth that he thinks that Marylyn was driven off in a green Jaguar car by a tall swarthy man," said Clare, "and the evidence of the porter at her apartments that a tall swarthy man called there sometime before ten o'clock that night and went away in a temper. He had a large signet ring. We also have finger-prints that aren't hers taken from her flat but in the circumstances they could be other mens."

"So you have something to go on," said Paula.

"Yes, not much but something, I agree."

Clare departed, promising to tell Paula should there be any further developments.

Paula buttonholed Gloria. "If you'd been brought up by your Gran, and you entertained men in your apartment, where would you leave any special things that you didn't want to risk other people seeing?"

"With my Gran," said Gloria. "I used to play with Mary when we were small and she was a secretive child; always hiding things. I wouldn't be surprised if she had things hidden in her room at Spring Cottage."

"Will you go and be nice to old Mrs Barton sometime tomorrow and ask her if Mary brought anything home and hid it away or asked her to look after?"

"Yes," said Gloria. "What sort of thing might we be looking for?"

"I haven't the slightest idea, it might be money or jewelry or, best of all, a diary, address book or letters."

The next morning Gloria walked along the village's one street and knocked on the door of Spring Cottage. Mrs Barton opened the door, she looked tired and years older than when she'd opened the door to Lady Hawkridge only a day or so ago.

"Hello Gloria."

"Hello, Mrs Barton, I've come to see that you're alright."

"I'm alright, dear. Everyone's been so kind, even that stuck-up Daisy Roberts came over yesterday to see if I wanted anything."

"That's alright then," said Gloria.

"Don't you worry about me, my dear, I've got my memories, you see."

"There is one thing, Mrs Barton, I remember how Mary used to hide things when she was small. Did she leave anything with you for safe keeping since she had a flat of her own?"

The old lady stopped smiling and she no longer looked Gloria in the eye. "She made me promise on God's honour that I wouldn't give it to no-one."

"Give what, Mrs Barton?"

"Her school book."

"She gave you her school book to keep, did she?"

"Yes, she said it was to keep her in her old age and that I mustn't give it to no one. Nor have I."

"Has anyone else asked you about her book?"

"No, only you."

"I don't want you to give me Mary's school book but seeing as how I was her school-friend, I wouldn't think she'd mind me having a little look at it, would you?"

"I don't know, Gloria. She said no one was to have it. She meant no one was to have what is writ in it, see?"

Gloria decided to change tack.

"Have you seen what is written in it, Mrs Barton?"

"When I knew that she'd never be coming here again I went into her room to the place she hid her special things. She didn't think that I knew where she hid things but she used the same place since she was about seven years old and she couldn't fool her old Gran, could she?"

Gloria agreed that she couldn't.

"So I brought them out here the next day. She'd kept every letter that her Ma had writ her and a few of mine, her school reports, some jewelry, an old tin she used to put her beads in, a savings book and her grey school book." The old woman went over to the dresser and pulled open a drawer, "There's the rest of them, I suppose that the money and things are mine now because there ain't anybody else, see?" She went on, "I ought to give them to a lawyer didn' I? Not the school book but the other stuff."

"Yes, Mrs Barton you should but I don't expect that it's more than you are allowed. Would you like my Will to ask the lawyer who looks after the estate's affairs to handle it for you?"

"Would it cost a lot?"

"I don't think so."

"I suppose it'd be alright then,"said the old woman.

"Will could take you in to the solicitor's offices in Dorchester. Do you have copies of Mary's death certificate?"

"No."

"Never mind, he'll know how to get them from the coroner's office. Shall I ask Will to make the arrangements?"

"I'd be ever so grateful."

"What about Mary's school-book?"

"Oh, I won't take that. I've put that and the tin in a safe place," she said with a cunning look.

And with that Gloria had to be content. She phoned Paula and told her that old Mrs Barton had a school-book that Mary had hidden at the cottage but that she hadn't been permitted to see it.

Chapter Seven

MR SWAIN, the Hawkridge family solicitor, could fit Mrs Barton in the following afternoon. Will saw that she had all the documents that she possessed concerning her granddaughter, put them in a big envelope and drove her to Dorchester. He waited while one of Mr Swain's younger colleagues dealt with the old lady, checked that they required no further information and drove her back to Tolbrite. He helped her out of the 4 x 4 and opened her front door and ushered her inside.

A scene of total chaos faced them. Every cupboard door was open and drawers pulled out and their contents tipped on the floor. Books had been taken from their shelves and dropped on the floor, cushions and mattresses were ripped open and even the oven door was open.

Mrs Barton shrieked and fainted. Will phoned Gloria and she hurried along, collecting her mother en route. They half carried the old woman to the 4 x 4 while Will called the police station at Bournemouth and asked for WDC Thornton. Fortunately Clare was there and Will explained what had happened at Spring Cottage. Clare said the usual things like 'don't touch anything' and 'she'd be right out'. In the event she was closely followed by the forensic team.

Gloria and Mrs Trowbridge took the shocked and weeping Mrs Barton to Will and Gloria's house. It annoyed Gloria that the house was still referred to in the village as the antique dealer's house, despite his being in a French prison for nearly three years with the prospect of further imprisonment when, or if, he returned to the UK where his brother and sister were also in jail for offences connected with the theft of antique furniture in France and England and the manufacture and sale of copies in the UK and France.

Gloria phoned Paula and told her the news. Paula drove out and instantly became Will's assistant looking after Mrs Barton's belongings and in particular, looking for a school book. Will phoned a friend of his and bought two new mattresses and some cushions for delivery the next day.

Alerted by the activity and the arrival of police cars, the sisters' Roberts came across to say that ever since her ladyship had asked them to keep an eye on old Mrs Barton they had been doing just that.

They had seen her drive off with young Will – a note of envy here – and had been surprised to see the workman arrive. He'd been dressed in blue overalls, he'd knocked on the front door and had then gone round the back. He'd re-appeared about fifteen minutes later and walked off down the road. Mary had insisted on going out and following him and had seen him get into a car and drive off. She'd thought it funny at the time that he hadn't had a van, all workmen have vans these days.

Pressed to identify the car, she'd confessed that to her cars broke down into two types, big –like daddies had been– and small and sometimes by colour. This one had been of biggish size and green, dark green.

Daisy said that they shouldn't rely on her sister, she had a poor sense of colour, remember that big American car who's owner had sat in the tea room for hours and Mary had insisted that the top was yellow and the bottom dark gray when it was plain to her that the top was charcoal and the bottom primrose. Or was it the other way round?

The forensic team had finished by nightfall and Paula found herself acting as Mrs Barton's companion while Will and Gloria were helping as usual at the Tolbrite Arms.

During the evening the old woman went through the various stages of disbelief that something like this could happen to her. An early enquiry of the police searchers had established that her savings, in a biscuit tin on the dresser, were still intact as were the things Marylyn had hidden away. Robbery hadn't been the motive. Paula told her that the robber had been after Mary's school-book. Had he got it?

The old woman looked cunning, "They won't find it, it's in my place now."

Paula said, "What would happen if something happened to you?"

The cunning look returned. "Then it wouldn't worry me, would it?"

"So you'd let Mary's killer get away with it?" countered Paula.

This gave the old woman cause for thought. Eventually she muttered, "I put it in a big envelope together with the beads tin and asked the Roberts sisters to look after it for me."

The following morning Will, Gloria and Paula attended upon the Cosy Tea Room. At the delicate tinkling of the door-bell the Roberts sisters thought that they had customers but were faced with a demand that they should surrender the package that old Mrs Barton had left with them. This they stoutly refused to do until Will did what he should have done at the outset and brought old Mrs Barton along to collect her package.

The school-book proved to be an exercise book with neatly ruled columns headed with date and amount and address. Not all the addresses were filled in. Will delved down into the envelope, took out the beads tin and shook it. Old Mrs Barton cackled, "I put that in as well. There bain't any beads in it, just a round metal thing with a hole through it and some powder, for her face, I expect." Will removed the lid with some difficulty and revealed the round thing and a small plastic satchet filled with white powder. He lifted the satchet and under it was a note on which was printed 'These fell out of his pocket. M.'

They took them back to the Estate Maintenance Depot and copied the book on the computer scanner. Then they phoned Clare Thornton and agreed that she would collect the items from Paula at the Southern Enquiries office at the radio station.

When she arrived she said that she'd have the drugs squad look at the powder in the sachet, she didn't know much about it but it looked like heroin to her. She and Paula then studied the book over a cup of coffee. She said,

"What was it the old woman said that Marylyn said, something about this keeping her in her old age? This is probably a record of her clients, or the clients she thought had money. From her remark, it sounds as if she planned to get more money for services rendered than perhaps her clients anticipated, a little extortion with a threat of blackmail. She may have started to ask for more or to drop hints about wanting more or what's in that sachet and that's what led to her murder."

"Seems like it, doesn't it?" said Paula. "Do the forensic people have any idea what was used to smother her?"

"They say that it was something like a traveling rug, a blue one, the sort of thing some people keep in their car."

"What do you think your inspector will do with this book?"

"Who can say?" said Clare, "if I say that it's important he's likely to dismiss it as irrelevant." She smiled ruefully. "The trouble is that if I say it's irrelevant he's likely to agree with me."

"Let's play it this way," said Paula. "Unless you tell me to back off, I'll take a look at each of the fifty or so people named in the school book, what they do for a living, where they live and in what style, what sort of car they drive and so on and tell you the results."

"Sounds OK to me, why don't you start with Mr Jackson, the newsagent who the porter recognized? He might be a bit more forthcoming with you than he would be with the police, you know, everything he says to us ends up in a statement but private detectives don't take statements, especially attractive ones like you"

They parted and later Paula set off to reconnoiter the Jackson offices and home.

She found that Mr Jackson owned six shops in Bournemouth and one in Poole. They had started out as newsagents, selling papers, periodicals, tobacco, cigarettes and sweets but now, in addition, sold foodstuffs, cosmetics, bottles of spirits, wine, beer and soft drinks and were open twenty-four hours a day. He operated from a unit on an industrial estate on the Christchurch side that consisted of warehousing and two offices, one of which was occupied by a middle-aged woman.

Paula went in to the outer office. The woman barely turned her head from her computer screen and said, "We're not recruiting."

"I've not come for a job," said Paula. "I'd like to see Mr Jackson please."

"He's busy. What do you want to see him about?"

"It's a personal matter."

"What sort of personal matter?"

"I'm afraid that's for his ears alone," said Paula, smiling sweetly.

"Oh no it's not," said the woman, "I'm his wife. Has he been up to his tricks again?"

"I don't know what you're talking about, Mrs Jackson, I can assure you that he hasn't been up to any tricks with me. I simply want to discuss something with him."

"Well, you can't. I run this business, not him and if you've got anything to discuss, you discuss it with me, understand?"

Paula decided to change tack.

"Tell me, Mrs Jackson, what sort of car do you drive?"

"It's none of your business but I've got a Ford Fiesta."

"And your husband?"

"He's got a Rover 75. What's this all about, we don't want to buy or rent any new cars. Just go away and leave us alone. Anyway, who are you?" A sudden thought , "Are you the police?"

"No, Mrs Jackson," said Paula as she left the office. "I'm not the police but I'm sure that they'll be along in a day or so."

She then embarked on the time-wasting task of driving to each of the other addresses in the school book and hanging about until she could see what sort of car the man of the house drove, the nature of his family life and where he worked.

It was late on the third day that she found a likely candidate. She'd already found two green Jaguars driven by short, fair skinned men. This one was taller, had dark hair and a Mediterranean look. An attractive female from the house collected two children from school in a Ford Galaxy. The house was substantial, set well back from the road in it's own grounds and approached by a short drive.

Paula was parked within sight of the house at seven the next morning. The green Jaguar came out of the gates at seven-thirty and Paula followed. The Jag joined a main road with Paula two cars behind. To Paula's surprise he seemed to be heading away from downtown Bournemouth. She hoped that he wasn't off on a long business trip. Soon she had the airport on her left. Her quarry passed the passenger entrance and entered the gate to the cargo area where he stopped, showed a pass and was waved through by the security guard who seemed to know him.

She stopped in a lay-by and watched the green car pull up outside what seemed to be one of a line of small warehouse units into which the car driver went. She photographed the place using her telescopic lens. About half an hour later the driver returned to the car and emerged from the cargo area gate where he turned away from Bournemouth and set off through the New Forest on the A31 to join the M27 Motorway at Cadnam. To Paula's relief he didn't transfer to the M3 but continued on the M27 and took the road to Southampton Airport where, again, he stopped at the entrance to the cargo area, showed a pass of some sort, had a word with the security guard and drove in. This time Paula couldn't see where he went and was unable to think of a plausible reason for seeking entry to the area.

She reasoned that the green Jaguar man must either be a regular customer of someone who imported goods by air freight or provided a service of some sort or perhaps he was himself an importer, with a unit at both airports, in which case he must operate on a reasonable scale. This last thought persuaded her that there was little point in waiting for him to come out –in one or two hours or more – and anyway she couldn't find a place to park her car, every road had double yellow lines. Her time would be better-spent back in the office finding out all that she could about him.

Paula was back in the Southern Enquiries office by early afternoon. From the Electoral Register she found that the rather nice house was occupied by a Mr George Swift and his wife Ellen. Further research revealed that in business he called himself Georgio Sabatini and was a wholesaler of flowers and continental garden supplies, a business that was centred on a shop in the better part of Bournemouth and a unit at the airport. But why had he been to both airports, surely he could have arranged to bring the flowers and things through the one place?

By dint of much hard work and seemingly innocent questioning, Paula found out that he had been born George Swift, the son of an English father and southern Italian mother from whom he had inherited his good looks and complexion, a quick mind and a host of Sicilian cousins. As a boy he had been closer to his mother than his schoolteacher father and had yearned to express his Italian-ness. He had worked in a flower business and had married the owner's daughter. The business had subsequently adopted an Italian name. It had worked, there is a touch of romance about flowers and a touch of romance about the Italians and the matrons of Bournemouth had subconsciously reacted to this and the business prospered.

In the back of Paula's mind was the question, why would a man like him, with an attractive wife and two small children, want to have an affair with Marylyn Barton? She assumed that it was for sex? In any case, was he the man who the American professor had seen? The best way would be to ask the professor to have a look at a photograph of the green Jag man.

She was in her car along the road from the Swift house with her telescopic lens fitted when the green Jaguar emerged the following morning. The morning was warm and, like Paula, he had the car windows down. She managed three shots while the Jaguar waited for a car to pass before driving out on to the highway and away. Back at

The Body in the Churchyard

the office she downloaded the shots into her computer. They weren't bad and the last one mirrored the situation in which the American professor had seen the green Jag, driving away. She studied the pictures; he did look swarthy and he did sit high in the car. Now to show the professor.

She tracked Stephen Hamsworth down that afternoon. He was sitting outside his hotel looking into space. She stopped beside him and gestured to a chair,

"May I?"

Stephen nodded and suppressed the remark about there being no charge that had leapt into his mind. He thought vaguely that he'd seen her before somewhere.

"I'm a private investigator," said Paula, giving him her card, "I've been retained to look into the murder of Marylyn Barton."

"Good Lord," said Stephen, "I thought that only happened on the movies."

"What?" said Paula.

"A private dick trying to beat the cops to the murderer," grinned Stephen and then warming to his theme, "and certainly good looking ones like you."

Paula grinned back. "It's not like that. Oh well, I suppose that it is in a way; the people who hired us don't think much of the police inspector who's in charge of the case."

"You mean Inspector Clouseau?" said Stephen.

"Ah, so you know," said Paula.

"I should, I'm his prime suspect, he put me in jail for the night."

"On what grounds?"

"Because I danced with her the night that she was killed or the night before the early morning she was killed," said Stephen.

"He's mad. Anyway, according to your evidence you saw her getting into what you think was a green Jaguar car driven by a swarthy man who sat high in the driving seat, correct?"

"That's what I told Inspector Clouseau," said Stephen with a big grin.

"Stop fooling please, this is serious. To the best of your knowledge that's what you saw?"

"Yes Ma'm."

"Did he look like this?" she spread the photographs out on the table.

Stephen picked one of them up and looked at it closely. He did the same with the other two. He said, "I think that the English expression is well-I'm-blowed."

"It might well be; my question is did he look like that?"

"It looks very much like the man looked that night."

"Thank you," said Paula.

"What does that mean, will you go to the police?"

"No and yes. No to Clouseau who would probably poh-poh the whole thing or go rushing in accusing the fellow and destroy any chance there might be of proving the case but yes, I will see that his assistant knows that you think that this is very much like the man looked that night."

"I couldn't have put it better myself."

"No, I don't think you could have, professor," said Paula pertly, getting up, "thanks for your help."

"Any time," said Stephen waving his hand and smiling at her. "We're going back to the States at the end of the week so you'd better make the most of it if you've got any more questions."

Paula left with a smile. He was a charmer.

Stephen went back to thinking of the various ways in which he could do the journey between New Haven, Conn. and Cambridge, Mass.

Paula was convinced that George Swift or Georgio Sabatini as he obviously liked to be called, was the man Stephen had seen that night. That was a long way from proving that he'd smothered the girl. If he had, it must have been because of something material, not passion, and that material reason might have to do with his business. Paula was suspicious of small importers, this one appeared to have an interest at two adjacent airports and what was in the small packet that Marylyn said would be her pension fund? She must discuss this with Clare Thornton.

Chapter Eight

GLORIA was pre-occupied. Her great aunt Maud had left her two houses in Bath that she had rented to students from Bath University. The present tenants were due to leave by the end of June. The actual date would depend upon the course of studies upon which they were engaged, some had already gone. Gloria's pre-occupation was on the matter of returning the student's deposits. This was her second year as a landlord. The first year she had given all eight of them, four from each house, their £300 back and then found that they had damaged the furniture, broken the plastic separators in the fridge, totally iced up the freezer, broken off the handle to the tumbler drier, broken plates and glasses and apparently carried off half the matching sets of cutlery. Much more damage than could be considered to be fair wear and tear. Most bedroom walls were daubed by a sort of blue plasticine used for putting posters and pictures on the walls and they had left the lavatory, bathroom and kitchen in a filthy state. Gloria's reaction, apart from horror at the amount of work required to restore the house to a live-in-able condition was to wonder what their homes were like? They were normal, well behaved, young people who clearly didn't know better.

The other thing was rubbish. It seemed that the students hadn't put any rubbish out for the dustmen or bottles and cans for the recycling people for weeks and had left it all for the landlord to get rid of. One set had piled a mountain of black sacks in the front garden while at the other house they were in the back yard and as for wine bottles and beer cans, no one who had today's students would believe the stories of how poor they are.

Last year it had taken many weekends and a weeks holiday to thoroughly clean the houses, emulsion the walls and touch up the paintwork and otherwise repair the damage. Gloria had spoken with Liz Mitchell who had been so helpful at the start when Gloria had suddenly found herself a property owner and Liz had told her that she shouldn't return any deposit until she'd been round each property with the last student to leave, checking the state of the house against the inventory attached to the tenancy agreement, reading the gas and electricity meters, collecting the door keys and locking the door as the last student left.

It was good advice but easier for Liz to do than for Gloria. Liz lived in Bath and could adjust her arrangements to suit any last minute change in student leaving arrangements. Many seemed to be vague right up to the last day. Then there were students from overseas who wanted to stay on through the summer. Liz had warned her about those as well.

This year Gloria was doing it properly, she'd sent each house a letter reminding them of the obligation – set out in the tenancy agreement – to leave the house in the same state as it was in when they had moved in a year ago, with more detailed advice on how this might be achieved and pointing out that the return of their deposit in full would depend on this. Liz had suggested that she should do this, remarking the fact already registered by those responsible for cleanliness and discipline in university halls of residence, that as the basis for entry to the university had been widened, the general intellectual and behavioral standard of the students had declined. Statistically almost inevitable, but sad.

Now she was at the crucial point, she must go to Bath tomorrow to see the last undergraduate out from each house. She knew and liked them both, a boy and a girl and she hoped fervently that the houses would be clean and undamaged and she'd be able to send them all their full deposit.

Will was keen to use the income from the houses in Bath to buy another house closer to Tolbrite, Poole preferably, to house students from Bournemouth University. There were two things in favour of this, the income from the Bath houses wouldn't be sufficient to service a mortgage on a house in Bath because property in Bath was ridiculously expensive but would be for a house in Poole. The other thing was the closeness to home. Indeed, they'd seriously discussed selling both the houses in Bath and buying more locally. As Will said, it made sense to do it while house prices in Bath were high.

In the back of Gloria's mind was what to do about her parents when they became too old to run the pub. Her parents didn't own it, only the goodwill, and they would wish to live locally. She was sure that the estate would find them something but perhaps she should be prepared.

All this was in her mind the next day as she drove up the A350 towards Bath. Will had been unable to take the day off to accompany her and she had no alternative to coming alone.

The Body in the Churchyard

She had arranged to deal with the house in Cynthia Road first and do the house in Faulkland Road after lunch. In each case she would walk round the house with the student, checking the contents and the state of the house against the inventory that the students had signed a year previously. She parked opposite the house, absently noticing that the man they paid to keep the gardens decent hadn't cut the front hedge recently.

Jason Smallwood, the student was waiting for her and was clearly keen to get it over with, his mother was coming at twelve to take him and his possessions away for good. He was pleased to tell her that he'd got a 2/1 in Business Studies and that the other three young men had also got 2/1's in their chosen courses.

Gloria had to admit that they had made an effort to clean the house. The three usually troublesome items, the electric cooker, the bathroom and toilets would need a good clean and there were blue tack marks on some bedroom walls but it wasn't bad at all. Indeed she thought, looking out of the window at the back garden, the boys had made more effort than had Mr Green, the gardener.

There were two broken plates and some missing items of cutlery. She sensed from their dusty state that most of the kitchen utensils that she had provided hadn't been used and pondered on the extra-ordinary diet that such young people thrived on. She expected that the girls in the house in Faulkland Road would have been more adventurous in their cooking.

They read the gas and electricity meters and entered the readings into the rent book. Gloria said that she would inform the suppliers and have the final bills sent to the responsible student. She checked that their addresses were correct in her copy of the rent book and told Jason that they would all get their deposit back in full. She had no doubt that she and Will would find walls to emulsion and paintwork to touch-up as well as a number of things that needed mending and cleaning when they pulled out the beds and drawers and so on but the boys had made an effort and what they found would be fair wear and tear.

Gloria had just checked that all the keys were there when Mrs Smallwood arrived. She was a friendly little person in a blue twin-set and navy trousers and obviously delighted with her son. Gloria marveled that such a small person should have such a tall, strapping son. She, and they, had the Bath problem, she was parked on double yellow lines outside the house, so they lost no time in packing Jason's bags and equipment in the car and off they went, to drive home to Hungerford.

Gloria had just made herself a cup of coffee when her phone went. It was her mother asking where she was and saying that the Bath police had been on the phone looking for her. It appeared that they'd like to see her in Faulkland Road. Ma would tell Will when he came in at lunchtime. She swallowed her coffee, decided to leave her car where it was rather than risk not finding a parking place in Faulkland Road and walked the few hundred yards to her other house.

That the police wished to see her was evident; there was a police-car squeezed into the last parking spot and a uniformed officer and a knot of onlookers outside her house. She found that a tearful Cicely Penrose, the student she had come to see-out, was one of the group. She was explaining, obviously for the n th time, that she was sure that she had locked the front door when she had just slipped out to go to the chemists in Moorland Road. She was sure that she *had* locked it, she always did.

It seems that she had returned to find a man busily changing the door lock. He had barred her entry claiming that the house was unoccupied and was now a squat for him and his partner and her child. A young woman with rings through her lip and ears had appeared behind him and screamed abuse at her. Cicely had rung the police.

The police had replied that, crazy though it seemed to any thinking person, under English law the squatters were within their rights in occupying unoccupied premises and in changing the locks. Cicely had pointed out that the house was not unoccupied, she was in residence and had just gone round to the shops. Furthermore she was sure that she had locked the front door. The person on the phone had still said that this was not a criminal act, to trespass on someone else's property was a civil offence. Cicely said that the trespassers must have forced an entry, shouldn't the police at least come and have a look, surely breaking and entering was a criminal offence, even in Bath. This had prompted a slight change in attitude, the voice had said that it is still most difficult to establish the law in such cases where squatters occupy unfurnished properties. Cicely pointed out that the property was both fully furnished and occupied and she had locked the door. The voice had said that it would ask one of the cars to come round and look.

A police car had arrived about fifteen minutes later and Cicely told her story once again, remarking that she was moving out that afternoon. The officers had inspected the door. It appeared that there were marks beside the Yale lock which could have been caused by it being forced but the occupants refused to obey the constable's request that they should open the door, instead, she of the pierced lip and ears appeared at the window and screamed that her son deserved to have a proper home like other kids and they wouldn't budge until the council gave her a house.

This was the situation when Gloria arrived. She remembered Helene's advice and made sure that her pocket recorder was switched on.

After establishing who she was, the officer said, "It appears that the door has been forced, that's breaking and entering. That, and then changing the lock, are criminal offences. However it's always difficult to remove mothers and children, makes the force look like bullies and since the young lady has said that she would be leaving the house this afternoon, couldn't the squatters be left in possession until the council could make other arrangements?"

Gloria said, "In no way, they're breaking the law and it's your duty to enforce it otherwise none of these people," she gestured towards the onlookers, "will be safe in their homes in future."

There were murmurs of assent from the crowd.

"I'll speak with the Inspector," said the constable and returned to the police car.

He came back and said, "The Inspector's coming."

It was twenty minutes before another blue and yellow arrived, bringing an Inspector and a woman police constable. The crowd grew and the Inspector instructed his underlings to keep the road clear.

Cicely and Gloria told their story again and Gloria voiced her strong objection to the suggestion that the first constable had made that the trespassers – the crooks – be left in possession until the local Council could provide suitable accommodation.

The Inspector said, "I understand your concern, Miss, but that might be the easiest solution and avoid us being seen manhandling a mother and child who, after all, are just seeking somewhere to shelter."

Gloria said, "I can't believe what I'm hearing. You're saying that in Bath, people can openly break the law and you, the police, will simply turn your backs on it?"

"Well, have you got a better idea," said the Inspector belligerently.

"Yes, I authorize you to force my door and remove those people in accordance with the law, they broke the lock to enter my property."

"Oh, I don't know about that, how do I know that you actually own the house?"

Gloria took the recorder from her pocket and waved it under the inspector's nose

"Look Inspector, as a matter of habit we carry these voice actuated recorders, see, it's recording what I'm saying now. Everything that you and your officers have said has been recorded." She made a great show of switching it off and went on, "Timmy Hawkridge who owns Hawkridge Radio is a great friend of mine and if you don't get those people out of there today, this recording will be played over all his stations to let the great British public hear how the Avon and Somerset police protect peoples property.

She switched the recorder on again and said,

"There are four police officers present, one of whom is a woman. You have two police cars and I, the owner of the house, have authorized you to break down the door to remove the man and woman who have blatantly committed a criminal act. What's stopping you, doesn't the law of the land apply in this part of Somerset? They say that an Englishman's home is his castle. After this, apparently, it isn't in Bath."

"I advise you to watch what you're saying," said the Inspector, "I could have you inside for saying that."

"For saying what? Inspector? I don't think you told me your name."

"For saying what you just said," said the Inspector.

"I don't think you told me your name," repeated Gloria.

"Inspector Molesworth and I've had about enough of this."

"I'm sorry, Inspector Molesworth," said Gloria. "What have you had enough of? Is it your house that's been broken into? Is it your furnished and occupied house that has been taken over by squatters? Tell us, what have you had enough of?"

"You and your arguing. This is a matter for the Bath Council's social services and as far as I'm concerned they can stay there until the Bath Council sorts it out."

"Have you informed Bath social services, Inspector Molesworth?"

"That's up to you. I intend to have nothing further to do with it," with which he got into his police car with his female assistant and drove off, followed by the other police car.

Gloria was thunderstruck, she hadn't bargained on the Inspector bailing out altogether.

"What shall I do," wailed Cicely, "all my money and credit cards are in there with my things and my dad's due at any minute to take me home."

"You heard what the police said. There's nothing that I can do at this minute, Cicely, you'd better let him take you home and I'll let you know when we've got rid of these people."

"What about my cheque book and credit cards?"

"Do you remember who they were with?"

"Yes but I don't know the numbers."

"Never mind, ring them all up, explain the circumstances and stop all further payments."

"Should I tell them about the Bath police refusing to do anything?"

"Certainly, in fact be sure to tell them that Bath police refused to take any action to arrest the crooks."

Cicely's parents duly arrived and heard the whole sad story. They drove off threatening blood and mayhem on the Bath police in general and on Inspector Molesworth in particular.

Gloria went back to the house in Cynthia Road and phoned Will. He told her to ring Helene. Helene asked her to dump the contents of her recorder on the line.

Thus it was that in it's major news spot at six p.m., the entire Hawkridge broadcasting network in the UK included an account of the occupation of an occupied, furnished house in Bath by breaking and entering. It opened with the simple statement,

It used to be said that an Englishman's home is his castle. No longer it seems if you live in Bath. This afternoon a young woman tenant left her house to pop round to the shops, locking the front door behind her. When she came back she found a man in process of

changing her front door lock. He said that he and his partner had taken it over as a 'squat' and refused to let her enter. She phoned the police and when they came they examined the now locked door and said that it appeared to have been forced. Meanwhile the owner of the house arrived. She happened to have a pocket recorder and this is what it recorded.

There followed the recording from Gloria's arrival and introducing herself to the first two police constables and ended with Inspector Molesworth saying that he intended to have nothing further to do with it and driving off. The announcer went on,

According to our legal experts the squatter's had committed at least two crimes, breaking and entering and illegal possession, both criminal acts for which they should have been instantly apprehended. Why weren't they? Is any citizen of Bath safe in their home any more?

Our experts are also of the view that the police might be liable for substantial damages should the intruders damage the property or the furnishings and chattels therein. And of course the Council taxpayers would have to foot the bill. We asked the Bath police to comment and they declined. We approached Bath and Northeast Somerset Council at four- thirty p.m. but they had gone home.

As Charles Smith, the Hawkridge Head of News, had anticipated, the national dailies got on to the story and set it up for their first editions. They asked for a quote from the Bath police and were told 'No comment.' Police headquarters at Portishead, which knew nothing about the incident, took a number of calls that evening from the press and asked the Bath station what was going on. Sensing that all-hell might break out in the morning, the inspector on duty told a patrol car to keep an eye on the house in Faulkland Road.

At five a.m. a police car turned into Faulkland Road from the top and met a blue van just pulling away from the house. There was no room to pass and the vehicles met bumper to bumper. In addition to the driver, the two squatters and the child were in the van. The policemen ordered them out of the van. The woman refused to get out and began shouting about the police ill-treating her child and continued to create a scene when on the pavement after the officers made her get out. The man and the male van driver got out sullenly. The police radioed for a WPC, two if possible, and the van driver took advantage of the diversion to run away down Faulkland Road, pursued by the second officer who was much fitter than he was and overtook him just round the corner. The officer handcuffed him and brought him back. The woman with the gold ring through her lip then attacked him, screaming that he was a dirty bastard deserting them and the child and trying to make her take the blame.

The officer who had not chased the man asked his colleague if he had heard the noise, he thought that the man had thrown something away when he ran.

By now there was an interested audience at bedroom windows and front doors and a few hardy neighbours were in the road in dressing gowns. One of the latter volunteered that he thought that the man had thrown something into the front garden of number two. The first police officer searched and found a pistol.

The man who had run immediately protested that the weapon wasn't his and they couldn't pin that one on him. The officers assured him cheerfully that he should have wiped off his fingerprints before he threw it away. The helpful neighbour in the dressing gown said that he had seen him throw it away and promptly had his name and address taken as a material witness. He retired to the entrance to his house and the officers could hear a woman telling him that he should have kept his mouth shut, now he'd have to go to court and give evidence and all that about our Edies's baby would probably come out, you couldn't trust lawyers these days.

The police officers had seen that there was luggage in the van and suspected that it might be stolen. Their concern was to keep the men and woman apart and in the road where anything they dropped would be instantly visible in the newly emerging day. The driver was protesting that this was nothing to do with him, he had simply been doing his friends a good turn and he didn't know that if any of the things they had put in his van were stolen. The woman screamed at him to shut-up and he retired to sit resignedly on the front garden wall of the nearest house, his handcuffed hands behind his back.

A second police car arrived with siren sounding and blue lights flashing. Two WPC's got out and had a word with their colleagues. They took charge of the screaming woman and the crying child, got them into their car and backed down the road before turning and driving away towards the center of Bath. A third police car, with three occupants, appeared shortly afterwards and the male squatter and the morose driver, he who had attempted to run away, were handed over for the new arrivals to take away One of the new arrivals stayed behind and after a brief talk with the first two policemen, which included all three of them peering into the back of the van, he backed the van down the road and turned towards the city center. The first officers on the scene went to the house that had been occupied and found the front door open. They made sure that it appeared safe and after a while a WPC arrived to guard the house until its owner could take responsibility for it.

Thus it was that, in Tolbrite, sometime after six that morning Will took a phone call for Gloria telling her that the squatters had left her house and would she please arrange to have it made safe. Will thanked the caller and said that they would be there within three hours. Will phoned the Sergeant and told him the news and asked him to tell the General that Will had gone to Bath to make the house secure while Gloria phoned Cicely and told her the news and that she should come to collect her belongings.

The Chief Constable heard about it on the morning news on Radio Bristol and stormed into his office demanding to know what it was all about. His staff officer placed before him the report from Bath that the squatters had thrown away a firearm as they attempted to make off with credit cards, a computer and other valuable equipment and were now in custody.

"There you are," said the CC, "there was no need for the radio people to make all that fuss last night, was there?"

"I understand that the prisoners said that it was hearing the broadcast that made them decide to do-a-runner Sir," said the staff officer. "It's a bad business about the gun, squatters with guns is a new one."

The CC snorted. He hoped that at least the bounders would give his force credit for catching them.

Will, with his tool-bag, and Gloria, relieved a grateful WPC before half past nine. The girl asked them to let police station know what was missing. The front door wasn't badly damaged and Will fitted a new Yale lock. The five-lever Chub lock had played no part in the affair and they agreed that the crooks hadn't got a key so it could remain and would be firmly locked when they left. The squatters hadn't done any physical damage – Will said that was only because they didn't have time – but clearly personal hygiene wasn't high on the woman's priority list.

Gloria bundled most of the mess in black sacks, washed up the dishes and floors, cleaned the bathroom and the WC, hoovered like mad and generally tidied up.

Cicely and her parents arrived before eleven. She went to her room and said that they had taken all the things that she had made ready to take home, her computer, monitor, scanner and printer, her Hi-fi and disks and a suitcase of clothes. She had lost her wallet containing her three credit cards and about twelve pounds. Will advised her to show no doubt about the amount to the police. "If you think it was twelve pounds, say you know it was twelve pounds because you counted it before you went to the chemist's shop yesterday morning, don't show any doubt because you can bet that the crooks will swear blind that the money is theirs." Cicely's mother thought that this made sense and her father made her write out a list of what was missing which he, personally, would take to the police station. His daughter suggested that he should go by bus, there is no parking at the police station and the adjacent NCP park is always full.

He returned two and a half hours later, worn out but triumphant, the police had found all of the missing articles in the van and had allowed him to bring away her wallet complete with the three credit cards and twelve pounds. The rest of the stolen items could be collected in a weeks time.

Gloria assured Cicely that they would all get their deposits back in full.

The Penrose's departed and Gloria and Will were not long behind them, after Gloria had made a point of telling the neighbours on each side that it was all over and the damage wasn't too bad. She phoned her friend Liz Mitchell and told her all about it.

"Was that you?" said Liz. "I heard it on the radio and thought that the voice putting the police in their place sounded familiar. I'm glad it turned out alright in the end, it could have been worse, couldn't it?"

Gloria agreed that, indeed, it could and she'd be in touch next week when she and Will would be up to ready the houses for next year's students.

The scene at Bath police station that morning was far from serene, both men and the woman with her child, had been put in cells pending questioning and the Council had been asked to send a social worker as a matter of urgency. No matter what the police did, the woman kept up a barrage of shouting, the tenor of which was that she knew her rights, squatting wasn't a crime, she hadn't had any breakfast, her baby needed a doctor, the policemen had molested her and she demanded to see a lawyer.

The van had proved to be stolen in Bristol the previous day and its driver would be charged with its theft. The police took his fingerprints and those of the man who had squatted. The gun proved to have a clear set of fingerprints of the van driver. . He was keeping very quiet.

To most of the officers the scene wasn't unusual except perhaps for the woman's persistent shouting. What was unusual and what created the most interest was the gun. No one had seen one like this before. It wasn't a revolver or an automatic; it would only take one bullet at a time, loaded into the breech. The other thing was that the barrel was plain, it wasn't rifled and was about 20mm calibre The resident fire-arms expert said that he hadn't seen a gun like that before but he understood from the Met that there was talk of a new supplier of shooters. Perhaps this was one, they should pass it to the Met. Pressed for an opinion he said that he didn't think that the barrel would be strong enough for a point four-five charge and perhaps the gun fired a smaller calibre round in a sabot. It wouldn't be very accurate beyond about fifteen feet, if that. The Inspector remarked that most shootings are at less than ten feet.

The gun was sent to London for examination by the experts who quickly found that it broke it down into four components, the barrel, the breech, the firing mechanism and the handle. The barrel and breech were made of steel and the firing mechanism and handle were of brass. In due course it came to the attention of the head of the anti-terrorist branch, Assistant Commissioner David Vowles who, at their weekly liaison meeting, showed it to his opposite number in the Ministry of Defence, Major General 'Tubby' Low, the Director of Military Security, who was accompanied by the head of the latter's special investigation unit, Captain Jackie Fraser. It was Jackie who remarked how ordinary the four pieces of metal looked when laid out on the Assistant Commissioner's desk and that "One wouldn't give them a second thought, would one?"

Vowles fastened on to this, "You mean that four people could board a plane, each carrying an innocent looking bit and put them together in the toilet to make a gun?"

The Body in the Churchyard

"Yes and not necessarily four people," said Jackie. "Look at the barrel, its threaded at one end where the breech screws on. There could be a separate cap screwed on, paint the whole white, stick a label on, fill it with aspirin and push in a cork. The passenger puts it in the tray with his keys and money as he goes through the metal detector and collects it when he's passed through and, bingo, the barrels' on board the plane."

"What about the other bits?" demanded Vowles.

"Oh, I suppose that I could dream up covers for those. For example, the firing mechanism could be part of a cigarette lighter. Remember, the security people are looking for things shaped like guns and daggers, not harmless looking small bits."

The Assistant Commissioner looked at Jackie, daughter of a colonel and niece of a general, slender, auburn haired with green eyes and a track record second to none in solving the MoD's security cases, be they attempted sabotage, detecting and catching spies, or simply the silly things or, sometimes the evil things, that sailors and soldiers did from time to time. Apart from liking her personally he knew that her training as a barrister had given her a razor sharp mind.

"I wonder how it came into the hands of that fellow in Bath?" said Tubby.

"It might sound silly but perhaps he stole it," said Vowles.

"It isn't likely that a member of Al-Qaeda would let someone steal his gun," said Tubby.

"Perhaps we're not reading the picture correctly," said Jackie. "Terrorism's the major threat and so we examine everything from that angle but perhaps the weapon's been made simple and easily broken down into pieces primarily for the purpose of smuggling it into Britain or any other country with strict gun laws."

"You mean a box of tubes screwed at the end comes in through Dover, a box of squareish bits comes through Harwich, a box labelled cigarette lighter mechanisms comes through Portsmouth and so on," said David Vowles, "I see what you mean. How about the charges?"

"I'll have to think about that. If the weapon was in my custody I'd have one of our research labs do tests with sabot mounted 7.5 and 9 mm rounds, starting with half charges and gradually increasing them, to see how it performed. Say that we find that it is strong enough to take ordinary 7.5mm or 9mm bullets, then all our supplier has to do is manufacture or import small brass cylinders with a 7.5mm or 9mm hole drilled in them and put bullets in them."

"Through Gatwick I presume in a box labeled rosaries," said her chief with a grin.

"If there's anything in this idea of yours, and I'm not saying that there is," said David Vowles, "I'd expect the boxes of bits to be imported by a firm that handles small quantities of metal objects and is run by only one or two people."

"What will you do next, David?" said Tubby.

"Try and find out where the chap in Bath got the gun from. I'll send Inspector Tom Burton down to question him." He looked at Tubby and grinned. "Since the Inspector is engaged to one of your sergeants it's as good as inviting you to collaborate with us, isn't it?" He turned to Jackie, grinned, and said, "Do you think your chief would let you help us on this one, if it's got a terrorist angle we're all in it together, aren't we?"

Jackie caught her general's little nod and said, "I think he might spare us for a little while, Commissioner."

Chapter Nine

KATHRYN decided that she should not allow the case of the murdered girl to distract her any longer from her self-imposed task, she must resume the search for her ancestors and where better to start than at that nice church at Tolbrite. Her students were now mixing freely with the team from Yale and could be relied on not to miss her in the afternoons.

She arrived in the village and drove straight to the church; she wouldn't let herself be distracted by the Roberts sisters. Perhaps she'd call in for a pot of tea later.

She walked round the well-kept churchyard. A whole area seemed to be devoted to Hawkridge graves. She remembered what the Roberts sisters had said about the squire owning the church and understood. After a while a pleasant faced woman approached her and said,

"I hope that you won't mind me asking but I noticed that you've been here for some time, are you looking for anything in particular?"

"Yes. I'm from the United States and I think that my ancestors came from Dorset."

"What was their name? By the way, I'm the vicar's wife, Mrs Ford."

"Hello Mrs Ford, I'm Professor Kathryn Glover from Harvard. The ancestor that I'm interested in is on my mother's side, called Pastor Francis Hawkins who arrived in New England in 1693. Some of the later records call him Friend Hawkins."

"There's no-one buried in the churchyard or in the neighbourhood of that name."

"I'd like to look at the old church registers of births and deaths if it's possible?"

"I'm afraid all of our old church records are in the diocesan library these days. They were getting damaged by people who had no feel for their value."

Mindful of the precautions that the Houghton Library at Harvard took to limit access to its rare books and manuscripts, Kathryn asked,

"How do I go about getting access to the diocesan library?"

"You'd better come and meet the vicar."

With which she turned on her heel and led the way to a gate in the churchyard wall that Kathryn hadn't noticed, that led directly into the vicarage garden, along a well-worn path and into a side door of the house, saying,

"You won't mind the mess, will you, it's always like this, what with Young Mother's meetings, Bible Study evenings, Parochial Church Council Meetings, the Scouts and so on."

As far as Kathryn could judge the place was spotless and uncluttered. If only her study at Harvard could be as uncluttered.

"Here we are," said her guide, opening a door and saying to the room's occupant, "I've brought you a visitor, dear, a Professor Glover from Harvard University." She turned to Kathryn and said, "Come on in and meet my husband, the Reverend Ford."

A tall man with a clerical collar and greying hair rose and looked at Kathryn over the top of his glasses. He extended his hand and said, "This is an unexpected pleasure, Harvard, eh, what brings you to these parts?"

Before Kathryn could speak Mrs Ford said,

"She's looking for her ancestors and wants to see the old registers in the diocesan library. I told her that you could arrange it for her."

"Thank you my dear." He turned back to Kathryn and beamed at her. "What is the family name that you're interested in, I don't think that you told me?"

Kathryn nearly pointed out that she hadn't had the chance, then she saw that his eyes were dancing and that he knew what she'd nearly said. She warmed to him and also to his wife who clearly protected him from what she considered to be unwelcome demands on his time.

"Hawkins, Pastor Francis Hawkins who emigrated to New England in 1693."

"There are no Hawkins' in the parish today and I don't recall any mention of that name in the records, but that doesn't mean that it's not there," said the vicar, "Have you looked elsewhere?"

"No" said Kathryn, "if you ignore my looking at tombstones in some villages near here."

"It was you who found that unfortunate girls body, wasn't it?" said Mrs Ford.

"Yes at that poor neglected church and that's why I decided to begin again with a nice, wholesome, lived in, church like yours."

"Thank you for the compliment," said the vicar. He turned to his wife, "Remind me to put that in my address next Sunday, my dear."

"We're fortunate to have a squire and his lady who support the church both spiritually and financially," said Mrs Ford. "The family has been here for centuries. The church is part of the estate and this living is within their gift."

Kathryn looked suitably puzzled.

"That means that the owner of the Manor House choses the vicar of this church," said the vicar, and added quickly, "and pays him his stipend, as well."

"We were lucky," said Mrs Ford. "Peter was a service chaplain and the General knew him and when the old vicar died he asked us if we'd like to come here."

"Yes," said the vicar, "we were very lucky to be chosen. Some of the earliest entries in this church's registers are to do with the Hawkridge family, marriages, baptisms and deaths."

"How far back do the records go?" asked Kathryn.

"To the late sixteenth century and, thanks to the interest shown by the family, they're practically complete, right up to the present time."

"And you don't recall a mention of Hawkins?"

"Afraid not but that doesn't mean that there's not one there, four hundred years is a lot of entries and some of the writing wasn't copper-plate in those days."

"Would the ancient registers from all the churches in Dorset be in the diocesan library?" asked Kathryn.

"Those that survived will be there or in a neighbouring diocese," adding quickly, "the diocese boundaries don't conform to the county boundaries added to which there have been some changes within the church over the centuries. We are in the Salisbury diocese; Bournemouth and the parishes to the east are in Winchester and a few places in the western part of the county are in the Exeter diocese, at the present time, that is." He thought for a moment and added, "Perhaps one or two are in Bristol."

"It would be a great convenience to historians like myself to have those sort of contemporary records all in the one place. How do I go about getting access to them? Would it be possible for you to give me a letter of introduction?"

"Willingly, but I warn you, it will take you a long time to peruse the frail and discoloured pages. How long are you here for?"

"I have to take my party of students to Exeter Cathedral in a weeks time to see the Exeter Book. It took a long time to arrange and we mustn't miss the date. We're researching the Anglo-Saxon Chronicles," said Kathryn. "From Exeter I plan to take them over the Somerset levels past where Alfred sheltered at Athelney, then to Edington where he defeated the Danes in one of the decisive battles that shaped English history, before we fly back to the States."

"A week isn't long," said Mrs Ford.

"No, it's not. In the back of my mind I've been toying with the notion of putting the kids on the plane but not going myself. It's some months before the next university session starts so there's no reason why I shouldn't stay in England a while longer."

"This is what I'll do," said the vicar. "I'll telephone the diocesan librarian, his name's Pudnor, and tell him that a professor from Harvard doing research would like to examine our old registers in the next day or so. You give me the number where I can contact you and I'll let you know what I've been able to arrange."

"That's most kind of you, I'll be always in your debt. I can't think of any other way to start my search."

"There must be some other contemporary papers," said Mrs Ford. "Have you tried the British Museum, or should it be the British Library these days? And some of the older families have written records that go back a good way."

"But seldom to 1693 my dear," said the vicar.

"The Hawkridge's do. Remember that professor who was researching the civil war, he spent so much time at the Manor House that Lady Hawkridge had to ask him to leave in the end."

Kathryn thanked the vicar and his wife for their help and drove back to her hotel feeling that at last she was making progress. The feeling persisted and when Stephen Hamsworth phoned and suggested that he should take her to dinner she said, "Yes."

Over dinner she described her day's activity and that she might stay-on in England for a week or so after her charges had gone home, depending on what the vicar might be able to arrange and what she might find in the documents in the church's custody. She remarked that she might have to visit the diocesan libraries in Winchester and Exeter as well as Salisbury and who knows where else.

After dinner they strolled hand in hand along the esplanade and when he delivered her back to her hotel, quite naturally he held her close and kissed her.

The Reverend Ford telephoned the next morning and told her that he had spoken with the curator of the Salisbury diocesan library, the Reverend Pudnor and he would be happy to have her visit his library. He gave her the library telephone number. Following her morning session with her students she told them that she was skipping lunch to drive to Salisbury to visit the cathedral library. This provoked a number of offers to accompany her which she declined with the argument that it was, perhaps, as well if she went alone to sound out the possibilities.

She took her hire-car and was soon passing through the New Forest to Ringwood and then Fordingbridge. The tallest cathedral spire in England was visible from afar, guiding her, as it had guided pilgrims over the centuries, to this, one of England's finest cathedral cities. She parked with some difficulty and entered the cathedral close with its rows of buildings for the choir-school, church offices, houses for diocesan officers and a museum to the county army regiment. She enquired the way from a hurrying cleric in flowing gown and after retracing some of her steps, presented herself at the dim portals of the library at two o'clock that same afternoon.

The Reverend Pudnor proved to be elderly, on the short side, of ample girth with a circle of gray hair around a bald pate and twinkling blue eyes, dressed in a black gown that had clearly seen better days. He welcomed her with becoming dignity, observing that it was a long time since his library had been honoured by a visitor from Pastor Harvard's school. He didn't say what was in his mind and that was that none of them had been as attractive as this one. How could he assist the professor?

Kathryn gave him a summary of her family history and that her interest was in tracing Pastor Francis or Friend Hawkins who had sailed to the American colonies with his wife and baby son in 1693.

"Interesting name that, Friend, used to be popular in Christian families and was taken up more and more by the non-conformists, the presbyterians and quakers and the like. That'd be about the time you're interested in, second half of the seventeenth century, after Oliver Cromwell's Commonwealth and the restoration of the monarchy. Remember, King James the second, who's adherence to the protestant faith was a bit suspect, was followed by Queen Mary who was openly a Roman Catholic. It could be that your ancestor wouldn't come near to a church that he'd consider was only one step removed from popery."

"Let's hope that his name wasn't that significant," ventured Kathryn. "Perhaps we could start at the registers for 1650 to 1700?"

"Tolbrite Church, you say?"

"Yes, " said Kathryn. "To start with."

The curator gave her an old-fashioned look. "You do appreciate that's about ten books each of about a couple of hundred pages, don't you and that each page will have about forty entries on it and has to be handled with kid-gloves?"

"Yes," said Kathryn. "If I don't get through them in the next five days I'll have to go away and return a week later, we've got a date to see the Exeter Book that we mustn't miss."

"That's an event you certainly shouldn't miss. I hope that your students recognize its place in history?"

"I can assure you that they do. They're nice young people. Now, when can I start on the first volume?"

"Not so fast, professor, if you please. Firstly, what evidence do you have that your ancestors came from Dorset?"

"Nothing concrete but there's a story that's been handed down from generation to generation that mother's people came from Dorset, England. Mummy was told it by her grandparents and I've grown up believing it."

"There's a lot to be said for folk-law," said the curator, "let's work out a plan. I suggest that first you look at the Tolbrite registers for 1685 to 1694 that I've had brought up."

"That sounds right," said Kathryn.

"If you don't find anything, what then?" asked the curator.

"I suppose that I'd like to look at the registers for the adjacent villages, they all seem to start with Winterborne."

"A lot of them do. OK I'll have my people bring them up. Is there anyone who might help you examine them? It's a big task that you've set yourself in a short timescale, seeing as how you've got to go home in time for the next university term."

"There is someone, a private enquiry agent who I know in Bournemouth. If I employed her would it be alright with you?"

"If you will vouch for her, I have no objection," said the curator, "but surely that would be quite expensive. I have no experience in such things but I gather that those people don't come cheaply. If you like I could ask one or two of the senior choristers if they would like to earn, what shall we say, ten pounds each, for an afternoons work looking through the manuscripts?"

"That would be splendid," said Kathryn, "I'd be most grateful if you could arrange something like that." She fished in her purse, "Here's a hundred pounds to start them off."

"You don't need to do that," said the Reverend Pudnor, taking the money and pleased that he'd have the money to pay as you go, so to speak.

He led Kathryn to a small room with a table and chair. On the table were a number of very old looking books with tooled leather covers.

"I got these ready for you," he said, "they're the Tolbrite registers for the years from 1685 to 1694. You mentioned a baby boy and in those days everyone had to be christened to avoid eternal damnation. So perhaps looking for a christening might be your best way."

"You are most kind," said Kathryn. "What time do you close?"

"The library is available only to visitors who make prior arrangements to call and they usually leave before six o'clock. Staying open after six raises all sorts of difficulties."

"I'll leave sometime before six. I've got to get back to my students in Bournemouth."

"That's settled then," he turned towards the door, "one final word, I suggest that you bring an overall in future, bibliography is dusty work at the best of times."

Kathryn settled down at the table and studied the small pile before her. She reasoned that the description 'baby son' would mean that he was less than a year old when he'd been taken to America and this probably meant that his parents had married in the two previous years, so she selected the book which covered the years from 1690 onwards.

She opened the book. The first pages were devoted to praise in religious terms for the king and church and the necessity to enter all births, marriages and deaths in the appropriate part of the register, that such entries must only be made by an ordained minister and correctly witnessed. She turned over the brittle pages, thinking that some charitable person should endow the library with the means to control the library storage areas with air conditioning to provide the best atmosphere to preserve such ancient documents. Was this yet another consequence of the English split between the church and state? Her mind switched to what a splendid job the anti-royalist and anti-Christ Soviet Authorities had done over the years in preserving their nation's royal and religious treasures. The same might be said for the French following their late eighteenth century revolution.

Kathryn brought her mind back to the matter in hand and turned over the pages. She ignored the pages dealing with deaths. That could come later. The births section had columns for date, Father and mother's names, the date of birth, child's sex, given names and Godparents. She turned to the section for marriages, columns for date of marriage, bridegroom's name and occupation, brides name and status (although it wasn't called that) and witnesses.

She was used to what she called old writing but it still took time to turn over the pages and decypher the faded writing. She was mildly surprised at the number of crossings-out and re-writing. At least once on every page of the births entries a name was crossed out and another substituted. She could imagine the scene where the mother or father insisted at the last moment on a name change. This led to speculation about the actual christening ceremony, if the priest has christened the child Gertrude at the font, could the parents change their minds at the registry and call her Gladys? If not, then why the crossings-out?

At half past five she had half-completed the first, and she thought, the most important, register without finding a single reference to the name, Hawkins. She had counted on finding something that might be followed up but there was nothing. The Reverend Pudnor was still in his room and she bade him goodnight and said that, with his permission, she'd be back the next afternoon.

Kathryn recovered her car and drove back to Bournemouth in good time for a shower before dinner with her students. She agreed that Salisbury was a place that they should visit and declined their offers to assist her in her research, preferring that they should spend their time exploring the city and it's cathedral and the old cathedral site set in an ancient hill fort at Old Sarum, a few miles north of the present city. This cathedral had been badly damaged in a storm a few days after its consecration and had been abandoned.

It was only after she had coffee and had decided to go to her room to call her mother and read a while that she saw the note in her pigeon-hole, 'What about dinner tonight?' She felt a trifle guilty. For not replying to his note, not for not having dinner with him, you understand, and then she felt righteous, he couldn't expect her to neglect her students, could he? And then she felt sorry.

She phoned her mother in Boston, Mass. to say that she had taken the first positive steps towards discovering who her ancestor was and from whence he came. She also mentioned, in passing as it were, that she hadn't found the note inviting her out to dinner until it was too late. She hadn't realized what she'd said until she heard her mother warning her to be careful and not to go out with strange men.

"Mummy, you've been telling me that since I was fourteen and now I'm twenty-eight. He's not a stranger, he's a professor from Yale and he was at Harvard in my time. Stop worrying, I'm a big girl now."

"I know you are baby but it worries us when you're so far away. You hear of such dreadful things happening over there."

"Don't be silly, Mother, it's just like America."

"Yes, darling, that's what worries me, if you see what I mean."

Kathryn gave up on that one and said,

"I'm searching through the old registers of Dorset churches that are kept in Salisbury cathedral, Mother, and it's going to take some time so I may stay here for another week or two. I'll complete the Anglo-Saxon Chronicles study as planned and see the students safely on the plane for Boston and then come right back here to Dorset to continue the search."

"What about the professor from Yale, is he staying on?"

"Mother, you are the limit. He hasn't the foggiest idea that I'm seriously thinking of staying on, I only decided to stay myself during dinner and anyway he's got a group of seven Yale English Lit. undergrads of his own to look after," and, she thought to herself, he probably can't afford to chop and change the way we spoilt Glovers can, poor dear.

"Well, you take care of yourself." Kathryn could almost hear her mother thinking and then it came. "I say, baby, would it help if I came over and looked at those old registers myself?"

From long experience Kathryn knew that a flat refusal would have her mother on the next flight to London, so she said, "When they bring them up from the vaults the registers are dirty Mother and the dust on them is probably hundreds of years old. I hesitate to say what old pollens and things it contains and knowing how many allergies you suffer from, it probably wouldn't be worthwhile, you wouldn't want to finish up in an English hospital, would you?"

"No I wouldn't. I'm sure that they've got some nice hospitals over there but I wouldn't want to try them especially with a whole new crop of allergies. Imagine trying to explain to an English doctor that the thing that's causing the trouble died three hundred years ago."

Kathryn felt herself being drawn into the red-herring debate that she herself had started. "They're probably used to dealing with old dust, Mother, but not," she hastened to add, "but not with the way it affects people from the States."

"Then I'd better not come, baby. You take care and let me know how you get on tomorrow, there's a dear. Goodnight dear."

When Kathryn entered the diocesan library the next afternoon there were already two serious looking schoolboys sitting at desks solemnly turning the pages of ancient registers. The Reverend Pudnor came forward to greet her and introduce Simon Biggs and Christopher Wade to her. Each was searching an earlier volume of the Tolbrite Church register for mention of Hawkins. The reverend followed her into the small room and watched as she donned an overall.

"That's better. Very becoming if I might say so," he paused. "I've been doing a little homework and I should warn you that you, we, are embarked on a formidable task."

"How formidable?" smiled Kathryn.

"Well, I hadn't really thought about it when we were chatting yesterday but last night I sat down with a map to prepare a list of the villages and towns who's registers we might wish to examine and discovered that there are more than three dozen within a six miles radius of Tolbrite. How many of these were there in the late seventeenth century and how many were big enough to have churches that kept registers, I don't know at the moment, my assistant is unearthing them for you at the present time." He edged a little closer, "I hope that you don't mind but I put him on the pay-roll as well."

"No, that's very sensible of you in the circumstances," said Kathryn.

The afternoon proved to be as fruitless as the previous day's, she and the two silent young men scanned page after page looking for the elusive name without success. Simon and Christopher left at five to resume their choir-school routine and prepare for evensong and Kathryn left at five-thirty, promising to be back on the morrow.

When she got back to her hotel, Stephen Hamsworth was sitting in the foyer. He rose to greet her, noticing her little frown of annoyance.

"It's alright, I won't bother you for more than a minute but since you didn't reply to yesterday's invitation to dinner and you're a well bred Boston girl, I assumed that it didn't get to you until it was too late, so I thought that I'd deliver tonight's invitation in person."

"I'm sorry," said Kathryn, "it's just that I've been looking at dusty old volumes all the afternoon and all the way back from Salisbury the only thing that I've been thinking of is relaxing in a nice long bath."

"I could volunteer to rub your back."

"I said relaxing."

"I get your point. What about dinner then, let's try somewhere else?"

"Very well, kind Sir, I'll be ready in the foyer at half past seven, and you shall take me to dinner and tell me how the Yale group's research on Thomas Hardy is progressing, how's that?"

"Excellent and you shall tell me about King Alfred and the Danes," said Stephen. "Now I can see where that idiot who said that scholarship is it's own reward, got his ideas from."

"My, my, is this an associate professor from Yale that I hear? Anyway, Stephen I'll be in the foyer at half past seven." With which she smiled sweetly, walked round him and made her way to the lift and a long relaxing bath.

After dressing she made her daily phone call to her mother.

"Hello Mother, just to tell you that I'm alright and that I've had no luck with the search for our ancestors so far. The curator tells me that there are nearly forty villages who's registers we've got to look at in this part of Dorset alone."

"I thought that there might be, baby, but in those days there weren't many people in the villages so the church registers can't be very big, can they?"

"No, I suppose you're right but we still have to look at them. They're very old and fragile," Kathryn remembered yesterday's call and added, "and the dust makes me sneeze."

"Don't the British have vacuum cleaners?"

"Yes, mother they have vacuum cleaners but these old registers are so brittle that they won't allow a vacuum cleaner near to them. Remember, they're over three hundred years old, older than the United States."

Kathryn could sense from her mother's slight hesitation that she was debating whether to advance the argument that the land mass that today comprises the United States is as old as time itself or to concede that, indeed, 1776 came after 1693. She was surprised, therefore when her mother said,

"And what about that professor from Yale, have you seen him since?"

"Yes mother and I'm having dinner with him tonight."

"Do I know his family?"

"I haven't the slightest idea, mother. I would guess not, his name's Stephen Hamsworth and he …he's in the English faculty." Kathryn had been about to say that Stephen had been the captain of the Harvard football side. That would have condemned him instantly to social outer darkness.

"Is that Stephen spelt with a ph or a v?"

"With a ph mother and stop meddling I'm only having dinner with the man, not marrying him."

As she uttered the words Kathryn realized that she had made an error.

"You're not thinking about marriage, baby, are you? Perhaps I'd better come over there after all."

"Don't be silly, mother, of course I'm not thinking of that. I just said it to show you how silly you are to worry about me having a meal with a fellow American professor. After all, he is a professor." She hoped that the word would conjure up the image of a stooped, grey haired, old man.

"They're often the worst," said her mother. "All that book-work leads to repression and sometimes it bursts out. There was a professor at Vassar when I was there who had a very roving eye." Her voice trailed away and Kathryn deduced that his attentions had not been entirely unwelcome, but you could never tell with her mother. Her voice resumed full strength and she said, with an air of finality, "That's how I know. You be careful, baby, they're still men."

Kathryn completed the call and went downstairs to meet Stephen.

Chapter Ten

THE following day the entire Harvard party went to Salisbury and spent an interesting morning exploring the cathedral and its close and the city. The museum contained some references to the Anglo-Saxons and to Wessex and the undergraduates voted it one of the best visits that they had made. After lunch Kathryn had excused herself, explaining, not for the first time, that she was searching the church registers for her family ancestors while the young people departed in their mini-bus for Old Sarem and back to Bournemouth via Avebury and Stonehenge.

The search of the registers continued that afternoon with the same disheartening result. Kathryn and the boys were now searching the 1685 to 1694 period in the registers of nearby parishes having drawn a blank in the Tolbrite volumes. By the end of the afternoon they had completed the registers that covered Almer, Winterborne Zelston, Whitefield, Bloxworth, East Bloxworth, Morden, West Morden and East Morden. The Reverend Pudnor cheered them up by remarking, in passing, that they wouldn't all be as easy as that.

Stephen dined with Kathryn and her group at the West Esplanade Hotel that night and afterwards they joined the many other couples strolling along the brightly lit esplanade. And perhaps her mother wouldn't have approved of the way she lingered in his strong arms when they said goodnight.

The next afternoon she was again in the diocesan library. She remembered to give the Reverend Pudnor a further two hundred pounds to tide him over, explaining that she was taking her group to Exeter the day after tomorrow and then by easy stages to Heathrow where she would see the students off on their way back to Boston before herself returning to Salisbury to continue the search. That afternoon she and the boys concluded that it appeared that no-one called Hawkins had been born, married or died between the years of 1685 and 1694 in the villages of Bere Regis, Tolpuddle, Athelhampton, Burlston, Puddletown, Milborne St Andrew and Winterborne Kingston.

Kathryn was beginning to think that her mother's mother's mother etc had got it wrong and that the Hawkins clan must have come from somewhere other than Dorset.

That evening she dined with the Yale group and on delivery back to the West Esplanade Hotel was kissed even more firmly and often She felt guilty because she enjoyed the awareness of his body and desire.

The last afternoon was the same. She and the boys did the registers that covered Winterborne Whitechurch, Lower Whatcombe, Higher Whatcombe, Milton Abbas, Binghams Melcombe, Winterborne Clenston and Winterborne Stickland where, Kathryn didn't need reminding, she'd found the girl's body. There was no recorded event that featured the Hawkins name. Kathryn departed after asking the Reverend Pudnor and the boys to continue looking and she'd settle up with them when she returned in three or four days time.

That night would be the last night in Bournemouth for both teams. Kathryn's group would leave early in their mini-bus for their afternoon rendezvous with the Exeter Book in Exeter Cathedral while Stephen's Yale group would make a more leisurely way to Heathrow for their return flight to New York. Reflecting the friendships made during the past week the members of the two teams mixed and there were a number of separate groups at dinner. Stephen made sure that he was in a party of two, himself and Kathryn. Before they said goodnight he said that he had to accompany his group back to the States but she shouldn't be surprised if he reappeared before she herself left the UK. She told him not to be silly and to save his money. He said that she was forgetting that they were both material witnesses in a case of murder right here in little old Dorset, England.

The journey to Exeter took longer than she had planned because the road was winding and single carriage for most of the way. At Bridport she took advice and followed the signs for Honiton where she joined the A303/A30 and made much better time on the final leg into Exeter. They checked into their hotel, had lunch and then repaired to the Cathedral from whence they were taken in a suitably solemn mood to see the rare manuscript.

They had read about it but seeing this manuscript, willed to the cathedral by Exeter's first bishop, Leofric in 1072, impressed the young people more than they had thought possible. They noted the tales and the disparate contents and, like most people, they were intrigued by the ninety riddles, some of which, they were told also feature in Scandanavian or Germanic documents of that time.

The Body in the Churchyard

They explored the ancient city that evening and left the following morning driving north on the M5 Motorway as far as Taunton where, after a couple of false turnings they joined the A361 for Glastonbury and Wells. The road crossed the motorway and within a few miles they were at Athelney, now vastly different (and drier) than when King Arthur sheltered there in 878. Kathryn reflected that at least the kids can say that they've been there and will know at first hand how low-lying and flat this part of the country is, criss-crossed by rivers and drainage ditches.

The church tower on top of Glastonbury Tor was visible from miles away. Glastonbury is famous for its ruined Abbey, destroyed by King Henry the Eighth when he broke with the church of Rome and declared himself head of the Catholic church in England. The monks were loyal to the Pope in Rome and so Henry destroyed their monasteries and abbeys, seized their wealth and dispersed the monks. The Harvard group walked through the ruined abbey and saw the thorn tree reputed to have grown from the staff that Joseph pushed into the ground at that spot. The tree blooms at Christmas and a branch is presented to the monarch. They were saddened at the excessive commercialization of this once charming place.

They drove on to the small cathedral town of Wells, nestling in the shadow of the Mendip Hills. This was different, the city fathers had succeeded in preserving most that is good. They had a late lunch and set out to explore this gem. Naturally they started with the cathedral, set in it's close with the choir-school and priests' houses nearby. They watched the ancient clock strike and admired the ornate stone carvings of the west front. Like most visitors they were surprised at how small the actual church was, hidden behind this imposing entrance. They admired the cloisters. Afterwards they went to the moat surrounding the Bishop's palace and saw, among other things, the bell with a rope attached to its clapper that hangs from the gatekeepers house and which the swans that live on the moat pull to ring the bell when they're hungry. They wondered if future generations of swans would learn the trick. Wells isn't all history, in the Market Square they saw the brass strip let into the pavement to show the distance that one of it's citizens, Mary Bignall Rand, had jumped to win an Olympic gold medal. Like many before them they marveled at its length. Further on they saw the stream that originates in springs in the Mendips and runs perpetually along the city's principal street.

Being so near, the young people pressed that they should visit Bath, arguing that although it didn't seem to have an Anglo-Saxon connection, the Romans were there. So Kathryn drove up the hill and over the Mendip Hills to Bath. They entered the city on the A367 and caught glimpses of the Georgian architecture as the road descended into the Avon valley. They followed the signs and passed quite near to the Abbey and, they gathered, the famous Roman Baths and Pump Room but they didn't spot them and that was as far as they got; they couldn't stop because there were always cars and buses impatiently hurrying them along and there didn't seem to be any parking places so, by unanimous consent, Kathryn went past the police station, the bus station and the railway station and back across the river to join the A4 to leave the city. After a quarter of an hour of vehicles shuffling forward a few feet at a time, she finally reached one of bath's landmarks, the Holbourne Museum, where one of the students pointed out that if they got into the right hand lane of traffic, they could get out of this slowly moving traffic jam and take the A36 which branched off to the south-east and would take them towards Edington and they would be back on Plan A. Kathryn did this with relief. That was Bath, that was, throttled by traffic.

Edington is a few miles east of the western escarpment of Salisbury Plain, close to the giant figure of a horse carved, it is said, in the middle ages, by removing the top-soil to reveal the chalk beneath and known as the Westbury White Horse, visible tens of miles away in West Wiltshire and Somerset.

They drove up the B3098 that climbs obliquely across the escarpment to make it's slope more manageable for people and vehicles and stopped close to the iron-age earthworks where the Danes had camped awaiting the arrival of Alfred's West Saxon army.

When she lectured on the subject, her theme always was that the people who led medieval armies were as intelligent as we are today but they had to make use of the materials and systems that were available. The fastest they could travel was on horse-back, the farthest an individual could strike was by bow and arrow and throwing spear and intelligence came by word of mouth or parchment on horse-back or on foot

Kathryn had done her homework on Alfred. When he had emerged from Athelney he had gathered an army that eventually numbered close to three thousand men. They hadn't all come at once but he had spent some forty days training a nucleus of them who would then train the others. Most of them would have some skill in the use of the weapons of the time, clubs, spears, axes and the bow and arrow and short sword; what Alfred had to do was to turn them into a disciplined force and he did this by making them exercise as units in the use of their shields, the message being that lines of men with overlapping shields can withstand the attacks of an enemy, be he on foot or mounted.

It also seemed that Alfred was aware of the Dane's movements; he hadn't followed the track towards Bristol and Bath but had struck out to the east, across the Somerset levels to pass south of the Polden Hills and the Mendip Hills along the route of the River Frome and on to Westbury, following the route that, centuries later, the Great Western Railway was to select for it's high-speed line from London to Devon and Cornwall.

Kathryn explained this as they sat in the mini-bus. One of the students said,

"If Alfred was stuck on an island in a vast lake, how did he know they were coming?"

"For years there had been skirmishes and inconclusive battles with Danish invaders," said Kathryn. "Alfred became king of the West Saxons in 871 when his brother died and there followed a period of peace but in 878 the Danes made a surprise advance westward. Alfred must have had warning of this because he withdrew to the island of Athelney while his followers harassed the invaders in a sort of guerilla warfare."

"Yes but how did he know where they were?" persisted the girl.

"Leaving aside the matter of Alfred and the Danes for the moment, that's always interested me," said Kathryn. "How did opposing armies find each other to do battle in those days? The countryside was much more wooded than is the case today, there was no aerial reconnaissance or radio and messages had to be carried by hand or mouth. Of course if one of the armies camped in one place for several weeks or months, the word would get around but if they were on the march the timescale is more difficult to comprehend."

"How so?" asked one of the boys, who, at an early age, had realized that as long as the teacher is explaining something, he or she isn't asking him and the rest of the class awkward questions.

She said,

"Take the case of Alfred in hiding on his island. He could hardly have had an army of informers on a radius of a hundred miles from his refuge, so, in the first place, his followers probably learnt of the coming of the Danes from travellers who passed by."

"The travellers would walk faster than an army loaded down with all the paraphernalia of war," said another girl.

"On the other hand," went on Kathryn, "it was probably on the basis of intelligence provided by travellers going the other way, that the Danish army was advancing westward seeking Alfred's army. In all probability they knew that he was somewhere in the Somerset wetlands."

The first girl said, "Sieges I can understand, one side isn't moving and the other side knows where they are, like in the Crusades. It's a wonder that there were any field battles at all. Take Gettysburg. My parents took me to the Gettysburg memorial site when I was small. I have never forgotten what the guide said, or what I think he said, that the battle only happened because scouts from the Union army, moving south down one valley went into a forest and chanced upon some scouts from the Confederate army moving north in an adjacent valley. It seemed to me that if those scouts hadn't met, the armies would have passed each other and the battle wouldn't have taken place. Well, not at Gettysburg, anyway."

"We could all have finished up as Confeds," said one of the boys.

"I thought that you were," grinned a girl, who went on, "So King Alfred chose the right way and beat the Danes."

"The evidence is that the Danes stopped at a place called Chippenham, about twelve miles East of Bath," said Kathryn. "Undoubtedly they had sent out scouts trying to find where Alfred was and, of course, they were being harassed by the Saxons."

"So Alfred knew where to aim for because the Danes had stopped in one place," said the girl who had mentioned the Crusades.

"Yes," said Kathryn, "Alfred got the word, perhaps he heard that they were about to move southwest, appreciated that the threat wouldn't go away and decided that the Danes had got to be stopped. He emerged and rallied men to his army. How long would that take?

The Body in the Churchyard

He'd need at least a hundred initially to attract others to his band. He allowed forty days for training and then he set out marching almost directly towards where the Danes were waiting. For the most part both armies would have been living off the land, which means raiding every smallholding and stealing their supplies of grain and slaughtering their livestock. Alfred's men, men of the land all, would have tired of that."

"They could still have missed each other," ventured one of the boys.

"Not really," said Kathryn. "The supposition is that the Danes knew of Alfred's advance and stopped on the high ground at Edington to await the West Saxon's arrival."

"And Alfred beat them" said a girl.

"Yes," said Kathryn, "by using methods used by the Romans centuries before. Perhaps he'd read about them in Rome. You've seen how steep the hill is; his soldiers advanced up it in lines with locked shields and absorbed everything that the Danes above them could throw at them. They drove the Danes back and eventually battle was joined here, on the plain above and Alfred's army won. I'm surprised that the English make so little of his achievement. If you ask English school children what took place in 1066 they will all say the battle of Hastings, which was when the Normans landed and defeated the English King Harold, but if you ask those same youngsters what happened in 878 no one will know, yet that victory, that stopped the Danes from conquering Wessex and then Mercia and then the rest of England, had as profound importance on the development of England as did the Norman invasion, two hundred years later." She added, "It was as a result of his victories that Alfred became king of all England."

"And they called him Alfred the Great," said a boy.

"The irony of it is," said Kathryn, "most of the 1066 Norman army were the descendants of Danes who had settled in northern France round about Alfred's time. This is all good background stuff but remember, our prime interest is in Alfred the scholar and the Anglo Saxon Chronicles that started to be circulated during his reign."

Her students wondered why, if it was as important as the prof. said, the British didn't preserve the battlefield like Gettysburg?

They spent the night at an airport hotel and Kathryn saw them safely into the departure lounge. She waited until the Boston flight had departed. There were no last minute panics and she took the hotel bus, collected the mini-bus and drove back to Bournemouth where she handed-in the mini-bus, collected her hire-car and drove to Salisbury and checked into a welcoming-looking hotel that had parking.

In London that morning Captain Jackie Fraser went to London District headquarters where her sergeants had an office and briefed them about the gun and their likely trip to Bath. Sandra Roberts and Kim Bourne had been with her for over two years and all three of them enjoyed working together. They were about Jackie's age and service wrongdoers were often surprised that such attractive girls could be so strong. As in all cases that involved her fiancée, Inspector Tom Burton, Kim would accompany Jackie while Sandra held the fort in London and carried on with the cases in hand. Inspector Burton, his Sergeant , Jackie and Kim traveled down to Bath by train and walked the few yards to the police station in Manvers Street. Jackie and Kim were not in uniform but nevertheless attracted some attention from the police officers.

The van driver was brought to an interview room. Inspector Burton introduced the girls as from the Special Investigation Branch omitting to say 'of the army'. The prisoner demanded that 'his brief' be present. The legal aid lawyer had been warned of their coming and arrived a few minutes later. He raised his eyebrows at the girls sitting behind Tom Burton and his sergeant but made no comment. Tom Burton opened,

"I understand that so far you have refused to co-operate with the authorities. You have been identified as Sidney Gilbert Jones of no fixed abode and you have six previous convictions for theft and stealing vehicles. We're not here to discuss the charges that have arisen as the result of what took place in Faulkland Road, Bath, earlier in the present week, we're here to discuss one thing and one thing alone, Mr Jones, and that is, 'where did you get the gun that you attempted to throw away that night?"

The prisoner studied his hands and said nothing.

Tom went on. "I think that even now you don't recognize the seriousness of your situation, Mr Jones. Hitherto you've been put on probation or given short terms of imprisonment for what you doubtless regard as trivial offences. So be it but this week you moved into the big league, didn't you?"

Still the prisoner studied his hands.

"Carrying a weapon in the execution of a crime and threatening an officer in the discharge of his duty are serious offences and you could go down for a long stretch this time, especially for threatening an officer with a firearm."

"I didn't threaten no officer, I was trying to throw the bleeding thing away," he burst out and turned to his lawyer. "They're trying to stitch me up."

"Then you're best course is to answer the questions, Mr Jones. And see that the authorities know the truth."

"They ain't asked me no questions," said Mr Jones.

"Well, I will now," said Tom. "Where did you get the gun from?"

The prisoner made a show of closing his lips and looked at his hands.

"Answer the question, please, Mr Jones, you don't want to be sent down to save someone else's bacon, do you? Where did you get the gun from?"

The prisoner roused himself and turned to the lawyer. "I wish I'd never seen the bleeding thing, it weren't no good, wouldn't take real bullets, see. A pal of mine lent me a bullet and it fell right through."

Jackie was thinking with horror that nowadays people like this were roaming the streets of Britain with real firearms.

Tom persisted, "Where did you get the gun. Mr Jones?"

Jones turned to the lawyer. "These silly buggers don't understand that I'm more scared o' the people I nicked the bleedin' gun from than I am of going down for a stretch."

"But they're going to find out anyway, aren't they, Mr Jones?" said Tom. "When this comes to court everybody will know that you had a funny gun, won't they?"

The prisoner closed his lips tightly and looked down at his hands.

There was a lengthening silence.

Jackie leant forward and said, "So you see, Mr Jones, it's up to you, if you tell us where the gun came from we won't need to describe the gun in detail in court. I don't know, if you help us enough we might even tell the CPS to forget that you had a gun at all. On the other hand, if you don't tell us where you got the gun from we'll have no alternative but to mention the gun and describe it in great detail, including how real bullets fall right through it."

The prisoner's lawyer raised his eyebrows but said nothing while the prisoner thought it over, then he turned to the lawyer and said,

"These bleeders are trying to stitch me up."

"No ones trying to stitch you up Mr Jones," said Tom, "we're simply pointing out the facts of your future life, either you tell us all that we want to know or we spell it all out in court and the people from whom you got or stole the gun will then carve you up in prison or when you come out."

"I don't know," said the prisoner.

"Or, of course they could take it out on that woman and her child," said Jackie.

The prisoner looked puzzled and then said, "You mean the bint in the squat, she's not his wife and that's not his kid. I never seen her afore a week last Sunday when he picked her up in the pub an' now I bet he wishes he'd never seen her at all. But he says that she was good in bed, I'll say that for her."

Kim, who didn't intend to have children, thought what fools some women are.

Tom returned to the question, "Where did you get the gun, Mr Jones, surely that's not a difficult question?"

"I found it, see." Jones sat back with the satisfied air of a man who had seen the light.

"Where did you find it, Mr Jones?"

"Not round here."

"Where then?" asked Jackie.

"If you must know, in Bournemouth."

"In Bournemouth, when was this?" asked Tom.

"Two or three weeks ago and I wasn't turning over a house, see." He turned to the lawyer and said, "Am I saying too much?"

The lawyer looked uncomfortable and said, "this interview is being recorded. Can I have an assurance that what my client may say will not be the subject of additional charges?"

Tom said, "You know that I can't give your client that sort of blanket clearance. What would we do for instance if he then confessed that he'd killed someone to get the gun. But what I can do is to assure him that if the gun came into his possession as the result of his looking into how somebody else lived, then we won't enquire into the circumstances."

The lawyer looked at them, felt re-assured and said to Jones, "No, you're not saying too much, they won't press additional charges."

"Well, it was like this, see, it was night and I was looking around," he looked at Jackie and said, "for somewhere to doss down, see and this house had a sort of workshop behind the garages. The house had burglar alarms, I could see the red light and I don't like houses with alarms, see, so I went round the back and looked in this workshop, see, an' in a cupboard I found this cardboard box. It was shut with that sticky brown paper, see and I tore it and looked inside. You could 'ave knocked me down wiv a feather when I seen that it was full o' guns."

He paused for effect, then went on,

"Well, I thought, seeing as 'ow there's so many they probably won't miss one, so I nicked it. I always fancied 'aving a shooter."

Tom was sure that the man was telling the truth, "Where was this house?"

"In Bournemouth, I'd walked a fair way from the front, on the outskirts, see."

"Was there anything near the house that you'd recognize?"

"Like what?" asked Mr Jones.

"Oh, I don't know," said Tom. "A pub or a cinema or, well, anything?"

"No it was dead quiet, what they call a quiet residential place, see."

"Where did you go afterwards?" asked Jackie.

"Well, I wanted to get as far away as possible and mix with other people, see and it was only afterwards that I remembered that I ought to have pinched some bullets as well. This was before I found out that bullets fell right through, see?"

"Yes," said Jackie. "Where did you go?"

"Down to the front and along to Poole Harbour."

"Was it a long walk?"

Jones thought about that and eventually said, "About half an hour, I'd say. It was late, see?"

"Did you walk fast, Mr Jones?"

"I did to start with 'cos I'd just nicked a shooter, then I slowed down and sort of strolled along. There was a gang of Americans kids sitting laughing and talking outside an hotel and some of them broke away and went my way and went into another hotel. They were lucky, they had beds to go to and I didn't."

"But you had a gun," said Kim.

"Yes, it gives you a good feeling to have a gun," said the prisoner.

Tom took over again,

"You're sure that you can't give us any more information about the house where you found the gun?"

"No, I didn't go near the house; like I said, it had burglar alarms."

"What about the garage?" asked Jackie.

"It was a big one for two cars."

"Did you happen to see the cars?"

"It was dark but I could make out a saloon, like a Merc or a BMW or a Jag and a big square car like a 4 x 4., There were some bikes in there as well."

"Thank you Mr Jones for your co-operation, you have our word that we won't make an issue in court of how you acquired the gun and we won't contest your story that you were throwing the useless thing away."

They thanked the lawyer for his helpfulness and told the Bath inspector the result of the interview and that the anti-terrorist branch would be following up the provenance of the weapon. Tom congratulated them for spotting the curious nature of the weapon and sending it to the Met. It could have terrorist potential.

In the train back to London they discussed how to go about finding the house with a big garage with a workshop behind within half an hours walk of the West Esplanade in Bournemouth. Jackie volunteered that she and the girls would go there and have a look round before the end of the week.

They went on Friday. As usual the sergeants took their white van and Jackie took her car, experience having proved the advantage of having more than one vehicle when on a case. Jackie had a second reason, whereas her sergeants would be off back to London at the end of the day, she intended to spend the weekend at the Tolbrite Arms where she had stayed at various times when engaged in cases in the Portland area and where her friends gathered on Saturday nights.

Chapter Eleven

WHEN Kathryn arrived at the library the next morning she was greeted by a jubilant Reverend Pudnor who hardly let her through the door before crying,

"We found it, well, actually young Christopher found it, believe it or not, in the Spetisbury register. I've put it in your room."

Kathryn was aware that it might be any old Hawkins but in her heart she knew that they had struck gold, this must be the one they were looking for.

"It's a christening at the end of 1692," said Pudnor, "they called the little boy James, James David Hawkins."

Kathryn felt icily calm, there was no hurry, she had all the time in the world. She took off her jacket and put on her overall before she turned to the open register. It lay before her written in copperplate letters,

> Nov 14, 1692. Boy, James David Hawkins. Father; Francis James Hawkins. Mother; Jane Mary Hawkins.

"This is wonderful," said Kathryn, "the date is about right. Now we should look for the marriage. When they arrived in New England they had just the one son who I assume is this one. This probably indicates that the parents were young and I'd think that their marriage wouldn't be more than two years before the birth of their first child, wouldn't you?"

Kathryn could see the reverend doing small calculations in his head. He said,

"Yes, I agree. In those days children seemed to come along fairly regularly and these two must have been just starting out."

"The rest were destined to be born the other side of the Atlantic," said Kathryn. "Did the boys look any further?"

"No, Chris found the entry last thing yesterday and went home like a dog with two tails."

She sat down and turned to the marriages part of the register, turned the pages until she came to November 1692 and slowly read the entries prior to that date. She found it half way down the previous page.

May 28, 1692 Francis James Hawkins, Gentleman.
Father, Gentleman. Jane Mary Sommers, Maidservant.
Father, Joseph Somers.

Kathryn studied the entry that said so much. Clearly Miss Jane Mary Somers was with child when she married. The Hawkins were described as Gentlemen and the bride as a Maidservant. Was this a case of the young master having his way with a maid? The boy's father's name was not spelt out, nor was the bride's father's profession.

She looked further and saw that the witnesses were the bride's father, who signed with a cross and, Kathryn caught her breath, Elizabeth Sarah Hawkridge (Lady)

She showed her discovery to the Reverend Pudnor. He too did a small calculation and said, "Ooh."

"I was looking at the witness, Lady Hawkridge," said Kathryn.

"I think that I've heard that name," said the reverend. "I believe that they're still landowners today."

"Yes they are," said Kathryn, remembering what she'd been told in the Tolbrite Arms and the vicarage, "they own the Manor House estate at Tolbrite, which includes the village and it's church, and one of the sons has some radio stations in the UK and America."

"That's where I've heard the name, on the wireless," said the Reverend. "I listen to their music programmes and their news, it's more balanced than the BBC's these days."

Kathryn photographed the entries and the front cover of the register with her digital camera and transferred them to her laptop to make sure. To make doubly sure she copied the register entries into her notebook. She'd come a long way to discover those entries.

She waited until the boys arrived after lunch, thanked them and the librarian for their help, brushed aside his suggestion that he should return the unspent part of the money that she had given him and left with their thanks ringing in her ears.

She returned to her hotel and spent the rest of the day looking around Salisbury.

Her phone call to her mother that evening was jubilant,

"I've found him Mummy, His name was Francis James, his wife's name was Jane Mary and their little boy was James David. I've photographed the register and I'll bring the pictures home to you."

"That's wonderful, baby, are you coming home tomorrow?"

"No, mother, there's a mystery about Francis James Hawkins, the father, that I want to investigate because, much as you might not like it, I don't think that was his real name."

"Of course it was, silly. Well, we know that people called him Friend Hawkins sometime after he got here but the Hawkins ended up owning a lot of Boston and you can't say fairer than that."

"I understand that, mother and that will always be his name in America. But in England, some time before he sailed, he may have had another name. I'll explain it all when I get back."

"He's not an illegitimate prince or duke is he?" asked her hopeful mother.

"No mother and I shouldn't have said anything because I have no facts just my over-active imagination."

"Is that professor from Yale still hanging around?"

"No mother that professor from Yale kissed me goodbye some days ago and as far as I know is back in New Haven at the present time."

"You let him kiss you, then?"

"Yes mother and if he'd wanted to take me to bed I might have let him. Does that satisfy your morbid curiosity?"

"When I think of all the money we spent on bringing you up and you say a thing like that. To your mother too."

"Oh come off it Mother, you know me better than that. But I admit that I do rather like the young professor from Yale. There I've said it."

"Then you must bring him home when you get back."

"We'll have to see," said Kathryn, thinking, not until I've really and thoroughly made my mind up.

"What do you plan to do now, baby?"

"I plan to return to South Dorset tomorrow. If there's room at the village inn, I'm going to move to Tolbrite and try and contact the squire to see if the family have any old letters and things, because a witness at the marriage of Francis James and Jane Mary in May 1692 was Lady Elizabeth Sarah Hawkridge and the Hawkridge family still live at Tolbrite, they own it, in fact."

"I've never heard of them."

"I'd be surprised if you had, mother, although the son has some radio stations in the mid-west and his company has made some good

TV documentaries that have been shown on TV in the States. Anyway, that's beside the point, what I want to ask the Hawkridge's for starters is, who was Lady Elizabeth Sarah Hawkridge?"

"Don't take too long about it baby, you've done what I asked you to do, you've found that he did come from Dorset."

"But that's not the end of it mother dear, surely you want me to find out all there is to know about them?"

"Yes baby, of course I do, it's just that I worry about you being so far away."

"I'm only a five hour flight away."

"That's a joke. After you've been through immigration and several security checks and customs and immigration on arrival, it's more like ten hours these days."

"Goodnight mother, I'll call you tomorrow."

The following morning Kathryn checked-out of the Salisbury hotel and drove through the down-land country and the New Forest to the Tolbrite Arms. Gloria and her mother were preparing the bars for the mid-day opening and the sound of bottle upon bottle indicated that landlord Trowbridge wasn't far away.

Gloria smiled her greeting, "Hello professor, we're not open yet but I could make you some coffee."

"Hello Gloria, I'd love some of your coffee but what I really want is a room for one or two nights and to pick your brains."

"We've got a nice room for you, one that we keep for our friends," said Gloria. "If you get your luggage I'll show you the way and when you come down your coffee'll be ready."

Kathryn got her bags and was duly installed in a very nice room at the back that looked over the pub's garden, complete with tables with sunshades, towards the gently flowing river and the meadows and woodland beyond. She knew from studying the map that Spetisbury was only a few miles away in that direction. She washed, repaired her make-up, went down to the bar and perched on a bar stool and Gloria's mother brought coffee for the three of them.

"What was it you wanted to pick our brains about?"

"In a nutshell I want to ask Mr or Lord or whatever he's called, Hawkridge, some questions about his ancestors."

"What for?" asked Mrs Trowbridge.

"Shh, Mum, that's none of our business," said Gloria.

"Well, the General wouldn't thank us if this lady was one of those American lawyers we see on the telly who sue people for millions of dollars, would he?"

"You're quite right, Mrs Trowbridge and there is no reason why you shouldn't know what I am interested in," said Kathryn. "Your daughter knows, because she was here that night when I told the police that the reason that I was in the churchyard at that place where I found the body was that I was looking for my ancestors."

"Yes, that's right, you think they came from round here," said Gloria.

"I now have proof positive that they did come from round here," said Kathryn, "and the reason that I'd like to speak with the present squire is that a Lady Elizabeth Sarah Hawkridge was a witness at my ancestor's wedding in May 1692, about a year before he sailed to the new world."

"Fancy that," said Gloria.

"I see," said Mrs Trowbridge, "You could write them a letter."

"But letters take so long to get there and they might not read it right away," said Kathryn.

"You write a letter and give it to me," said Gloria. "My Will's the estate maintenance manager and he'll give it to Lady Hawkridge this afternoon and bring you her answer at tea-time. How's that?"

"She might even ring you if Will explains that you don't have much time," said Mrs Trowbridge.

And thus it was. Margaret Hawkridge phoned Kathryn and invited her to tea that afternoon.

When she pulled up outside the front door of the Manor House a tall erect figure came down the steps to open her car door and said, "Her ladyship's in the small sitting room."

He led the way and a tallish, slender woman with greying hair rose and took her hand and said "I'm Margaret Hawkridge, Have some tea and tell me all about it. This is the Sergeant, by the way, who looks after us, with his wife, of course."

Kathryn told her hostess the whole story, how the Hawkins had made good in the new world, the Glovers building railways and the two families coming together by marriage and her family interest in finding out from whence Friend Hawkins had come. She then showed

Margaret the copies of the entries in the Spetisbury Church register dated 1692 and the witness signature, Lady Elizabeth Sarah Hawkridge.

Margaret agreed that it was interesting and asked how she might help.

"Well, there are a number of things that might be inferred from what we now know," said Kathryn. "First, Jane Mary was pregnant when they were married. She is described as a maidservant and her husband a gentleman. It may be that she worked for his parents and they fell in love or worse. Then there is Lady Hawkridge signing as a witness. This must mean something. Was the girl her maid? The girl has her father as a witness and it looks as if Lady Hawkridge was the boy's witness. If so, is there a family bond? Could Hawkins be a contrived name for a Hawkridge. In short do you have any old family records?"

"Yes we have but I couldn't say what state they're in. Our son Timmy found them all carefully put away in an old cupboard when he and his brother and sister were exploring in the roof about twenty years ago. A few years ago he and the Sergeant brought them down and put them in one of the outhouses in which Timmy installed a machine to keep them in the correct environment. He had an idea that he might find time to write a book or a television play about them one day. It's just occurred to me, you must be the young woman who found poor Mary Barton's body."

"Yes, I'm afraid so," said Kathryn. "I was looking at the gravestones."

"She grew up in the village, you know, such a sweet child. Her father was a drunkard who died young and her mother drove herself into an early grave struggling to make both ends meet. The grandmother who brought her up is still in the village. Such a shame."

"Life can be very cruel," said Kathryn.

"Sorry, I'm digressing," said Margaret. "You want to look at those old papers. I'll have to ask Timmy. Don't get me wrong, of course you shall look at them but Timmy will tell us what to do about his humidifier, or is it de-humidifier? And how to handle the manuscripts."

"Thank you. Do you know if the Hawkridge family had any connection with the parish of Spetisbury in those days?"

"Yes, even today the Hawkridge Manor estate borders on Spetisbury and in the seventeenth century the estate was bigger than it is today and included Spetisbury," said Margaret. "The Dower House was there."

"The Dower House being where the widow of the lord of the manor moved to when the heir and his wife took over?"

"Yes, that's it, where they packed the new squire's mother off to. It sounds a trifle heartless but it was a sensible enough system, she took her furniture and servants."

"I suppose so but in a house as big as this you'd have thought they might have found her a wing to live in," ventured Kathryn.

"You have to remember that they had many more children and servants in those days and also would have had visitors who brought their personal servants. There weren't any metalled roads, just rutted tracks and the visitors may have taken some days to get here. They wouldn't expect to turn round and go straight back even if their horses had been fresh enough, so they would stay for a while. The house would have been fairly fully occupied for most of the time."

"So it's possible that Lady Elizabeth Sarah Hawkridge was the Dowager Lady Elizabeth Hawkridge?" suggested Kathryn.

"Yes, quite possible," said Margaret.

"I'm beginning to think that I should have spent more time going through the old church registers."

"Why so?"

"I should have gone back about thirty years before 1692 and looked for the birth of a Francis James Hawkins or perhaps Francis James Hawkridge," said Kathryn. "Sociologists and detectives tell us that people change their surnames but seldom alter their given names."

"Timmy's family records might include an early family tree," said Margaret, "I'll ring him and see what he says."

She picked up the phone, waited a moment and said, "Oh Sergeant, please get me Mr Timmy."

The phone rang after a minute. "Hello Penny, is Timmy there?" "Oh, no don't disturb him, it's not that urgent, it's just that I have with me a professor from the United States who would like to consult the old Hawkridge papers that he put in the stables." She listened to what Timmy's secretary was saying and raised an eyebrow at Kathryn. "You're not planning to go back to America tomorrow, are you?"

Kathryn shook her head and mouthed, "No."

"Alright Penny, ask him or Helene to call me when their meeting's over, there's a dear."

She turned to Kathryn and said, "That girl's a marvel. She's married to Timmy's Production Manager. You heard, she'll have him call me when he's free. There's no point in your waiting because I'm sure that you'd prefer to start all bright and fresh tomorrow morning, if that's possible. You're staying at the Tolbrite Arms, aren't you?"

Kathryn said that she was and wrote down her digital telephone number. Lady Hawkridge escorted her to her car and watched her drive off.

She re-entered the house and asked the Sergeant to get Charles Howard at the US Embassy in London. When he was on, she said,

"Charles, I hope that I haven't taken you away from something important. I've just had a visit from a Harvard professor, a charming girl who says that she's looking for her ancestors, name of Kathryn Glover; do you happen to know her?"

"Yes Lady Hawkridge I know her. She's one of the Boston Glovers, only child, in fact. The girl's lovely and totally unspoiled notwithstanding that they own half of Boston and the state of Massachusetts. Her mother's a DAR. How did you meet her?"

"In the church archives she's found references to the ancestor called Hawkins who emigrated to the new world in 1693 and there is a reference to a Lady Elizabeth Hawkridge being a witness at the wedding."

"So that led her to you?" said Charles.

"Yes and I hope to let her examine our old family papers tomorrow. Thanks for your help Charles, I hope that you didn't mind me asking but one really can't be too careful these days, can one?"

Timmy called later. "Hello mother, I understand that you've got an American professor who wants to look at our family history. I'm embarrassed, really, because I should have had the papers indexed but didn't get round to it. The professor will have to browse about trying to find what he is interested in. There's no objection to removing the documents for perusal, a pack at a time, that won't do any harm. Helene would like to know how the professor gets on when we come down for the weekend. Gosh, that's tomorrow, if the professor works on Saturdays we'll see him. Must go now. Love you."

Margaret just had time to say, "He's a girl," when Timmy rang off.

Chapter Twelve

AT ABOUT the time that Kathryn was seeing her undergraduates off from Heathrow, Paula was closeted with WDC Clare Thornton in the Southern Enquiries office.

Paula reported on her search for swarthy looking men who drove green Jaguar cars and how she had followed George Swift alias Georgio Sabatini to two airports and had showed his picture to Professor Stephen Hamsworth.

"Did he recognize him as the man he'd seen?" asked Clare

"Yes and no, he said that it could have been him."

"Well, that's something," said Clare. "He might have said No."

"Have you found out what the white powder is that was in Marylyn's bead tin?"

"Yes, practically pure heroin."

"And what about the list of names in her exercise book?"

"The Inspector's left that to me and I'm working my way through them. I have to be careful because one can't go to their homes and as good as suggest the reason why their name should be in a prostitute's notebook, I have to get them alone and ask them to tell me. I've had some funny replies, I can tell you."

"I assume that you're doing background checks?"

"Yes, practically all of them have no police record and most of them have a good credit rating. One of them is a church-elder and two are school governors."

"Of girls schools, I'll be bound," said Paula and then regretted saying it. She added "So far then, there's no evidence against anyone mentioned in her book?"

"That's so," said Clare. "It's funny but you do realize that he's in the book under the name Swift, that's what led you to him. Sabatini isn't among the names mentioned in it. I know it sounds silly but what do you intend to do now, Paula?"

"In the circumstances he seems to be my only lead so I'll try and find out if there's anything funny about his business and then think about whether there's scope for crime in it, worth murdering a girl for."

"Don't go all psychological on me, please. In my job I see people committing serious crimes for the most trivial reasons."

"Ah but are they the sort of people who live in nice houses, run two cars and a business and appear to have interests at two airports?" said Paula.

"Believe it or not, sometimes they are. There seems to be no limit to people's greed and vanity."

"The problem is that I can't spend all my time watching Sabatini, I've got to help Fred on the credit card investigation."

"Do we know about that?" asked Clare.

"I wouldn't know. We are commissioned by a bank and I don't know whether they've called you people in. It's supposed to be all very hush-hush in order not to scare the customers."

"Are they stealing credit cards?"

"Some are but it also seems that someone has found a way of taking money out of the customer's account without actually stealing their card and, before you ask me, no, it's not a computer fraud, what appears to be the customer's credit card is being used to draw money from cash machines."

"You mean, they've got duplicate cards?" asked Clare.

"Something like that. Fred thinks that all they need to do is to copy the strip on the back."

"What about the PIN number?"

"He thinks that it's encoded in the strip at the back and the crooks have found a way to read it," said Paula. "Failing that, we also have ideas on how it can be read. This would mean that all the victims have visited a certain business where a credit card is the usual means of payment."

Clare thought for a moment and said, "Like a filling station."

"Clever girl," said Paula. "Fred's asked the bank for a list of the localities where the victims live because we think that people tend to use the local garage, that sort of thing, and if we get a cluster in one locality we'll take appropriate action."

"Such as?" asked Clare.

"My idea is that the bank prepare a credit card with a special character in the magnetic strip. I would use this at the suspect business and only at that business and we wait and see if it turns up."

"That wouldn't necessarily catch the crooks," said policewoman Clare.

"It might if the use of the card with the special character rings an alarm in the bank or triggers a camera placed behind the cash machine."

"But you can't be sure that the cash is being taken from particular cash machines in Bournemouth," said Clare, "and you can't equip all the cash machines on the South Coast."

"If I was doing it I'd spread it about by drawing money in neighbouring places," said Paula, "but so far the thefts have all taken place in the target town. In the present case, Bournemouth."

"Please keep me in touch."

Kathryn was at the Manor House at nine the following morning. She judged that the family would have breakfasted by then and the butler, Sergeant, would be able to spare her a moment to start her on her search. To her surprise Lady Hawkridge came out with the Sergeant. After greeting Kathryn she turned to the left and led the way, saying,

"I've put you in the Rumpus Room. It's really the ballroom annex but David and I turned it into a place where the children could play when it was raining, hence it's name. Children need somewhere to let off steam without adults constantly saying don't and our grandchildren use it now. The Sergeant's cleaned a big table and a comfortable chair and he'll show you where the archives are kept. Timmy, our son, says that it will do no harm if you take out a package at a time and put them back when you get the next pack out. He also apologizes for the fact that the papers have not been indexed. We'll give you a key to this outside door to the Rumpus Room so that you can come and go as you please without coming through the house and the sergeant's got a key to the storeroom for you. Would you care to join us for lunch?"

"Don't think me rude but I seldom eat lunch." Kathryn smiled, "it gets in the way of work. I'm enormously grateful to you for allowing me access to your family papers and for giving me the use of the Rumpus Room and I'll try to be no bother."

"At least you'll let the Sergeant bring you an occasional cup of coffee?"

"That would be most kind."

The Sergeant opened the door and gave Kathryn the key. Lady Hawkridge left them with a smile and the Sergeant took Kathryn to the stables block where one of the stalls had been turned into a room with a controlled environment for the papers. The Sergeant gave

Kathryn the second key and reminded her to be sure to keep the door shut.

He looked along the row where two hunters had their heads over their stable doors looking enquiringly at the visitors and said, "Do you ride, Miss?"

"Yes, when I'm at home."

"The General seldom rides these days, her Ladyship stopped after a fall some years ago and the groom has arthritis. The boys and Miss Elizabeth ride when they have the time and meanwhile these two get what exercise I and the vicar's wife can give them. Don't mistake me Miss, the General loves them and comes to talk to his horses every day, he says that they're all getting old together."

"Do they spend any time in the paddock?"

"Oh yes, the groom sees to that. Perhaps you'd care to ride while you're here, I'm sure the General would be grateful, we've got the kit."

"I'll wear my jeans tomorrow and perhaps I'll be able to take one of them out for half an hour or so."

"Very good, Miss, I'll look forward to that. I'll leave you to get on with your work"

Kathryn was wondering how long it would take an experienced young horseman man to ride across country to Spetisbury. She might try it tomorrow, provided the horse they gave her was docile.

She went into the storeroom. The papers were tied in bundles on wooden racks. She hoped that the papers of each bundle had some relevance to the other papers in the same bundle and were not just bundles of papers thrown randomly together. She took down each bundle in turn and made a note of the date and subject of the first paper to have a date. She made her way along each shelf in turn until she had dealt with all fourteen bundles. Some long departed person had taken care of them. The packs were in date order. She speculated that this was probably a priest employed by a squire as his secretary.

The very first pack covered the period 1600 to 1700. The next two each covered a half century, !701 to 1750 and 1751 to 1800, the next one covered the twenty years 1801 to 1820 and the next nine each covered ten years from 1821 to 1910. The final pack had clearly not been assembled by the priest and was simply a mass of more recent correspondence pushed together.

Kathryn carefully took down the 1600 to 1700 bundle and took it to the table in the Rumpus Room. She would have preferred to call it the Ballroom Annex with mental images of young couples flirting during a respite from dancing but concluded that, with the children's bicycles and toys all around, Rumpus Room said it all.

The bundle consisted of about seventy pages. Kathryn realized that they might be gold dust covering some of the most turbulent years in English history, the Stuarts, the Civil War, and the restoration of the monarchy. A century with an always present undertone of protestants versus catholics. She was in a quandary, she had a passing familiarity with old English script but it took time for her to properly understand what the writer meant. The ideal solution would be to carry the documents back to Harvard or failing that to somewhere in England where an expert might work on them but that wasn't on. An alternative would be to photograph each sheet and study the pictures or have someone study the pictures, at leisure back at Harvard. To do this she'd need a better light than was available in the Rumpus Room and would have to expose the old documents to it for the minimum time. Probably have to take the pages out of the store-room five or so at a time. She decided that today she'd go through the pages tabulating their subject and date if she could de-cypher them and would raise the possibility of photographing them with her hostess before she left that afternoon.

Jackie and her sergeants rendezvoused at the radio station. They had met and worked with Fred Smart and Paula Simms before and were sure of a friendly welcome, the use of the toilet and a cup of coffee.

On the way down the M3 Jackie had decided that it hadn't been very sensible of her to bring the girls on the day before the weekend, at the most they'd get only a few hours in before returning to London but they would appreciate being out of the office and at the very least they'd get a feel for the task ahead.

Jackie explained to Fred and Paula that a thief had been caught in possession of a gun of a sort not seen before and which might be of use to terrorists and when questioned had said that he stole it from a shed behind the garage of a house in Bournemouth. They had come to find that house.

"There is a large number of houses in Bournemouth with a shed behind a garage," said Fred, helpfully.

"Yes, we know," said Jackie, "but we've got two other clues. When he made off with the gun the thief says that he passed an hotel where lots of young Americans were talking and some of the Americans broke away and walked in front of him and went into another hotel. Overall it took him about half an hour to reach the seafront from where the thief walked to Poole looking for somewhere to sleep out for the night."

"That's more like it," said Fred. "Find the hotels that had young Americans in the past few weeks, draw a line through them. Measure about half a mile from the esplanade and the house you want will be the one at the inland end of the line."

"Isn't it good that we have a man to tell us poor girls how to suck eggs?" smiled Paula.

"Yes, I don't know where we'd be without them," said Jackie.

"I can give you a starter," said Paula. "An American professor and some students from Harvard were staying at the West Esplanade Hotel until recently. I know that because she found the body."

"What body?" asked Kim.

"A call-girl called Marylyn Barton," said Paula. "Her body was left in a village churchyard and the prof found it when she was looking for her ancestors. That sounds vaguely Chinese, doesn't it? We're involved because when he learnt that the case was in the hands of Inspector Clouseau , Tim Hawkridge asked us to keep an eye on things because the murdered girl was brought-up by her grandmother in Tolbrite and the old lady still lives there."

"Paula's co-operating with the policewoman who does all the work," said Fred. "Which reminds me, there is another American professor involved, this time from Yale and he was put in jail for a night by the Inspector because he danced with the murdered girl at the Half Moon club the night she was murdered."

"Bournemouth's a veritable hot bed of crime, isn't it?" said Sandra.

"It's certainly livened up in the past month," said Fred. "Our major preoccupation at the moment is credit card fraud, someone's worked out a new angle to relieve other people's bank accounts of cash."

The Body in the Churchyard

"Are you going to be at the pub tomorrow night?" asked Jackie.

"Yes, are you coming?"

"If they've got a room I intend to stay the night. I'd better ring them now."

Jackie walked out of the room while dialing on her mobile phone. She came back to say that it was OK, they could put her up but that an American professor was in her usual room.

"It must be the girl who's looking for her ancestors," said Paula. "She fled to the lights of the pub the night she found the body and Will went up and told the police where she was."

"Do you know the names of the hotels at which the Americans were staying?" asked Jackie.

"The Harvard group was at the West Esplanade Hotel. I'm sorry but I don't know where the Yale students were."

"Never mind," said Jackie. "Thanks for you help, we'll be off on our search. With luck, I'll see you tomorrow night. We'll leave the van in the parking lot, if we may."

They set off in Jackie's car and found the West Esplanade Hotel. The receptionist confirmed that a party of American students and their professor had stayed there but had now returned to America. Questioned, they happened to know that another party of American students had been staying at Harvey's Hotel in Old Christchurch Road.

Jackie and her sergeants sat in the car and studied the street plan. Old Christchurch Road was fairly long. They drove slowly along it until they came to Harvey's Hotel. Sandra went in and confirmed that a Professor Stephen Hamsworth and a party from Yale University had stayed there.

They studied the map and drew half-mile lines on it. The thief could have come down a number of streets before he joined the Old Christchurch Road and turned towards the sea front. Still, they reasoned they would only have to search a band about a quarter of a mile wide, paralleling the sea front for a distance of about half a mile.

With the aid of the street map they listed all the roads in this area and divided it into three shares. On Monday they would each take their third share and do the footwork.

They drove along the possible roads to get a feel for the types of houses and then went back to the radio station where Sandra and Kim departed cheerfully on the way back to London. Jackie drove to Tolbrite and was welcomed as an old friend.

She came down at about six-thirty to find another girl sitting on a stool at the bar.

Gloria said, "This is Professor Kathryn Glover and this is Captain Jackie Fraser." She produced two glasses of Bouchier Red wine and put it before them.

The girls touched hands and Kathryn said, "Captain in the Army?"

"Yes," said Jackie. "Army police."

"Gosh," said Kathryn. "You're young to be an army police captain."

"I'm older than I look," said Jackie modestly. "I know all about you, professor, how you found a body while looking for your ancestors."

"It sounds so silly, now, doesn't it, to be wandering round a churchyard looking at tombstones? But it was all I could think of doing at the time. I'd started in the church along the road but there wasn't anyone about so I went churchyard hunting. Wish that I hadn't."

"I gather that our local Inspector Clouseau put a colleague of yours in jail."

Kathryn took a moment to let this sink in. "Oh, you mean Stephen. He's not exactly a colleague, he's at Yale but we were at Harvard together as students. Answering your question, yes, he was kept in jail for one night until the Embassy got him out. How do you know that the Inspector's called Clouseau?"

"I've had a number of cases in Dorset and in each of them I've had to prevent him messing things up. He's a menace."

"Why don't his superiors sack him?"

"That's a mystery to everyone in Dorset," said Jackie. "How is the search for your ancestors going?"

"I've had the most amazing luck." She proceeded to tell Jackie about the search in Salisbury and the discoveries in the Spetisbury registers and her approach to Lady Hawkridge, and said, "Do you know her?"

"Yes," said Jackie, "we're old friends but I know her daughter-in-law Helene better, we spent four years together doing the same law course at the London School of Economics."

"I understand that she's married to the son who's in the media business?" said Kathryn. "Everybody keeps mentioning Timmy."

"Yes." She lowered her voice, "he's the one who's money has kept the estate going, his and Helene's." Then in a normal tone, "Helene is half French, this wine is produced in her mother's vineyards in Burgundy. Where is your home in the States?"

"Boston."

"So you work just across the Charles River from your home," said Jackie.

"Yes, in Cambridge. Mass. But I try and keep work and home separate. I live on the campus and visit my parents most weekends. What do you do?"

"Much the same, I've got a flat in London where I spend all the week when I'm not away on a job and I have lunch with my parents most Sundays."

"Where do they live?"

"Oh, in London, too," smiled Jackie. "They moved there when my father retired from the army and became a banker."

Mrs Trowbridge came along behind the bar and said, "Would you like to share a table for dinner?"

"Yes please," said Kathryn.

They spent the evening together and Jackie learnt many things she'd never known before about Anglo-Saxon Britain and Massachusetts.

The following morning Jackie drove into Bournemouth to do a little preliminary reconnaissance along the West Esplanade-Harveys Hotels line. Kathryn went to the Manor House, dressed in jeans, shirt and sweater. She hoped that the Sergeant would be able to provide her with a pair of riding boots. He and the groom saw her mounted on the oldest of the hunters and said that there was no reason why she shouldn't cross the river and ride across country to Spetisbury, being sure to close all field gates behind her, of course. She crossed the river, and followed the track across the water meadows and through the Long Wood and was then away, across country to reach the A350 and Spetisbury. It was a ride that any young gentleman would have thought nothing of. She rode back and insisted on rubbing the horse down and watering him. He had enjoyed the outing as much as she had. She then returned to her self-imposed task of examining the papers. She had asked Lady Hawkridge's permission to photograph the four oldest bundles of papers which covered the period from 1600 to 1820 and Margaret had in turn consulted Timmy. Kathryn explained that, being a historian, she had included the 1801 to 1820 bundle to cover the Napoleonic wars because there was bound to be a Hawkridge somewhere in Wellington's army if not with Nelson at Trafalgar. Timmy and Helene could see the good sense of what Kathryn proposed to do and asked only that they be allowed to see whatever she wrote before it was published. This assurance she willingly gave. Thus it was that, aided by a bright light that the Sergeant provided, Kathryn photographed the papers and downloaded them onto a disk by way of her laptop.

Chapter Thirteen

PAULA decided that it was time that she learnt more about the Sabatini business interests at the airports. She assumed that the airport cargo area would be less busy on a Saturday than on a weekday. She assumed a role she had used several times in the past, that of a roving reporter for Hawkridge Radio. In the past, in the Bristol area, the material she had recorded during investigations had been the subject of two useful broadcasts, one of which had been a series on the work of various departments of the City Council. The Bournmouth station manager, Jill Jones, had given her access to a set of portable recording equipment, a station pass and business cards and the use of a car with Radio Bournemouth painted on the door. She was, to all intents and purposes, a radio reporter, albeit unpaid.

Jill phoned the airport managers and said that they were considering making a half hour programme on how the cargo business is handled and she would like to send one of her reporters to take a preliminary look with the actual recordings to follow. At each airport the manager was absent and the person looking out for him said that he supposed that it would be all right. Yes, he'd tell the security people on the gate. Paula blessed that unknown soul who had said that there is no such thing as bad publicity.

She drove up to the cargo entrance of Bournemouth airport, stopped the car and got out with a considerable show of legs. The security guard helped her sign in, gave her a temporary pass and watched those same long legs get back in the radio car. He directed her to a parking spot in the central area. She got out and slung the recording equipment over her shoulder and walked along the rows of importers units. There was an intermittent stream of small tractors towing trailers loaded with goods, presumably from aircraft, to the units and a lesser number taking loads from units, presumably to be loaded into aircraft. All mixed with normal trade lorries bringing and collecting goods. Closer to the passenger terminal, a separate number of tractors and trailers was ready to deal with the baggage of arriving and departing passengers.

Lest someone should be watching and also because she was genuinely interested, Paula described the scene into her microphone, complete with the noise of passing traffic. For possible follow-up action she noted and recorded the names of the unit holders and what they did. They all had big roller shutter doors and many were open, revealing, in many cases, stacks of cardboard boxes ready for dispatch, one way or the other. She came to the unit that bore the painted legend Georgio Sabatini, Importer of Fresh Flowers, Garden Equipment and Supplies, above the door. The door was shut.

The next unit door was open and two men in overalls were leaning on the adjacent wall smoking cigarettes and watching Paula. When she moved in their direction the younger of the two shouted, "Want me to sing for you, darling?"

Paula smiled and walked up to them. "You'd better be careful, I might take you up on that. Tell me, what do you do?" She pushed the microphone in front of the man's face and switched on.

"We're import-export agents, we handle anything except for refrigerated cargo. You want something shipped somewhere, we'll handle it for you with speed and efficiency."

"Like it says in the firm's adverts," said the other man, half scornfully.

"Say I want to send something to, say, Taiwan. Planes don't fly to Taiwan from Bournemouth, do they?"

"We get it to an airport which flies cargo to Taiwan," said the younger man. "Actually there is quite a trade in air cargo from Taiwan." He laughed, "You should have picked Outer Mongolia."

"And how would you have got my goods to Outer Mongolia?" asked Paula, intrigued.

"Sent it to Schipol, the Dutch have a run to all the ex-Soviet republics along the southern border that ends at Ulan Bator."

"Thanks," said Paula, then changed the subject. "Doesn't the flower man open on Saturdays?"

"He's been and gone. His stuff comes in early in the morning and is away in the shops by the time they open. Comes from the Channel Islands, Scilly Islands and Holland mainly. Then they shut shop, it's air conditioned to preserve what they don't sell. He didn't open at all on a Sunday but then he got a contract from one of the big supermarkets and now sends out a van load at eight o 'clock Sunday morning regular as clockwork. The owner does it himself."

"What about garden equipment, does he deal in things like lawnmowers?"

"Yes, but not as much as he used to. A small man like him can't compete for price with the big stores."

"Some of his hardware arrives through us and I know that he has stuff arriving at Southampton," said the second man. "I was making a delivery to our unit there one day and there he was, raising merry hell because a delivery he was expecting hadn't arrived. In the end they found it, it wasn't much bigger than, say, two shoe boxes and I thought hardly worth Georgio coming himself to collect it."

"Perhaps the contents were valuable?" said Paula.

"They weren't, the reason for them being mislaid was that the Customs had opened the box for inspection and I saw in it. They were brass fittings, looked like some sort of latch mechanism."

"I suppose they were important to him," said Paula.

She thanked the men and concluded her visit to the Bournemouth airport cargo area with an interview by the security guard on the gate.

She then drove to Southampton airport. She did her flashing legs act in front of the security guard on the gate to put him in a receptive mood and was given a temporary pass and told where to park.

Southampton was much busier than Bournemouth. They had the same equipment but it seemed to be being used more intensively because there were more flights arriving and departing. She walked past the units, there was no unit for Georgio Sabatini or, as an afterthought on Paula's part, George Swift. He had clearly been at the airport to collect a shipment. Thus his business consisted of the shop and airport unit at Bournemouth. In a way Paula felt relieved, having a unit at two adjacent airports had seemed crazy.

She interviewed the security guard and drove back to the radio station to hand in the car and equipment.

That evening she arrived at the Tolbrite Arms to find Jackie Fraser there with Kathryn Glover. They had just dined together. Their three way conversation, with a glass polishing Gloria making up a fourth, explained what each of them was doing in the neighbourhood at that time. Fred and Angela were the next to arrive and to learn why Jackie and Kathryn were there, followed by Timmy and Helene who required no explanation because Jackie had spoken with Helene on the phone and both Timmy and Helene and their children had spent part of the afternoon in the Rumpus Room with Kathryn.

Eventually the conversation turned to the investigations that the various participants were engaged in.

"How's the murder enquiry going?" asked Timmy. "Is friend Clouseau still intent on fouling everything up?"

Paula spoke of her discussions with Clare and her own enquiry into George Swift alias Georgio Sabatini, simply on the grounds that he owned a green Jaguar and, according to the other American professor, looked like the man he claimed to have seen driving off with Marylyn Barton. She described her visits to the two airport cargo areas, thanks to her roving reporter guise and her conclusion that Mr Swift had just the shop and the unit at Bournemouth airport.

"Why did he go to the Southampton airport cargo area?" thought Timmy aloud.

"On the occasion that was described to me by a man from the import/export company that's next to the Sabatini unit at Bournemouth airport, he went to collect some goods that were consigned to him at their Southampton unit."

Fred said that at last the banks had seen the sense of giving him the data that he'd asked for. The credit-card robbers were getting away with twenty thousand pounds a week and there was a cluster of losers in the Branksome and Ferndown areas. He was now looking at the petrol stations in these areas.

"Did you suggest to them that they should set up a dummy account in your or Paula's name and provide a credit card with a doctored magnetic strip?" asked Helene.

"Yes," said Fred, "and the idea went down like a lead balloon. The area manager could see all sorts of problems, none of which detracted from the good sense of the idea but had to do with convincing head office and setting precedents."

Helene looked at Timmy. "Do you think that Bill Lawrence could produce a card with a doctored strip?" She turned to Jackie and Kathryn and explained, "Bill's Timmy's Technical Manager and is a genius at electronics."

"I'm sure that he could, Angel, but there's no point in it unless the bank co-operates, the phoney card would have to leave a unique record in the cash machine print-out to identify it."

"You're making difficulties, lover," said Helene. "Perhaps we don't need a phoney card at all. Fred opens a new account and gets a new card. It's used just the once at the suspect shop or filling station and we wait and see what turns up."

"To hurry things along we'd need two cards, one for the Branksome area and another for the Ferndown area," said the practical Paula.

"Yes," said Fred. "In Paula's name, she gets out and about more than I do."

"What he means is that I'm more gullible looking," grinned Paula.

"Have you had any ideas about what they do with the money?" asked Timmy.

"No, not really," said Fred. "But twenty thousand a week rather scuppers your idea that the perpetrators simply spend it or save it for a rainy day, doesn't it?"

Helene turned to Kathryn and said, "In Britain banks and other businesses have to ascertain where large sums have come from as a precaution against money laundering."

"It's the same in the States," said Kathryn. "We tightened up quite a bit after the 11th of September."

"You don't think that this could be terrorists collecting money, do you?" asked Angela.

"I'd doubt that," said Jackie. "The last thing they would risk is being caught for stealing money. They get their money from overseas, paid into a hidden account, usually associated in some way with a religious organization."

"I suggest that you persuade the bank manager to open two accounts in Paula's name," said Helene, "put, say, a thousand pounds in each and to let you see a print-out of each account daily. In each case the print-out would show Paula's legitimate purchase and, if the business is involved in a credit card fraud, the sum withdrawn from a cash machine or otherwise spent."

"The fraud won't show up in the print-out until three or four days afterwards," said Fred.

"That's why each account has to have a thousand pounds," said Helene. "The bank official shouldn't have a fit, he's losing money anyway but you'll have to repay him the value of Paula's legitimate purchases."

"Bang goes my hopes of a diamond necklace," grinned Paula.

Not to be outdone Will gave a graphic account of the squatters in Gloria's house in Bath. Gloria pointed out that he hadn't been there but she had.

"Well," she admitted, "I wasn't actually there in the night when the squatters had tried to get away with a lot of stolen property. One of them had a gun, too, and tried to throw it away when the police caught him."

Jackie hadn't realized until that moment that the house at the Bath end of the gun affair was Gloria's. She said, "It's a small world."

"And what does that cryptic remark mean?" grinned Helene.

"Well, two coincidences," said Jackie. "Kathryn's search for her ancestors has revealed an association with the Hawkridge family and the gun that Gloria mentioned is the reason that I'm here tonight – in addition to the fact that I love coming here."

"Are we permitted to know any more?" asked Timmy.

"I don't see why not, as long as you keep it to yourselves. The Bath police realized that there was something unusual about the gun and sent it to Scotland Yard. Their experts decided that it could be useful to terrorists and that brought us in."

"And Bournemouth?" prompted Timmy.

"When we interviewed the man who tried to throw it away, he said that he stole it from a place in Bournemouth," said Jackie. "Incidentally, in his statement he mentioned passing two hotels at which there were young Americans."

"Small world indeed," said Kathryn. "If it was my young people and the team from Yale that he saw, we were only here together for about two weeks when the paths crossed."

"Since that's the only clue we have to where the gun came from we have little choice but to follow it up. My sergeants will be back on Monday and we'll be searching inland along a line joining the hotels."

"What will you be looking for?" asked Paula.

"A detached house with a burglar alarm which shows a red light in the dark, a large garage with a saloon car, like a Mercedez Benz, BMW or Jaguar, and a square looking 4 x 4, and a shed behind the garage."

"And the best of British luck," said Will.

"Why terrorists?" asked Timmy, "is it non-metallic?"

"No, it's metallic but different," said Jackie, picking up her drink and partly turning away.

Gloria decided that they had had enough of what she considered to be 'man's talk' and asked Angela if she would play for them.

Walking back across the park with his arm around her waist, Helene said, "You're intrigued by the gun, aren't you?"

"Yes, Angel, it must be quite a threat for them to have brought in Jackie's unit. The fact is that the words terrorists and guns makes me think of smuggling them aboard air liners. This brings up two further thoughts, non-magnetic to avoid the detectors and reduced charges to make the weapons safer for use in a pressurized aircraft."

"Jackie said that they are metallic and quickly changed the subject, didn't she?" said Helene sleepily.

"Perhaps it's aluminium or brass," mused Timmy.

"They used to make cannons out of brass in olden times."

"If it's meant to take reduced charges it needn't be as strong as a gun to take full charges, need it?"

"Look, lover, she's going to bring Kathryn to church tomorrow morning and you can put your theories to her then. I invited them to lunch but they declined, didn't want to be a nuisance. Kathryn said that she'd like to carry on looking at the old papers in the afternoon and I said that it would be all right for Jackie to come with her. They seem to have hit it off, don't they? "

On the way across the park the following morning, Helene told the General and Margaret that Jackie and Kathryn might be at church and that they had declined an invitation to lunch at the Manor House. They all met outside the church when the service was over. Kathryn sought out the vicar's wife and told her of the find at the diocesan library and how she was continuing the search at the Manor House. Mrs Ford thought it nice that the American girl had come to church and brought a friend. She rather thought that she had seen the auburn haired girl before and when she was introduced as Captain Jackie Fraser she remembered, she was the girl who was on the TV catching spies and terrorists and being shot at and threatened with knives. She thought that Tolbrite Church was coming up in the world.

Kathryn and Jackie were in the Rumpus Room in mid-afternoon when Timmy and Helene and the children came in to say goodbye. Kathryn said that she would probably be going home later in the week and would work back at Harvard on the papers that she had photographed. She would keep them informed on what she might discover or deduce. She thought that for each sheet she would provide the best possible picture and a translation in modern-day English. A lot of the papers, including those in the earliest bundle, were accounts, records of what the tenant small-holders paid to their squire but there was some correspondence and, it seemed to Kathryn, mention of births and deaths. Someone had compiled family trees from the mid-eighteenth century and Kathryn hoped to be able to do the same for the last decade of the seventeenth, even if it meant employing Simon Biggs and Christopher Wade to go through every church register in the Diocese of Salisbury looking for Hawkridge's.

They went their separate ways on the Monday morning, By the time that Kathryn arrived in the Rumpus Room, Jackie was parked at the radio station and sitting in Paula's room. She had booked rooms for the sergeants before leaving the Tolbrite Arms and was awaiting their arrival. When they arrived they agreed who should do which area and were taken there by Paula in Jackie's car.

Sandra's experience was typical, she walked along each street in her section picking out detached houses that had a garage big enough for two cars and an evident burglar alarm on the wall. That was the easy bit. The problem was the shed, which houses had a shed behind the garage? Or for that matter, had a shed at all? Out came her trusty clip-board and she was instantly transformed into Sandra Roberts, garden shed sales-person. She'd have to call at all the possible houses.

She walked up the path of the first house and pressed on the bellpush. No sound could be heard so she knocked on the door . After a moment the door was opened by a man who said in a loud indignant voice, "Alright, I heard the bell, no need to knock the door down."

"Sorry, I couldn't hear it ring."

"It's not intended for you to hear, you know you've rung 'cos you've pushed the bellpush, it's for us to hear, understand?"

"Yes, I'm sorry but many bells don't work."

"Well, ours does. What do you want?"

"I represent the Secure Garden Shed Company," lied Sandra. "We'd like to know if you'd be interested in our 2004 range?"

"No I wouldn't" said the man beginning to shut the door.

"Why not?" said Sandra despairingly.

"Because I wouldn't, that's why." and the door closed.

Sandra retreated wondering where she'd gone wrong, there must be an approach that would reveal whether a householder had a shed.

The Body in the Churchyard

The answer was plain. She walked up to the next house and pushed the bellpush. At the end of two minutes she hammered on the door.

The door was opened by a woman. She said, "I thought that I heard somebody."

"I rang the bell," said Sandra.

"That thing hasn't worked for ages," scoffed the woman. "Fancy pressing that."

"Do you have a shed?" asked Sandra.

"Who wants to know?" asked the woman.

"The Secure Garden Shed Company," said Sandra.

"What I've got and what I haven't got is my business," said the woman.

"But this is your business," said Sandra. "Is your shed old, does it leak?"

"No to both questions," said the woman.

Sandra could have throttled her.

"So your shed isn't old?" said Sandra.

"I didn't say that," said the woman.

"Then what is it," screamed Sandra.

"No need to raise your voice," said the woman. "I'm not deaf."

Only stupid you silly old cow, thought the normally imperturbable Sandra.

The woman went on "What was your question?"

"Do you have a shed or workshop?"

"That isn't what you said."

"I thought that I'd make it easier for you to answer," said Sandra.

"I'm not senile, if you want to know if I've got a shed you've only got to ask"

"Very well then, do you have a garden shed?" said Sandra.

"No," said the woman and slammed the door in Sandra's face.

Sandra tried three more houses. One had no shed, the second had a shed at the bottom of the garden and the third told her that it was no business of hers what they had, you didn't have to pay Council Tax on sheds. She retired to the pub where they had agreed to meet for lunch to find Kim already there and Jackie not far behind. Each had a similar story to tell.

"Look Cap, why don't we ask the boys at Middle Wallop to photograph all these gardens, then we can knock on the doors or ring the bells." She added hastily, "with confidence."

"That's not a bad idea, let's skip lunch, collect the van and go and ask them this afternoon."

Thus it was that by three o'clock she was closeted with the commanding officer, Lieutenant Colonel Ben Priestley and Major Hargreaves who commanded flying training at the base.

"What you're saying is that for some hush-hush reason the SIB would like to have pictures of the back gardens of a third of Bournemouth?"

"That's about it, Sir," said Jackie, crossing her legs and smoothing her skirt, "it would be useful training."

"Something to do with terrorists, eh?"

"Terrorists can't be excluded, Major."

"When would you like this information?"

"By tomorrow afternoon."

He grinned at her and said, "OK my dear Jackie you shall have the enlargements by six tomorrow, how's that? In the mess we still talk about the day you had us tracking those Belarussian agents who kidnapped the MoD's nuclear weapons expert. Did us no end of good in high places."

Jackie thanked them and promised to be back at six tomorrow and stay to dinner. She'd leave the sergeants at Tolbrite and come alone, in uniform.

Chapter Fourteen

KATHRYN stole an hour during the morning to ride the horse that she had ridden before. She followed the same track through the Long Wood and then veered to the north-west, coming eventually to Winterborne Whitechurch. She carefully crossed the main road and followed the line of the lane that led to Winterborne Stickland, where it had all begun. She corrected the thought. Winterborne Stickland was where her adventure had begun but she suspected that, for the Clan Hawkins it had all begun at or near the Dowager's House at Spetisbury in 1692.

As she trotted back she decided that she'd have completed checking the photographs by the end of the day, by tomorrow lunchtime for sure, and that she'd go back to Boston on Thursday. It wasn't until she was rubbing down her mount that she remembered that she might not be the final arbiter on that; perhaps the British police would try to insist that she stay to give evidence of finding the body. It then occurred to her that if she simply left, the British police couldn't do much about it. With this comforting thought she watered the horse.

It was when she was again engrossed in her work in the Rumpus Room that it occurred to her that simply going back to Boston without telling anyone might not be too clever. If the police really wanted her to stay and she went without permission, they might put her on a black list and when she next wanted to come to England, as she most certainly would to follow up what she had collected on this trip, she might be stopped at Heathrow. She knew that were the positions reversed, the FBI would surely have her name on a computer black list. She decided that she'd ask Clare Thornton.

She phoned the Bournemouth police station and eventually Clare was on the line.

"Clare, this is Kathryn Glover. I've finished what I came to England for and I plan to go home to America on Thursday. Since I found that girl's body I might be wanted to give evidence at an inquest but I'd hope that in the circumstances, me being American and having no connection with the girl or any of the other participants, my statement would suffice. I don't want to get crossed lines with the

English police but you can't expect me to stay here until the murderer is caught."

"I agree that you can't be expected to kick your heels until we decide to hold an inquest and I'd think that your statement would do. There is just one thing, a word of warning from a friend, you must watch what you say, you just said that you had no connection with the girl or any of the other participants..."

"Nor have I," interrupted Kathryn.

"What about Professor Hamsworth?" asked Clare.

"Oh, er yes, I suppose that he might be called a participant," said Kathryn and then recovered, "but he's in the same position as I am and anyway he's already back in the States. If I go you'll have to treat us both the same. The only reason that I'm asking is because I'm frequently in Britain and I don't want to find that I'm on some sort of police black-list when I next come."

"Will you promise to return if we want you? You might be able to make it coincide with a business trip."

"Yes, I'll come back if needed."

"Then that's good enough. It's been nice to know you Kathryn."

"Likewise, Clare. I've met some nice people this trip."

The credit card investigation was on hold while Fred went to ask the area manager to create two new accounts in Paula's name and deposit a thousand pounds in each. He had to explain the purpose twice and then in the simplest words. The fact that the crooks might make three maximum allowable daily withdrawals from each account was the sticking point, "after all the crooks don't know how much money your operative has in her accounts, do they? And if they try to withdraw £250 on the third day and it fails, so what?"

They compromised on £500 in each account. Fred asked that they shouldn't be round numbers.

Paula decided that she'd spend the day on the Barton murder case and played once more her recording of what the friends had said in the bar of the Tolbrite Arms on Saturday. She wondered if Tim and Helene had their recorders with them; they'd introduced her to the idea and she couldn't understand why more people didn't do it.

What was it that Timmy had said? 'Why did he go to the Southampton cargo area?'

She thought about it. Swift / Sabatini had a unit at Bournemouth airport next to the import / export company and received packages there. In the normal course of events the import / export people would naturally route things for him to Bournemouth. What possible reason could there be for Swift / Sabatini to collect things from the Southampton unit instead of letting the importer bring them to Bournemouth?

From her work in divorce cases Paula didn't need reminding that unfaithful husbands and wives often used accommodation addresses to conceal letters and other things from their other half. Is this what Swift / Sabatini was doing and if so, who was he concealing whatever it is, from? The customs, the tax man and the drug squad came to mind.

But what was it the man outside the Bournemouth unit had said, something about a box as big as two shoe boxes containing brass fittings that the customs had opened for inspection. That dealt with the customs and the drug squad and she didn't think that the tax man would lose much sleep over a box of brass fittings. So why the special treatment?

Paula had long ago decided that one day she'd write a private detective's handbook embodying all the ploys and stratagems that a clever operator might use. She used one of them now. She looked up all the Swift / Sabatini telephone numbers, dialed 141 to conceal her own number and phoned the shop. When the phone was answered she said,

"Could I speak with Senor Sabatini please?"

"Who's calling, please?"

"The Windsor fertilizer company."

"I'm afraid that Mr Sabatini isn't here at the moment."

"Do you happen to know where I can catch him?"

"No." very sharply.

"Very well, I'll ring this afternoon."

"He won't be here."

And the phone was put down.

Paula phoned the unit at the airport,

"Could I speak with Mr Sabatini please?"

"He's not here."

"Oh, I'm sorry, do you happen to know where he is?"

"Who wants him?"

"I'm from TNT and I've got a package for him."

"Not another one! He had one on Friday, came in at Luton, where's yours from?"

"It doesn't say," said Paula, "but it looks Dutch."

"That figures," said the voice, "he's probably working at home and he'll be off to London tomorrow but don't tell him I said so."

"I'll try there then," said Paula having no intention of doing any such thing, she now had a lot to think about but she knew where she'd be at the crack of dawn on the morrow, outside Swift's house with a full tank of fuel.

It being Monday, it was Will and Gloria's night-off from the pub and the night for Wills chat show. They followed their usual routine, a quiet meal, a visit to the cinema and then to the radio station at about a quarter to ten for a chat with the station manager, Jill Jones before Will went on the air immediately following the news from Hawkridge Media Central. Jill always produced his show and made the split-second decisions on what to allow to go out on the air. Gloria sat beside her on the other side of a low glass screen from Will with a white board on which she wrote the callers name in big black letters. They had found that callers, especially female ones, don't like being called by the wrong name.

Will opened the show,

"Hello callers, this is your weekly chance to air your views on current affairs or to share with other people a past experience, be it happy or sad or simply embarrassing. You will have heard on the news some days ago of the discovery of a girl's body in a local village churchyard. She grew up in our village and was a very nice person. Her Gran who brought her up after her parents died, still lives there. I mention this not only as a small tribute to Mary but also to ask if anyone can help the police to find the person who killed her. It's known that she left the Half Moon Club alone and on foot at 10.00 o'clock on the 23rd of May. It has been reported that she was seen to get into the passenger seat of a green Jaguar car in the club's car park. Did anyone else see this or see a girl walking away from the vicinity of the club alone or with a taller man at about this time?

Remember, you can speak freely, you don't have to tell us your name but it's helpful if you give me a name that I can call you by."

He looked through the glass screen and Jill nodded, she had a caller, probably someone who hadn't been called– back before they ran out of time the week before.

"Hello caller, what do you want to discuss?"

"My names Shirley and I don't agree with what you said about using buses last week. There's some of us as lives in the country as have to go by car."

"I realize that Shirley, what I was saying was that there ought to be more buses on the country routes to make it not necessary for people to use their cars."

"But you heard what your other callers said about there not being enough people to make it pay."

"Yes, it would have to be subsidized and then people like you, Shirley, would be able to save money by going by bus."

"But it wouldn't be as convenient, would it?"

"It depends on what you consider convenient. If you mean getting to the shops or to the dentist, no the bus wouldn't be as convenient but if you take the longer view a lot of people wouldn't die from the effect of pollution and global warming, would they?"

Jill was making wrap it up signs. Will said,

"Goodnight Shirley, thank you for your call."

He took off his headphones and grinned through the screen where Gloria was wiping SHIRLEY off her board. He could faintly hear the music that filled the time between calls. After two minutes Jill was gesturing him to put them on again.

"Hello caller, what do I call you?"

"My names Bill and I don't agree that the taxpayers should pay for country people to ride on buses, they should move into town."

"But many can't, Bill," said Will, "perhaps they work in the country or perhaps they can't afford a house in the town. Some of us have to live there to keep the country going."

"You could have buses to take people to work in the country," said Bill as if he'd solved the problem.

"You do know that the farmers are getting ready for the early milking at 4 o'clock in the morning, don't you Bill? Would all your country workers have to leave home sometime after three a.m. to catch the bus taking the early-morning dairymen?"

"'Course they wouldn't, they'd have to change the time they milk the cows."

Will decided that he'd had enough of this idiot.

"Thanks Bill for your interesting views, I hope our country friends were listening."

He took off his earphones and the music swelled. But not for long.

"Hello caller, what do you want to talk about?"

"The last caller. I've never heard such rubbish, all move into town, indeed and change the time of milking!"

"I gather that you live in the country," said Will.

"No I don't, I'm a schoolteacher in Poole."

"What do I call you, I can't keep saying Miss, can I?"

"I don't see why not, the children do but you may call me Heather."

"You feel strongly about the environment?"

"Of course, all thinking people do."

"What would you do, Heather?"

"I understand that anything that we do in Britain would be a drop in the ocean of pollution but someone's got to start and perhaps the rest of Europe would follow. First I'd put the price of petrol and diesel up to, say, twenty pounds a gallon. Then I'd bring in coloured petrol and diesel at five pounds a gallon for essential users, like buses and lorries delivering food and things."

"What about all the Mums taking little Bobbie to school?"

"That's a problem because too many of them are making a quick school-run before themselves going off to work to pay the mortgage or fund a second holiday in Florida. They'd have to decide on their priorities. If it meant that more parents would walk their children to school it would be good for the school and good for the children, reduce obesity and bullying for one thing."

"Thank you for your call, Heather, I'm sure that, like me, a lot of our listeners agree with you."

Will took off his earphones and looked at Gloria who had written 'NOT ME, BATH' on her board, from which he deduced that schoolteacher Heather's proposal to put the price of petrol up for non-essential users would hurt absentee property owners like Gloria. They grinned at each other. After two minutes Jill made her earphones-on motion,

The Body in the Churchyard

"*Hello caller, who am I talking with?*"

A very quiet voice said, "*Are you talking to me?*"

"*Yes,*" said Will.

"*It was a lady who called me back.*"

"*Yes,*" said Will. "*That was our producer, Jill, who does all the hard work around here. She manages Radio Bournemouth.*" He grinned at Jill.

"*Oh I see. Is what I say being broadcast?*"

"*Yes.*"

"*Oh, fancy that. I can't hear myself because the lady, Jill did you say her name was, she told me that I mustn't have my radio on.*"

"*That's right,*" He looked at Gloria's blank board and said, "*I don't think that you've told us your name.*"

"*Oh, I don't want to, people would know who I am, wouldn't they?*"

"*I shall call you Violet,*" said Will hoping that his more erudite listeners would get the inference to shrinking violets. "*What exactly did you want to speak about?*"

"*Oh yes, it was about what you said at the beginning, about Marylyn getting murdered.*"

Will's heart beat a little faster. He wished that he hadn't been clever about the name,

"*Can you help us?*"

"*Well, I know her, knew her I suppose I should say, and I saw her that night.*"

"*Where did you see her?*"

"*Well, I was going in to the club with a friend when she came out.*"

"*What time was that?*"

"*About ten. I'd just met my friend and he said let's go to the club and I looked at the time.*"

"*Was Marylyn alone?*"

"*Yes, she said Hello but didn't stop, it sometimes embarrasses men friends you see.*"

"*Did you see where she went?*"

"*She went across the car park and got into a car. I saw it because a man came out of the club and sort of stood in the doorway, looking after her and me and my friend couldn't get past him to go in.*"

"Did the car drive away?"

"Yes, it made a noise."

"What about the man who blocked your way. What did he do?"

"He went back into the foyer and said something to Chalky, he's the door-keeper, and then he walked out of the club. I got the idea that he was interested in Marylyn."

"Can you remember anything else about the car and who was in it?"

"No, it was getting dark by then but it made a noise."

"Could you see the colour?"

"It wasn't a light colour, more like green, dark green, the colour they paint Jaguars."

"Was it a Jaguar?"

"Now you make me think about it, I suppose it was; it sounded like one."

Will looked at the girls and saw that Gloria had written 'Jill has phone number' on her board. He blessed the system by which the producer never puts a caller directly on the air but always calls them back.

"Thank you for your call, dear, I'm sure that what you've told us will be of the greatest use in helping to solve the mystery of Marylyn's death."

Will took off his headphones and sipped at the cup of coffee that Gloria handed him. He thought that any subsequent calls would be an anti-climax.

Jill let the coffee break last a full three minutes and then motioned him that a caller was waiting.

"Hello caller, can I have your name?"

"It's Steve and I want to talk about the electricity and gas people."

"The utilities," said Estate Maintenance Manager Will.

"Yes, the electric and gas people," said Steve.

"What about them?"

"Well, the trouble you have in getting any sense out of them."

"In what way?"

"The people in the papers say that we should look round for the cheapest supplier. They're right, of course, because it's the same gas or volts that come out of the pipe or wire no matter who you pay your bill to."

The Body in the Churchyard

"That's true, Steve."

"So we should chose the supplier who gives the best service, usually on the telephone. So what do they do if you ring up, they keep you sitting there listening to canned music with a girl butting in every two minutes telling you that all their operators are busy. And you're paying for the call. Then when you finally get through they play dumb and make things as difficult as possible especially if you're trying to change your supplier."

"I thought that the new supplier did all the work for you?"

"They're often as difficult as the people you're leaving."

"Thanks for your call, Steve, perhaps other listeners have had the same sort of unhappy experience with the utilities."

The evening followed it's usual pattern. There were the expected calls about the price of houses, he looked at Gloria through the glass, and students and the general incompetence of the utilities. Will thought that the utilities might be a good topic next week.

Jill voted the session a good one. Will asked her to let Paula listen to the recording of the call about Marylyn Barton when she came in tomorrow.

But Paula didn't come in on Tuesday morning; at half past six she was parked within sight of the Swift house and able to follow the green Jaguar when it emerged from the drive and turned towards the main road. She fell into place and allowed two other cars to get between her and her quarry. He made for the A31 through the forest, joined the M27 and took the slip road to the M3. Paula sensed that she was probably on her way to London.

She and Sabatini were not in Bournemouth when an army helicopter on a training mission scheduled to cover Poole, Portland and Bovington, hovered slowly over Bournemouth.

Paula followed Sabatini to the car park of a supermarket in Sunbury. Most customers park as close to the actual entrance to the store as possible but Sabatini parked away from the majority of cars and next to a blue BMW. He parked his car and sat there for a few minutes, then got out, opened the boot of his car and took out a box. He closed the car boot and looked casually around. He then opened the boot of the blue BMW and put the box in and closed the boot. He then got back into his own car and drove off. Paula photographed the whole thing from her parking place some distance away.

She decided that she would wait and see who came for the blue BMW. Sure enough, two minutes later, a swarthy man walked up to the car, started the engine and drove off with Paula a sensible distance behind. With great difficulty she followed the BMW until it stopped outside a café in Lewisham. There was no room to park and so the BMW was double parked and holding up the traffic, including Paula. The driver got out unhurriedly, walked round to the rear of the car opened the boot, took out the box and, with a gesture to the cars that he was holding-up, went into the café. Almost immediately he reappeared and got into the car and drove off. Trapped in a line of impatient drivers Paula had no option but to follow him, noting the name of the café, 'The Palermo Bar' in passing. She followed the blue BMW until it parked in front of one of a row of large terrace houses at Blackheath. She photographed the car and the house.

She drove back to Bournemouth feeling that she was making progress. She must tell Clare; honest people didn't do what Swift / Sabatini and the swarthy man had done in the supermarket car park.

Jackie's exit from the Tolbrite Arms in uniform was not without comment. She drove to Middle Wallop at teatime to receive the blow-ups of the film that the helicopter had taken and stayed to dinner as the guest of Major Hargreaves. It was late when she arrived back at the pub.

Chapter Fourteen

THE following morning at the radio station, she settled down with the girls to look for garden sheds behind garages. They identified seventeen houses that had a sizeable shed behind a largish garage and these were laid out on Paula's desk when she came in. Sandra made haste to gather them up but Paula stopped her, asking, "What are those?"

"We got fed-up with trying to find out what people had in their back gardens so the Cap got some friends of hers to take aerial pictures," said Kim.

"We've identified seventeen possibles for where that chap stole the gun," said Sandra, "always assuming that he was telling the truth."

"You mean about the American youngsters and the half hour walk to the sea front?" said Paula. She turned to Jackie who was sitting nearby, "I was thinking on the way home on Saturday night that the Swift house must be somewhere near there. I wonder if he's one of your possibles?"

Sandra laid the pictures out one by one. As she looked at them Paula mentioned that, for want of a better lead in the murder enquiry and because of the two-airport cargo puzzle, she had been keeping an eye on Swift / Sabatini and had followed him the previous day. She described the strange goings-on that she had witnessed in the supermarket car park and following the blue BMW to the bar in Lewisham and the house in Blackheath.

Jackie was now fully alert. She made Paula say it all again into her pocket recorder, echoing her comment that honest people didn't behave like that. Mr Swift / Sabatini was up to something and it wasn't to do with flowers.

She said, "I've got a feeling that this could be serious crime and perhaps dangerous. You've done extremely well Paula but I suggest that from now on you keep away from Mr Swift or whatever he calls himself and leave it to the police. No, not the locals, Scotland Yard. It's time I reported to our General and I'll also see that Scotland Yard hears about this."

Paula had continued looking at the pictures taken by the helicopter and she stopped at one and said, "That's it, that's the Swift house.

See, it's got a largish shed behind a large garage, like the van driver said."

Sandra put the photograph to one side and said, "We'll have to find a way of examining what's in that shed."

"No we won't, Sandra," said Jackie. "Well leave any breaking and entering to the experts. If Swift's a wrong-un you can bet that by now the shed and garage are wired and David Vowles would never forgive us if we alerted Swift to the fact that someone's interested in him."

"That van driver in Bath got in without sounding any alarms," said Sandra.

"True," said Jackie, "but we're not going to. That theft may have alerted Swift. We'll leave it to Tom Burton."

Inspector Tom Burton of the Special Branch worked in a unit answerable directly to the Assistant Commissioner in a way similar to the way Jackie and her girls worked directly for Major General Tubby Lowe. He was also engaged to Kim and, Jackie guessed, always knew much of what her team was doing. She didn't mind, they worked well together.

Jackie drove to London that evening, spent the night at her flat and by 10a.m. she and General Lowe were with David Vowles and Inspector Tom Burton. For the senior officers' benefit she recapitulated the story of finding the peculiar gun and the decision that her team should try to find the house in Bournemouth from which it had allegedly been stolen. She then described the murder of Marylyn Barton and the American who stated that he thought that she had been driven away in a green Jaguar car and was kept in prison for a night by Inspector Clouseau leading to Tim Hawkridge's instruction to Southern Enquiries to find out all that they could, that in turn led to Paula's arrangement with WDC Thornton to share information.

For want of other clues, and with WDC Thornton's agreement, Paula had visited all the addresses written in the murdered girl's private notebook to see which of her clients, if any, had a green Jaguar car, a swarthy complexion and was tall.

She had found that a Mr George Swift had these attributes so she followed him. She found that he went to a unit at the Bournemouth airport cargo area, trading under the name Georgio Sabatini, and dealing in flower and garden supplies. The day she followed him, when he left the airport he went to the Southampton airport cargo area.

Paula had posed as a Hawkridge radio reporter and spoke with workmen at the import / export agency that had a unit next to the Sabatini one. She found that Swift / Sabatini had a shop in one of the better parts of Bournemouth and also supplied the trade. Asked about Southampton, one of the men had said that Sabatini had garden supplies consigned to Bournemouth and to Southampton and always collected them himself. The man had seen one of the Southampton consignments that had been opened by the Customs, a box the size of two shoe boxes, filled with brass things.

In an attempt to discover who had garden sheds, she and her sergeants had backtracked along the route that they thought the original gun thief had walked. This had proved most difficult and so friends in the Army Air Corps had done a training photographic mission over that part of Bournemouth which resulted in them finding seventeen houses with a sizeable garden shed behind a large garage.

David Vowles remarked "It's useful to have friends."

"In high places," said Tubby.

Jackie said, "Yes, it is, you see we were using our friends Fred and Paula's office as our base in Bournemouth and had all the photographs laid out yesterday when Paula came in. She'd been following Sabatini the previous day and what she told us is the reason that I asked for this meeting."

"You have us on the edge of our seats," grinned the Assistant Commissioner.

"Sabatini left home at about seven a.m. and took the M3 to London. He stopped in a supermarket car park in Sunbury, parking next to a blue BMW, some distance from the other shopper's cars. He got out and removed a box the size of two shoe boxes from the boot of his car and put it in the boot of the BMW which was conveniently unlocked. Sabatini then got into his car and drove away, presumably back to Bournemouth. Paula has a video of all this. She sat tight and after a few minutes a swarthy man came to the BMW, got in and drove off with Paula some distance behind. She managed to follow him, despite traffic lights and other hazards and saw him stop, open his boot and take the box into a café called The Palermo Bar in Lewisham then drive on to an address in Blackheath."

"Well done Paula," said Tubby.

"Yes, she deserves a medal," said Jackie. "I've told her that she may have uncovered something serious and she's to keep clear of Swift / Sabatini from now on because I thought that Scotland Yard would now take over. Incidentally, Paula picked out Swift's house from our aerial photographs, he's got a big shed behind his garage, just like the van man in Bath said."

"We've got the things we spoke about last time," said David Vowles "metal shipments coming in at different places. The significance of the words Sabatini and Palermo shouldn't escape us, either. Sabatini was one of the old style godfathers in New York and Palermo's in Sicily."

"So it might not be terrorists?" said Tom.

"I never thought that I'd live to see the day I was relieved that the villains might only be the Mafiosi," said David Vowles. "At least they mainly kill one-another."

"All things are relative," said Tubby Lowe.

"This is all speculation," cautioned Jackie. "We haven't got any hard evidence, couldn't we get the Customs to open the next box that appears consigned to Sabatini, so that we might compare whatever's in it with the four pieces of the gun that we have?"

"Five pieces if we include our imagined sabot," said the General.

"We've got enough already to justify investigating further, don't you think so, Sir?" said Inspector Tom Burton. "Starting with asking South East division what they know about the Palermo Bar."

"Yes I think so, we'll leave the Customs thing for the moment, there's always the risk that he'll get suspicious." David Vowles turned to the Major-General and grinned, " Can we continue to have your help, after all, they might be terrorists?"

The General turned to Jackie, "What do you think?"

Jackie said, "I didn't cancel our accommodation at the Tolbrite Arms."

"Good then, do all you can help Tom at the Bournemouth end."

When they were back in the MoD and the General had gone through his 'Come in and have a cup of tea' routine and she was seated in his room, Jackie told the General about Kathryn Glover and the search for her Hawkins ancestors that had led to her investigation

The Body in the Churchyard

into the old Hawkridge papers. His reaction was "I must tell Jane, she's distantly related to the Hawkridges." He thought a bit and added, "Come to think of it, they've been there for so long that half the county of Dorset must be related to them in one way or the other."

At his request Jackie recounted the story of how another American professor had danced with the victim the night she was murdered and how Kathryn Glover had found the body and it transpired that both professors were leading teams of undergraduates and knew one another from their student days at Harvard.

"But none of this has any bearing on the gun business?" queried Tubby.

"Only coincidentally," said Jackie. "If Paula hadn't got it into her head that Swift / Sabatini fitted the bill for the man the American professor thought that he saw driving away from the Half Moon club that night in a green Jaguar car, she wouldn't have followed him. Secondly the van driver who stole the gun probably wouldn't have remembered passing those two hotels if it hadn't been for noticing the American students."

"It's amazing how we depend on chance in this business, isn't it?"

"Yes and No, General; the trick is to recognize the significance of pieces of information when they pass before you."

"What will you do now?"

"Discuss with Tom Burton what he'd like us to do at the Bournemouth end while he looks at the bar in Lewisham, where, I suspect, most of the action will centre."

"Off you go then and please be careful, I don't want your uncle asking me why I let you go back there."

Paula had woken up wondering what else she could do to solve the murder case. When she got to the office she found that the priorities had changed, the bank had created two new accounts for Miss Paula Smith and Fred was determined that she should try them forthwith. A study of the accounts of the bank's customers who's funds had been raided showed that they had purchased something using their credit card at a garage, either in the Branksome area or Ferndown.

Paula would buy some petrol at each garage, using a different card for each. As she drove into the first garage, Paula could see a snag.

How would she know whether a copy of her card was being used? The bank might not know until the clearing process was complete and that might be in three or four days time. She reminded herself that it didn't matter, what's three days in a lifetime?

She drove into the suspect garage at Ferndown, got out and filled her car's tank with fuel, intent on stopping at a nice round, easily remembered sum. She stopped at £23. She turned away then looked back and saw that the meter now said £23.01. She'd noticed this at other garages, you stop filling and then the pump adds a penny. She locked the car and went into the shop, busy calculating how much profit garages across the country make each day from the 'added penny' racket.

The cheerful young man behind the counter took her card, said £23.01 and passed it through a Switch device on the counter just below her line of sight to check her credit worthiness, explaining ingenuously, "You've no idea how many people come in here with someone else's card." He then invited Paula to sign the usual slip of paper.

She drove back to the radio station and changed into Fred's car. She repeated the performance at the Branksome filling station. She put £19 worth of fuel in the tank, locked the car and walked into the garage shop. The blonde girl behind the counter said, "Nineteen pounds and a penny please." Paula handed her the second credit card and a penny. The card disappeared from Paula's view and was returned a moment later. She signed the slip, received her receipt, went back to Fred's car and drove back to the radio station.

This was where Jill Jones caught up with her and gave her a tape recording of Will's shy girl caller who had seen Marylyn get into a car on the fateful night.

Paula phoned Clare Thornton who came over later to hear it.

"So it was exactly as the American professor said," said Clare.

"Yes, now let me tell you what happened when I followed Sabatini yesterday."

Paula told the WDC about the parcel switch and the bar in Lewisham and the aerial survey, finishing with Jackie's admonition that they may have stumbled upon serious crime. She took Clare into a nearby room into which the SIB team had moved. Sandra and Kim were there. Paula said,

"You all know each other don't you?"

"Yes," said Clare, "the last time was at Bovington, wasn't it?"

"I've been filling Clare in on yesterday's happenings and Jackie's warning to tread softly as far as Sabatini's concerned. Do you know what happened in London this morning?"

"The Cap phoned to say that Scotland Yard were taking over the London end and that we are to keep a watching brief here," said Sandra. "That's to do with the mysterious boxes and guns. She didn't mention the murder enquiry."

"We've no alternative but to continue with our enquiries into the murder," said Clare, "and if that involves questioning Mr Swift, then we will question Mr Swift."

"But you mustn't at any price mention the boxes or guns," said Kim, "otherwise you may put a giant spanner in whatever Scotland Yard is doing."

"It might come out in the questioning," said Clare.

"If there's anything dishonest about his activities you can hardly expect him to raise the matter, can you? So we shouldn't," said Sandra.

"I don't know if my Inspector will accept that."

"Look, Clare, I told you about the boxes and the gun because we agreed to share all information that might have a bearing on the murder," said Paula. "Don't let me down. You know and I know that if he knew what I've just told you, Inspector Clouseau would be likely to bring Swift / Sabatini in and question him about his activities and destroy any hope of the authorities ever getting to the bottom of things."

"Well, you can see that it puts me in a funny position, can't you?"

"Yes, but you'll have to accept it. If Jackie had heard this conversation and knew that you had even thought of telling Clouseau what I've told you, she'd kill me."

"Even if we are using your offices," said Kim.

"No, I mean it, we have to keep the two cases separate," said Paula. "Swift / Sabatini must be given no inkling that anyone is interested in the boxes that he receives through the import / export agency or what he does with the contents. I for one have no idea what's in them but I rather think that Jackie has."

The sergeants kept their eyes on the papers that they had been studying when Paula brought Clare in.

"Oh, alright," said Clare, "I know that you're right."

"Then let's hear what your next move might be in the Marylyn Barton murder case."

"I'd think that on the strength of having two witnesses statements that they saw Marylyn being driven away in a green Jaguar car we might ask the drivers of such cars who are named in her school-book where they were at 10 p.m. on the night in question."

"Good," said Paula "and we mustn't forget the men who called at her flat that evening nor the man who went there the next night."

"Who had a big signet ring," said Kim. "You could get some photo's and show them to the porter at her apartment block."

"There's just one thing," said Clare. "I'll have to go and see the second witness who Will called Violet, where does she live?"

"I'll have to ask Jill but I can see that it'll present a problem."

"How's that?

"The station gives a guarantee of anonymity to all the people who call-in."

"Surely they would waive that in the case of a murder enquiry?" said Clare.

"They'd be fools if they did," said Sandra. "The whole success of the chat-show depends on people speaking without fear of exposure."

"But that's ridiculous," said Clare. "It's like a confessional."

"I'll have a word with Jill Jones and see what we can come up with," said Paula.

"If you question someone, can you take their finger-prints and a DNA sample?" asked Kim.

"No," said Clare, "only with their consent until they're actually charged."

"But they can't blame you if you happen to get it accidentally," said Kim "I've always imagined myself going into a camp barbers shop and picking up a sample of hair that the barber has just cut off my suspect."

"When does hair cease to be part of a person's person?" tried Sandra. "Who owns the hair on the barber's floor?"

"I can see that there's some fertile minds working on the DNA problem," said Clare. "What about finger prints?"

"Leave that to us," said Kim, having no idea how she would get them.

"I'll have to go," said Clare, "but before I do let's agree that for the purposes of the murder investigation, the man we suspect is a Mr Swift. That's the name on his birth certificate and if he's ever charged, that will be the name he'll be charged under. For the other investigation," she grinned at Paula, "the one that I've forgotten already, he can be called Sabatini."

"That's good," said Sandra. "We'll tell the Cap."

They adjourned and the sergeants drove to Tolbrite where Jackie joined them. They had a brief discussion before dinner, during which they played the recording of the afternoons discussion, and discussed how to get fingerprints and a DNA sample.

Kim remarked that if he was a womanizer there was one obvious way and she wasn't volunteering. She wondered where he got his hair cut?

Sandra said, "I wonder if Swift-called-Sabatini serves in his shop. If he does I'll buy a smooth surfaced vase." She pointed out, "It's alright to decide to call him Swift but it's difficult when he's standing in the middle of a shop called Sabatini's isn't it?"

Jackie didn't think it difficult at all and directed that on the morrow Kim should do a clipboard enquiry at the Swift home and Sandra should reconnoiter the shop.

"And what will you do Cap?"

"I thought that I might let Mr Swift see me."

Dinner that evening was a bitter-sweet occasion because Kathryn was leaving the following day to fly back to Boston carrying the precious photographs of the Hawkridge papers. In the last two days she had pored over the first batch and picked out three letters that seemed to end with what might have been 'Your loving mother, Elizabeth' but the text would require a lot of deciphering. There were other letters in what appeared to Kathryn to be a younger hand but she reminded herself, not for the first time, that facts were what counted, not wishes.

As Gloria said to her mother in the kitchen the following morning, "I always knew that Jackie was lovely but go and have a look this morning, she's absolutely gorgeous."

After breakfast, Jackie and the sergeants, mine host and his wife, Will and Gloria were there to see Kathryn on her way. She promised that she'd be back when the experts had deciphered the old letters that she'd photographed. One of the last things brought tears to her eyes when Will gave her a note from Lady Hawkridge wishing her a safe journey and a speedy return.

In mid–morning Jackie drove into Bournemouth and stopped practically in front of the Sabatini flower shop. She got out and walked languidly into the shop. The flowers were lovely and her admiration of them was not part of the act. Jackie wandered round the shop with a sales assistant hovering behind. In a few minutes a tallish man appeared and muttered something to the assistant who melted away. He contrived to capture Jackie's attention and asked,

"Did madam have anything particular in mind?"

"Not really," drawled Jackie, "Lady Hawkins told me about your shop and I thought that, since I was passing, I'd look in."

"Always pleased to oblige," said Swift alias Sabatini.

Jackie raised an eyebrow, looked arch, stretched, and said, "So I understand."

"Our blooms are of the finest quality."

"So I see, perhaps I'll come back tomorrow about eleven."

With which she sauntered out of the shop.

She joined Sandra and Kim at the radio station.

"I didn't see you at the flower shop," said Jackie.

"But I saw you," said Sandra. "He watched you till your car was out of sight."

"Was he suspicious?"

"No, just drooling with desire."

Kim said, "We're wasting our time down here, Cap."

"From that I gather that you didn't have a successful morning?"

"Correct, I didn't have a successful morning. The Swifts don't need any wooden garden furniture and they've got a shed, practically new as sheds go. Let's go back to London."

"She's got a point, Cap," said Sandra, "there's nothing that we can do down here in Bournemouth on the gun thing; when it breaks it'll break in London."

"You're right, of course," said Jackie "I'd like to see if I can get Sabatini's finger-prints tomorrow and, if I'm lucky, a sample for DNA testing but there's no reason why you should stay. Why don't you go back to the pub and check out this lunch time?"

That night she ate a solitary dinner at the Tolbrite Arms and retired to her room. As Gloria remarked, the place seemed empty.

Chapter Fifteen

THAT Thursday Inspector Tom Burton went to Lewisham to ask the locals what they knew about the Palermo Bar.

He had spent some time examining the previous year's crime figures for the area. It was a sad story and he had much sympathy with the officers who were at the sharp end, who daily had to deal with a miscellany of filth and crime. There were pages of attempted robberies and assaults by dope filled morons wielding knives and baseball wielding thugs, cases of gross bodily harm and murder. Most of the murders were domestic where the victim was related to the killer, few of these were premeditated. But there was an increased number where a weapon had been used against an apparent stranger, usually a knife but occasionally a firearm. He noted that the use of firearms was on the increase particularly by gangs.

The license to sell intoxicating liquors in the Palermo Bar was in the names of Luigi Sabatini and Benito Sabatini, who, it was understood, were brothers and owned the premises. They had held the license for over ten years and the police had never had cause to oppose its renewal. The Sabatini brothers worked hard, one of them was always there and an elderly woman whom the brothers called Moma presided over the cash register with the eyes of a hawk from morning till night. They wouldn't allow rowdiness and excess, in fact as far as the authorities were concerned, the bar was among the best run in Lewisham, if not London.

Tom asked who the clientele were? Did any known villains frequent the place?

He learnt that because it was so well run and caused no trouble, the police largely ignored it, they had enough to do, dealing with the afro-Caribbean's who seemed to be taking over the adjacent suburbs.

The station sergeant said that he used to walk that beat. It hadn't always been quiet. The previous owner had been a nice man of Italian extraction who lived with his wife and many children above the Neapolitan Café, as it was called in those days and made a modest living. Then all sorts of things started happening to the café. Eventually the eldest daughter called at the police station and poured out the story of demands for protection money but her father refused to say a word, said that his daughter was imagining things. She didn't imagine the Molotov cocktail that was thrown through the window one night and set fire to the café. The family was rescued from the upstairs windows in the nick of time. That was the end of the Neapolitan Café, the shell of the building was bought for a song by the Sabatini's and had since prospered. They hadn't had any trouble, no one had thrown a fire-bomb through their window.

The sergeant thought that the Palermo Bar's regulars were mainly Italians, natural enough since the bar specialized in Italian dishes. The environment was friendly and intimate with booths along the walls and soft music played. In the early days it had been rougher. As a young copper, sheltering from the rain in a doorway, he'd noticed that the Palermo Bar stayed open later than the other café's and that men came in cars long after other people were abed. He'd thought at the time that there might be hostesses there. He'd mentioned it in his report but no one did anything. Then he'd been shifted to a different beat. In those days young policemen weren't supposed to think.

"What do you think of it now, Sarge?" asked Tom.

"I really ought to ask you why you're interested in it Inspector but I can guess, you suspect an Italian connection."

"Let's just say that there are straws in the wind," said Tom.

"The only thing that I can see that hints at that, is that it's so damned quiet and respectable," smiled the sergeant.

Tom said that he had a point and went next to Inspector Patel.

"As you know I'm from the anti-terrorist cum special branch unit attached to the Assistant Commissioner's office," said Tom.

"My, my, we are honoured," smiled Patel, "We thought that you people had forgotten that we existed."

"You'd be surprised what David Vowles knows. People sometimes forget that he started as a copper on the beat."

"How can I help you, Tom?" said Patel.

"We want to know something about the Palermo Bar."

"Why?"

"A suspect of Italian extraction from Bournemouth put a box in the boot of Luigi Sabatini's car in a supermarket car park at Sunbury two days ago and Luigi delivered it to the Palermo Bar before driving to his home in Blackheath."

"What was in the box, drugs?"

"We don't know but we suspect guns."

"Are they stolen? I'm surprised to find you on such a case."

"We think that they're peculiar guns capable of being taken on to an airliner without detection."

"Oh, I see, hence the AC's concern. How can we help?"

"I agreed with your desk sergeant that the only thing that's peculiar about the Palermo Bar is that it's so quiet and law-abiding."

"That's a thought," said Inspector Patel. "I hadn't looked at it that way."

"Now that means that the rowdy element in this borough know to steer clear of the Palermo when they've had a skin full."

"I suppose so."

"My question is why and how do they know that the Palermo's off-limits?"

"I suppose that the word gets around," said Patel.

"Well, for starters, I want to know what that word is," said Tom, "and that shouldn't be too difficult."

"How?"

"Your division has a large ethnic population to police and a difficult problem with afro-Caribbean Yardies and the like. They're trouble makers who have created disturbances and terrified people in most café's and bars. Why do they leave the Palermo alone? You have some excellent afro-Caribbean officers who have their ear to the ground. Ask them to find out why this is, without mentioning the guns, of course."

"There's no harm in trying," said Inspector Patel, "I suppose that you want the answer yesterday?"

"Or earlier," grinned Tom. Then he became serious, "I was looking at your divisional crime figures before I came down. Stripped of the Home Office's statistical adjustments...."

"Swindles," said Patel.

"Stripped of the swindles there has been a sharp-ish increase in the use of firearms."

"It's the same in all the big cities," said Patel.

"I was wondering if there is any evidence that a particular group or nationality has provided the victim or the attacker?"

"There's rivalry among the West Indian gangs. Most of them seem to be getting guns from somewhere and frankly as long as they're shooting each other we don't mind too much. Of course if we catch them with a gun we do them for possession and if the bullets match a shooting we do them for that. But we don't play at heroics."

"What about the others?" asked Tom, "any particular nationality singled out?"

"Well," said Patel slowly, "there were a number of Italians, usually knife wounds."

"Let us know when you get anything, Patty and thanks for your help."

He edged his car out into the stream of traffic and drove slowly past the Palermo Bar. It looked innocent enough. He thought about that, innocent enough for what? He'd give Patty until Monday before hastening him.

The next day Jackie took care with her make-up and put on an outfit that she knew that she looked good in.

At breakfast Mrs Trowbridge asked her if she was going somewhere special and she replied, "Yes, but not the way that you mean."

She checked out of the pub saying that she'd spend the weekend at her flat and would be back on Monday evening. If she couldn't come, she would telephone.

She sauntered into the Sabatini flower shop at ten past eleven. Sabatini had evidently been looking out of the door and was instantly at her side. "Buon giorno signorina."

"Good morning" replied Jackie, gesturing with a gloved hand. "Your flowers are beautiful." She walked slowly round the store with Sabatini describing and naming the varieties. He kept touching her to draw attention to particular blossoms and contrived to get ahead of her at the narrow places so that she must pass close by him. She affected not to notice. At the end of the tour she went back to the roses and said that she would like a dozen for her mother. Sabatini called an assistant to wrap them.

Jackie gave the assistant her credit card and was about to drop her lipstick in its smooth shiny case when Sabatini made an elaborate show of presenting her with a red rose in a small glass phial. Jackie accepted with a show of appreciation at the gesture. She came close and looked him in the eyes and removed some hair that was on the shoulder of his jacket. He was so engrossed in looking at her and perhaps wondering what she would do that she didn't think that he noticed.

Mission accomplished she took her purchase, made sure that she didn't rub the phial or drop the hairs, thanked Sabatini for his excellent service and that she'd probably be in tomorrow and walked out of the shop. To her horror, he came too. She now had the problem of unlocking her car and getting in complete with the roses without smudging his fingerprints on the phial or losing the two hairs that she had taken from his coat. She managed it by giving Sabatini the roses to hold while his gaze was riveted on her legs swinging into the car. She accepted the roses back through the car window.

"Perhaps the signorina would honour me by having lunch with me one day?"

"Perhaps," replied Jackie with a come-hither look as she put the car into gear and moved off.

She stopped round the corner and put the phial and hairs in separate plastic envelopes and phoned WDC Clare Thornton to meet her at the radio station.

When Clare arrived, Jackie explained how she had obtained Sabatini's prints and strands of hair from which his DNA might be obtained.

"I'm not sure that evidence obtained in that way would be admissible in court," said Clare. "Defence lawyers can often have that sort of thing thrown out."

"Clare for goodness sake join the real world. Stop worrying about the rules. That can come later. What I've given you should give you the confidence to take the man in for questioning. Then you can take his prints and get your DNA sample."

"It's alright for you, Jackie, but before we can bring Sabatini in for questioning I have to persuade Inspector Stevens and I never know which way he'll jump."

"What's the name of Inspector Clouseau's boss?"

"Detective Superintendent Harding."

"Then I'll have a word with him. Don't worry, I won't land you in it. In any case, we'll have to get Scotland Yard's OK before we move."

"Why's that?" asked Clare.

"As you know they are working on something that involves Mr Swift / Sabatini that could be more important than the murder in the immediate future. It's simply a question of timing."

"What should I do then?"

"Take these samples and have your experts deal with them. I'll have a word with the Super and explain. Don't worry, you're doing fine."

Jackie called on Detective Superintendent Harding that afternoon. She had phoned ahead and arranged the appointment but she still had to wait a few minutes until the Superintendent's secretary came to get her. During this period she was aware that she was the object of much male scrutiny. She had met the Super before and he knew of Jackie's reputation. She briefed him on the Swift / Sabatini scene, how she was convinced that he had something to do with Marylyn Barton's death and how she had obtained his fingerprints and a DNA sample which should provide the local force with reason for bringing Swift / Sabatini in for questioning. She described the bigger scenario in which Sabatini appeared to be implicated and that Scotland Yard were now virtually in charge of the timescale of events and that bringing in Georgio Sabatini for questioning should first be cleared with the Assistant Commissioner. She stressed the part that WDC Clare Thornton had played under difficult circumstances and that Inspector Stevens mustn't be allowed to interfere. Superintendent Harding said that he understood completely, his force would assemble all the evidence and await the go-ahead from Scotland Yard.

When she'd left he sent for Clare Thornton.

"I've just had a visit by Captain Fraser. She spoke very highly of your work."

"That was kind of her, Sir."

"She's a remarkable young woman."

"Yes, she gets results. Perhaps because she's allowed to get on with things."

He gave her an old-fashioned look and grinned. He went on,

"Have you passed on the finger-print and DNA samples?"

"Yes Sir."

Harding picked up the phone and told his secretary to tell the boffins that the two samples that WDC Thornton had handed to them were to be given top priority and the results reported directly to him.

Clare departed well satisfied.
By which time Jackie was on her way to London.

That afternoon Inspector Patel saw PC Brian Johnson.

Brian and his wife Sadie had survived the insults leveled at a coloured police officer from both sides and had earned respect in the community. It had been hard and there had been times when she had wept on Brian's shoulder when someone had been beastly to her in the supermarket because she'd married that symbol of oppression, a policeman. But they'd weathered the storm, in part by Brian's patient work with the schools. He was now qualified for promotion and would have his sergeants stripes soon.

"Brian, Scotland Yard want to know why the tear-aways never rough-up the Palermo Bar?"

He thought for a bit and said, "Now that you mention it, it is odd, isn't it? I suppose it's because it's Italian."

"Why should that make a difference?" Patel was testing him.

"Because those sort of Italians are hard men and stick together, they haven't been absorbed the way the Poles have."

Patel absorbed this, perhaps that was because the Poles that Brian was referring to hadn't got anywhere to go back to in communist Poland.

"Have a sniff round this weekend, will you, see what the word on the street is?"

The bar at the Tolbrite arms was less crowded on Saturday. It seemed half empty to Will and Gloria. Fred, Angela and Paula were there but Timmy and Helene were in France with Claire-Marie, and Kathryn and Jackie had gone.

On Monday morning the bank informed Fred that a sum of £250 had been withdrawn from each of Paula's two phantom accounts. He and Paula thought that they knew how it was done, the problem now was to find out by whom? Paula was sure that as Monday wore on, further withdrawals, made the previous Friday and Saturday would emerge. The delay in processing cheque and cash machine withdrawals inherent in the British banking system was more than a nuisance. She guessed that it would be an uphill fight to persuade the area manager of the bank to extend her line of credit to encourage the crooks to make more withdrawals, he was already talking of calling the police in and shutting the filling stations.

They would have to determine whether these were company frauds or the work of individuals. As regards the latter it was difficult to imagine that two individuals could work themselves into a position of trust in garages in Oxford, Brighton and Bournemouth in such a short time and that other employees wouldn't have noticed. She regretted that she'd not worn a button-hole camera when she bought the petrol. She would next time but at the moment both their tanks were full. She asked Jill if she could borrow her car and fixed a diminutive camera to her jacket. Driving towards the Ferndown filling station she decided that she'd first see if the same person was taking the money as on Thursday; it would be pointless filling Jill's tank for nothing. Then it occurred to her that if she recognized the person taking the money she needn't buy any petrol, all she had to do was buy a newspaper and click the camera. She thought, the area bank manager should be proud of her, saving him money. At the Ferndown station the newspapers were arranged in a tabloid sized egg-crate structure outside the shop. Paula stood there apparently torn between the Sun, Mirror, Express and Mail while she attempted to see if the same cheerful young man was on till-duty. He was and she snapped his profile through the window before joining the queue with her copy of the Daily Mail to snap him full faced.

She drove to the Branksome petrol station. The newspapers were arranged the same and Paula could see through the window that a man was on the till. She drove away resolved to come back late in the afternoon when the blonde girl might be on duty. Meanwhile she downloaded into her computer the shots that she had taken of the young man. There was no point in watching the young man, she hadn't used the credit card to purchase the Daily Mail.

The blonde girl was on duty by teatime and was duly photographed as Paula paid by credit card for the fuel that she put into Jill's car. That cost would probably appear in the bank statement on Thursday. Paula made a comment to the girl about being scared to have a night shift with all these robbers about and the girl replied that it wasn't too bad, she was off at ten.

Paula was parked where she could see the filling station shop at fifteen minutes to ten. She saw a man arrive in an old car and park it round the side. He went in and could be seen chatting and taking over from the girl. A bigger and more modern car, driven by a man drove onto the forecourt and she put on her coat, came out and got into the car. Paula could see her lean over and kiss the driver who then turned his head to look out of the driver's window preparatory to driving off. Paula gave a start and then smiled as things started to fall into place. The driver of the car, the man the blonde girl had just kissed, was the cheerful young man from the Ferndown filling station.

She followed them to a caravan on a site on the western side of Poole. They parked and went in. Lights came on and curtains were pulled. Paula could see shadows moving inside. She pondered, was it likely that they would come out again that night to draw money, she corrected that, to steal money, out of cash machines? She thought about it. Unless the devices they had at the filling stations were very sophisticated, they still wouldn't know the PIN numbers that went with the cards. They would have to read the magnetic strips to get the numbers. Given the right equipment, that might only take a matter of minutes, but on balance Paula decided that they would probably have a meal, decypher the PIN numbers ready for the next day and go to bed. She waited and the lights went out at eleven.

She was back at the caravan site early the next morning complete with her Radio Bournemouth reporter's equipment should anyone challenge her. The cheerful young man emerged and was waved off by the blonde girl in a dressing gown. Paula reckoned that it would be a good hour before the girl was dressed and ready to go out, so she followed the man. He went directly to the filling station at Ferndown and opened it at seven o'clock. Paula drove back to the caravan park and waited.

The girl emerged at nine-thirty and walked to the bus stop opposite the camp entrance. Now Paula had a problem, if she hadn't got the radio station's recording gear she would have parked her car and joined the queue for the bus. But she couldn't risk someone stealing Jill's equipment. She watched the girl get onto a bus, read the route number and drove towards the radio station while explaining the situation to Fred by phone. Would he please be ready to drive her to the West Cliff along which the bus was sure to come? Fred climbed into the car and dropped Paula on the bus route. The bus with the blonde girl came along and Paula joined it.

Paula filmed the girl getting cash from seven machines and followed her as she went round the shops, buying food and household goods before going to three separate building societies and paying money in. Eventually she caught the bus and returned to the caravan site.

Back at the radio station office, Paula downloaded the pictures that she had taken and wrote her report. In all, she thought, things had turned out well.

That afternoon, she and Fred took the report to the area bank manager and laid the facts before him. Paula noted that he seemed to be more interested in the possibility of getting 'his' money back from the three building societies than in the apprehension of the suspected criminals.

The manager agreed that they should take the material that they had gathered to the police. They asked to see Inspector Wyatt. He listened to what they had to say with a copy of Paula's report in front of him and said, "Why didn't the bank come to us?"

Fred said, "You know banks, they don't want to admit that they've got a problem until it stands up and hits them in the face and using us was a convenient, quiet, way of seeing what their problem was."

"You reckon that they'll still have some of these phoney credit cards?"

"Yes," said Paula, "they probably keep them until they've got all they can from the accounts. There can't be many places to hide them in a caravan."

"You say that they're both there at night?" asked the Inspector.

"They were last night and I expect that their duty roster at the filling stations will be the same all-week."

"I'll bring them in for questioning tonight, get them just as they reach their caravan and have someone search the vehicle while they're away. What are we looking for?"

"You're looking for a store of credit card sized plain pieces of plastic with a magnetic strip on them," said Paula, "that's the raw materials. Somewhere there will be those that they've used, they will probably have a three or four-figure number written on them. Collect all of them. Then, and most importantly, there'll be some clever electronic equipment, chips and transistors on green baseboards. In fact a copy of the electronics inside a cash machine that reads the magnetic strip on the card you push in. It may be wired to a computer monitor or a laptop."

"So we ought to take one of the back-room boys with us?"

"Without a doubt," said Fred. "There's also the electronic device that they used to copy the cards at the filling stations, to transfer what's written on the real card's strip on to one of the phoney cards. It's puzzled us how they do it without anyone questioning what they're doing. Do they leave it there and risk someone being curious or do they bring the devices home each night?"

"If they do the girl will have it on her when we bring them in," said Wyatt, "could you be here tonight, say at eleven, to listen to the initial questioning?"

Fred said, "Paula's the expert who did all the work." He turned to her "Can you be here, say, to represent the bank?"

"Wouldn't miss it for the world," said Paula. She turned to the Inspector. "That's another thing your searchers must look for, Building Society books, I saw her deposit stolen money in three."

When the cheerful young man and the blonde girl got out of their car that night they were illuminated in the headlights of an unmarked police car. The girl dropped a packet under the caravan. This was seen by the occupants of a second police car stationed the other side to prevent them driving off. The packet contained copies of credit cards. They were taken separately to the police station. Searchers moved into the caravan and in due course found all the things that Paula had suggested that they should look out for.

The following morning detectives were at the two filling stations. There was a certain amount of difficulty at Ferndown since the cheerful young man was supposed to be there to open the station for business. This was resolved.

At each place the detectives found what appeared to be a switch device connected to the phone line. The filling station staff said that it was to check the credit rating of cardholders, if it showed a green light when you passed a credit card through it, then the card was good. In fact the device wasn't really connected to the telephone line and it always showed a green light if a card was passed through it. If a button on the side was pressed it copied what was encoded on the card's magnetic strip. The police took them away.

Under examination it emerged that the young man's previous employment had been installing and maintaining cash machines. Next day, after more questioning and fingerprinting, the couple were charged with theft and released on police bail

Chapter Sixteen

PC BRIAN JOHNSON knocked on Inspector Patel's door, opened it and poked his head round. He was aware that the Inspector liked to deal with his correspondence first thing and didn't welcome intrusions.

"Convenient to have a word, Inspector?"

Wyatt looked up irritably, saw who it was, smiled and said, "Come on in, Brian, have you got anything for me?"

"Yes, Gov' and it's queer."

"Sit down and let's have it then."

Brian perched on the edge of a chair and said,

"I asked around over the weekend. It was about three years ago and the local gang, who call themselves the Marauders, decided that it was about time they made the Italians trading in Lewisham contribute to their well-being by paying for protection. Two of the leading lights called Ace Jones and Snowball Summers said they'd look after it and rode off on Ace's moped wearing helmets. There were witnesses who confirmed that the two of them parked the bike outside the Palermo Bar and went in."

Brian paused for effect.

"Go on man, get on with it," said Patel, eventually.

"Officially, that's it, Gov', they went in and they were never seen again – alive, that is. Their bodies and the moped were recovered from the Thames a month later. Since then the Yardies and the Marauders have left the Italians alone."

"Sounds a wise decision. Were the two tear-aways reported missing?"

"Ace was, by his mother. She's a nice little woman who brought him up without the benefit of a father. She's probably better off without him. Snowballs mother said good riddance, she openly said that she hoped that he'd gone for good."

"Any evidence how they died?"

"I looked-up the coroner's report, their injuries were consistent with having collided with something but the coroner was puzzled by the moped. It was undamaged."

"It looks as if the owners of the Palermo Bar know how to look after themselves. Any rumours about them?"

The Body in the Churchyard

"The usual stuff, they're Italian so they must belong to the mafia. But there's absolutely no evidence that they've done anything illegal."

"Thank's Brian," said Patel. "Let me know if you hear anything else."

Patel continued to deal with his incoming mail while at the back of his mind he thought about how he might find out more about the Sabatini family and their bar.

He debated the alternative approaches. He could use his precious manpower – he supposed that he should say person power to be politically correct – to undertake 24 hour surveillance of the bar and see if any of the customers had 'form'. On the other hand he could use his precious money to have some handbills printed saying that there are rumours of a protection racket and inviting the recipients to ring a telephone number, anonymity guaranteed, they needn't give their names and addresses. The handbills would be pushed through the letterbox of every shop or house with an Italian name. He grinned at that, a couple who had honeymooned in Naples and called their house Capri, would get one.

He'd half-decided to put the handbill idea to his superiors when he paused. Who had said anything about a protection racket? Brian had referred to the Yardies and Marauders and the desk sergeant had as good as suggested that the Sabatini's had been operating a protection racket that had led to them fire-bombing the previous owner to get their hands on the premises. For the past ten years there had been nothing, not a hint. You didn't need guns for a protection racket, well, not in Lewisham and if the Sabatini's wanted guns it was probably for something bigger than extorting money from neighbouring shopkeepers.

Of course, if they were running a string of girls up-west and someone was trying to muscle-in, then they might need guns. So he was back at surveillance, not of the bar but of the brothers Sabatini. If they were running call-girls they'd have to have a minder or two on the spot, as it were, to watch over the girls and collect the money. Who would mind the minders? Would they come to the bar to hand over the money or would a Sabatini go to collect it? In either case, how often? Weekly was Patel's guess.

It then occurred to him that he wasn't alone in this, perhaps Tom Burton had some officers who could help and they wouldn't be known to anyone in Lewisham. He phoned Tom and Tom said that he'd be down that afternoon.

When he came, Inspector Patel rehearsed all the arguments and offered his conclusion that the Sabatini's were probably in a moneymaking racket in the West-End and needed the guns for their 'foot soldiers' lest or because someone might threaten to steal their business. The most probable business was girls or drugs and somehow Patel favoured the former. He concluded with, "What do we do about it?"

"I think that you're right," said Tom, "the guns are for their associates. The vice-squad has reported that there have recently been three unexplained killings of men who ran girls in Mayfair and that the girls have been threatened by the killers. They are terrified and say that the newcomers are Albanians who are importing their own girls from Eastern Europe."

"Would the vice-squad have any idea if the Sabatini's are involved, you know what I mean, are seen making weekly visits to suspected 'pimps' or girls flats?"

"I don't know. Can you get pictures of them?"

"I'll arrange it, might take a few days."

"Get one of the old woman as well and meanwhile see if there are any men who call there regularly, the same time, same day, each week."

"Since it's a restaurant and people have regular habits that's practically everyone who goes there," said Patel.

"There is one more thing," said Tom Burton, thinking aloud, "Forensic say that two of the dead men were shot by the same gun but that the bullet that killed the third man and lodged in his body, didn't appear to have been fired from a gun."

"What did they mean by that?" said Inspector Patel.

"That it didn't have any rifling marks,"

Tom Burton left and Patel issued instructions that the Sabatini brothers and their mother were to be covertly photographed.

The results of the fingerprint and DNA samples provided by Jackie for comparison with the prints found in Marylyn Barton's room and on a cigarette end found close to the body at Winterborne Stickland came to Superintendent Harding that afternoon. He sent for Clare Thornton. When she came he said

"We've got a yes and a no with the samples the army captain provided."

"Which is the yes, Sir?"

"The fingerprints show that Swift was in the murdered girl's room and in her room at her grandmothers place."

"And what about the DNA?"

"The cigarette end wasn't left there by him."

"Frankly, Sir, I didn't expect that it would be. Swift doesn't smoke."

"What else is there to check?"

"There are the fibres that were found in her mouth and nose. There's a rug that colour in Mrs Swift's car. I'd like to have that tested."

"I'll have a talk with Scotland Yard. I can't imagine that his relationship with the murdered girl, whatever it was, had anything to do with the gun thing. If we pull him in on a suspected murder charge we needn't make any reference to guns."

"Except, Sir, it might have been her knowledge of the guns that caused him to kill her."

"But that needn't come out until the trial by which time our colleagues in London may have let us off the leash," said Superintendent Harding. "What evidence have we got?"

"We know that he'd been in her room," said Clare. "The porter has identified him as the man who came there at about nine-thirty on the night that she was killed and again on the night after. We have two witnesses who saw her being driven off in a car like his, driven by a man who looked like him, at ten o'clock on the night she was murdered."

"And you think that the rug that's now in the wife's car may have been the one that smothered her?"

"Yes, Sir."

"Then go ahead and bring him in for questioning, constable."

"Yes, Sir," said Clare with rising enthusiasm, then her face fell, "What about Inspector Stevens?"

"I'll deal with the Inspector. I've taken charge of this case. Take a patrol car and bring Mr Swift in for questioning."

A patrol car with two stalwart policemen took Clare to the Sabatini flower shop where she arrested a shocked George Swift, in front of some even more shocked assistants and customers, on suspicion of being responsible for the death of Mary Barton, sometime known as Marylyn Barton. Having delivered Swift into the hands of her colleagues at the police station, Clare and the patrol car sped to the Swift home where she took the rug from Mrs Swift's car and then informed her that her husband had been taken to the police station for questioning in connection with the murder of Mary or Marylyn Barton.

George Swift, as the police insisted on calling him, demanded that his lawyer be called. The law practice that dealt with his business affairs sent their partner, Mr Smallpiece, who dealt with court cases. When he learnt that the questioning concerned the death of a young woman he didn't know whether to seize it as realizing a lifelong ambition or to decline as gracefully as he could. His criminal experience to date had been cases like driving without due care, petty theft and burglary. He put a bold face on it and took his place beside his client in the interview room, opposite Superintendent Harding and WDC Thornton. Clare switched on the recorder and made the required statement regarding time and who was present.

"You are George Swift alias Georgio Sabatini?"

"Yes but I object to the use of the word alias, Sabatini is my business name."

"Very well but we shall call you by the name on your birth certificate, Mr Swift."

"I prefer Sabatini."

The Superintendent continued, "We are enquiring into the death of Mary or Marylyn Barton, who I believe you knew."

"I've never heard of her," said Swift.

"We have witnesses who saw you at her apartment block the day she was killed and the day afterwards."

"I was probably delivering flowers to somebody in the building."

"Half past nine at night is an unusual time to be delivering flowers. I thought that you had an employee who did your deliveries."

"Not the special late night ones," said Swift, smugly.

"If you didn't know the deceased, perhaps you'd explain how you fingerprints were found on objects in her room."

"I can't, I've never been inside her room. In fact I've never been inside Boscome Heights."

"If you didn't know Marylyn Barton, how is it that you know that she had an apartment at Boscome Heights, we didn't mention it?"

"I don't know, you're trying to trick me," he turned to the lawyer and said, "It's your job to stop them tricking me."

"As far as I can see, Mr Swift, the police questioning has been fair and straightforward."

"Fat lot of use you are," said Swift.

"Since you find it difficult to remember your visits to Miss Barton's flat, let me change the subject, Where were you at nine-thirty p.m. on 23rd May?"

"How should I know, that's a fortnight ago, some of us lead busy lives and are out and about all the time," he warmed to his theme, "we have to, to pay the taxes to support people like you."

"Just answer the question, Mr Swift, where were you at that time on May 23rd?"

"I don't remember."

"Let me refresh your memory then, we have a witness who saw you go upstairs at Branksome Heights at nine-thirty that evening"

"They're mistaken, that's it, they're mistaken," said Swift, "people do get things wrong, you know."

"Let's try ten o'clock then. Where were you at ten o'clock the same night?"

"You're just fishing about, trying to trap me," he turned to the lawyer. "There must be some law that prevents this sort of harassment, do something."

"This isn't harassment, Mr Sabatini, er, Swift," said the lawyer, "just answer the questions and I'm sure that the Superintendent will let you go home."

""Where were you at 10 o'clock on the evening of 23rd May?" repeated Superintendent Harding.

"At home, I suppose."

"Perhaps your wife will be able to confirm that?"

"You leave my wife out of this," shouted Swift.

"Surely she'll be concerned that you've been brought in for questioning?"

"Of course she will, she's my wife, isn't she?"

Clare slipped a piece of paper in front of the Superintendent who said,

"I see that she's already here, asking why her husband is being questioned."

"You leave her out of this, I don't want her worried."

"But she's worried already, you'd expect her to be, wouldn't you?" said the Superintendent.

"There's no need for her to know, well, you know," said Swift.

"No, we don't know, Mr Swift, tell us what we should know."

Swift had just been about to say something about going with a call-girl but saw the danger in time. Instead he said,

"Well, if you don't know I'm certainly not going to tell you."

"We'll have to question your wife, you know, there's no escaping that because your alibi will depend on her won't it?"

"I was home, she'll confirm that."

"Tell me, Mr Swift, do you and your wife have a normal sexual relationship?"

The lawyer drew in his breath, the Super might be treading on thin ice here.

"Depends what you regard as normal," said Swift. "Some people need sex more than others." He hurried on, "we Italians are more hot blooded than you English."

"And you're wife's English?"

"Yes."

"I wonder what her reply will be when I put the same question to her?"

"She won't know what you're talking about," Swift smirked.

"Oh I doubt that," said the Super, "just because a woman goes cold after the birth, shall we say, of her second child, it doesn't mean that she's unaware of her husbands desires."

"Who said anything about my wife not wanting me to make love with her?"

"No one, Mr Swift, but men who have a normal loving sexual relationship with their wife usually don't make use of the services of prostitutes."

"She had a difficult birth with our last child and she's scared of having another baby."

"Why couldn't you have told us that before," said the Super in a smiling fatherly way. "So you had to go with someone like Marylyn Barton?"

"Yes, I had to, didn't I? Otherwise I'd have had to divorce her, wouldn't I?"

"That's one way of looking at it, I suppose," said the Superintendent, "so you now admit that you knew Marylyn Barton?"

"I didn't say that, I said that I had other women." He turned to the lawyer and asked. "Didn't I, they're trying to put words into my mouth?"

"Yes Mr Swift, you didn't say that you made use of the services of any particular girl."

Clare thought that Swift had got his second wind, a sort of if-this-is-all-the-police-have-got-to-go-on-then-I've-got-nothing-to-worry-about. She took the metal cylinder with a hole through it that had been found in Marylyn's bead box and absently rolled it between her fingers on the table.

Swift who was looking at the Superintendent and saying, "I want to go home now," caught sight of it out of the corner of his eye and stopped in mid-sentence, recovered and finished the sentence with a total change of facial expression, he couldn't stop himself looking at the object that Clare was fingering.

"What's up, Mr Swift?"

"Nothing," said Swift.

"It looked as if something WPC Thornton was doing disturbed you."

"I can't stand people fidgeting with things when I'm talking," said Swift.

Clare allowed the cylinder to roll across the table to where Swift picked it up.

"What's that you've got, Thornton?"

"Sorry, Super it's a piece of a roller bearing from my bike, I didn't realize what I was doing."

"Well don't fidget again, it disturbs Mr Swift."

Clare carefully took her metal thing back.

Harding turned back to the prisoner. "I'd like to have my people take your fingerprints and a DNA sample and then you can go, but don't leave the country."

"I refuse, you haven't charged me with a crime, why are you treating me like a criminal. I won't have it." He turned again to his lawyer. "They can't make me, can they?"

"The police want them for elimination purposes. If you give them it would help eliminate you from the police enquiries," said the lawyer.

"No I won't. This is a democracy and I know my rights; better than you do, apparently."

"Very well, Mr Swift," said the Superintendent. "Your refusal to assist the police has been noted. You may go now but don't leave town. We will most certainly want to ask you some more questions. Now we'll question your wife."

"I object, you can't question her without my permission, I'll sue you, yes, that's what I'll do, I'll sue you."

"Mr Swift," said the Superintendent patiently, "we've finished with you for the time being, now we're going to interview your wife. If you'd like your solicitor to be present, we have no objection, in fact we'd welcome it."

"I don't want any lawyer to be present, I'll be there myself."

"I'm sorry, Mr Swift but that's not permissible, it's your lawyer or no one."

Swift muttered and fumed and eventually agreed that the lawyer should be present.

With great difficulty he was removed from the interview area, still demanding to speak with his wife before she was interviewed by 'those twisters.'

Clare begged a moment to take her piece of metal with Swift's finger prints on it, to the fingerprint people. They already had them, thanks to Jackie Fraser but Clare thought it wise to make sure.

The lawyer asked if he might have a word with Mrs Swift before she was interviewed by the police.

He brought her into the interview room and as they arranged themselves opposite the Superintendent and Clare, Mr Smallpiece, the lawyer, said that he had explained to Mrs Swift the reason why her husband was being questioned by the police.

"I'm sorry, Mrs Swift, but I'm afraid this is going to be unpleasant for you," said the Superintendent.

"Mr Smallpiece has told me that you are enquiring into the death of a prostitute and that you think that my husband may have known her," said Mrs Swift. "This doesn't come as a shock to me – the bit about the prostitute – because I have long suspected, nay, known, that he went with them. Perhaps I should explain?"

"Please do," said the Super.

"It started, no, I don't even know if that's true. I'll start again. I first began to suspect that he was being unfaithful when I was carrying our second child. I don't know how long before that he'd been carrying-on but I was sure of it by the time the baby was born and so, when I came home from the nursing home, I told him that I'd had a difficult childbirth and wouldn't want to go through that again. Accordingly, he could sleep in the second bedroom. And that's how it's been for the past five or more years."

"Did you consider divorcing him?" asked Clare.

"I'm a Roman Catholic and so is my husband and he wouldn't want to risk penury."

The Superintendent thought that she meant purgatory, and said, "pergatory?"

"No, penury."

"Penury, why so, Mrs Swift?" asked the Superintendent.

"I own the business. I owned the shop and George was my employee. I married him and we renamed the shop and he's made a success of it. But Daddy saw that it remained in my name and if anything happens to me it goes to the boys with Mr Smallpiece's firm as executors."

"Mrs Swift's father is the solicitor who founded our practice," said Mr Smallpiece.

"Thank you Mrs Swift, that's most helpful. Now, if I may, I'd like to turn to the night of 23rd May. Do you happen to remember where you and your husband were that evening?"

"I know where I was, I was at home. I'm home every night of the year except when I take the children to visit my parents in July and at Christmas. It's no hardship, staying home with the children, I help them with their homework, we play games, we watch video's and the television and I read to them. What could be nicer than that?"

Clare thought what a nice person she was.

"And your husband, was he home before half-past nine?"

"I've been thinking about that. He's out most evenings and because we have separate rooms I seldom know whether he's in or out. I'm afraid that I can't help you. Sorry."

"Oh but you have, Mrs Swift, you can't say for certain that he was at home."

"He may have been but it would be unlikely." She paused and wrinkled her forehead and then said, "He was out. I remember now. The reason that I remember is that his cousin Luigi rang from Lewisham. I'd gone to bed about eleven and had just got undressed and in bed when the phone rang. It rang and rang and I thought that it would wake the children. In the end I went down into the hall and answered it. It was Luigi asking where Georgio was and whether the consignment they expected from Antwerp on the 22nd had arrived. I said that I'd no idea. He said 'That was yesterday. Be sure to tell Georgio that things are getting dangerous up West and they badly needed the goods.' I wrote down what he said, word for word, on the pad beside the telephone and went back to bed."

"I know that this must be difficult but did anything else happen around that time?"

"Not that I can remember. He had made a great fuss a fortnight or three weeks earlier when he said that something was missing from the garden shed and either I or the boys must have taken it."

"Did he say what it was?"

"No, I asked him repeatedly, how can we look for something when you don't know what you're looking for?"

"Did he report the theft to the police?"

"That's what I said, report it to the police, that'll prove that the boys hadn't taken whatever it was. He wouldn't call in you folk or say what it was that had gone missing but he swore us to silence not to say a word to the two cousins in Lewisham if they asked."

"He sounds a difficult person to get on with," said Clare.

"Let me put it this way, it's no hardship to keep my bedroom door firmly shut at night. All that we have in common now is our two boys."

"Was there any other odd thing that happened about that time?" asked the Superintendent.

"What about cars?" added Clare.

"Well," doubtfully, "there was the rug."

"What about the rug?"

"I found it in George's car. It belongs in the back of my car to keep the boys warm when I bring them home from school games or swimming. Then it disappeared and some days later I found it in the boot of the Jaguar so I took it and put it back in my car."

"Did you wash it or send it to the cleaners?"

"Good Lord no, why would I do that? I didn't give it a thought until now. Your policemen took it, you don't think that it has got something to do with that poor girl's death, do you?"

"At the present time we don't know," said the Superintendent.

She looked shocked and said quietly, "But you suspect that it does, don't you?"

"Thank you Mrs Swift for coming to us and being so helpful," said the Superintendent. "We'll type this up and WPC Thornton here, will give it to Mr Smallpiece for him to get your signature if you agree."

"What has happened to my husband?"

"We've let him go for the moment."

"So when I get home I can expect to be questioned about what I've told you?"

"Say that you told us nothing, say that you couldn't remember."

Mr Smallpiece, the lawyer, nodded vigorously and said, "That's by far the best course."

"What about the blue rug?"

"Say that you're mystified because the police came and took the blue rug away. Ask him if he knows of any reason why they should do that?"

"Alright but I'm going to say as little as possible from now on."

" If you have any problems ring us and we'll be there in a matter of minutes," said the Superintendent.

"Thank you, I might do that."

Chapter Seventeen

KATHRYN settled into the familiar surroundings of her study at Harvard and opened her Hawkins pack. She'd been met at the airport by her mother and had scarcely had a moment to herself all the weekend. At least half a dozen times she'd told her mother, her aunts and various friends of her mother the story of her research into the church registers and the Hawkridge papers. She'd shown them the photocopies of the entries and the pictures that she had taken of Salisbury Cathedral, the Manor House and the churches at Tolbrite and Spetisbury.

Her mother was intensely interested in it all. Kathryn had the impression that her aunts, her father's sisters, were more interested in the story of her discovery of Marylyn Barton's body and the subsequent investigation by the British police.

"The British police don't carry guns, you know," said Aunty Doris.

"Some of them do, after September 11th," said Aunty Susan.

"Coming through Heathrow," said Kathryn, "it seemed that all the policemen had enough weapons to equip an army."

"Well, they would, wouldn't they?" said Aunty Doris.

Kathryn had looked at her father who grinned and changed the subject. Dear Dad, he'd been listening to his mother's search for her ancestors ever since Kathryn could talk and had smiled and said things like, 'if you say so my dear' and let it all wash over his head. Now it seemed it might begin to have some substance. He hadn't said much but Kathryn knew that he'd taken it all in.

Now it was Monday. She sorted through the photographs of the 1600 to 1700 pack and took out the ones that had captured her attention in the Rumpus Room; brief letters, one of which had a date that looked like 1692 that seemed to have been penned by the same hand.

Her work with old English and German documents had given her some familiarity with the script and an awareness of how much the language used by the scholars who penned the manuscripts and their form of writing had altered down the centuries. She had two requirements, an expert who might be able to conjure up the words on the document that had faded with time and another expert who could confirm her reading of them. She was certain she knew people in her university who had the expertise, the question was were they still on vacation? She went to the library that was devoted to history and consulted the librarian. He recommended that she consult Associate Professor Schultz about techniques for resolution and her own Professor Halliwell for translation. Failing that she might ask Yale, which numbers the Boswell papers in its massive 10 million volume library or Princeton's Firestone library, the home of many original manuscripts.

Professor Schultz was back from vacation and could see her that afternoon.

He turned out to be middle aged, with grey hair and pebble glasses over which he peered at her while he shook her hand and saw that she was comfortably seated.

Kathryn explained that she wanted to read and understand some 17th Century letters that she had found in England and photographed. She showed him the photographs that he took and held a few inches in front of his nose.

He tut, tutted. "Is no good, all we have is what the camera saw. We need originals if we are to try to bring up lost words and look behind them."

"Can't you do that from the photographs?"

"No, fraulein Professor, your camera dealt with only one part of the spectrum, we have to try other parts of the spectrum if we are to have the paper reveal it's secrets."

"You mean that I have to bring the manuscripts here?"

"Or to somewhere where they have the required equipment." As an afterthought he added, "and knowledge."

"Where would that be in England?"

"Oh, all the good places, Cambridge, Oxford, London...."

"I see. I don't know if the owners of the originals would let them be taken away, they're kept in a controlled environment. Would it be possible to take the instruments to the documents instead of the documents to the instruments?"

"I don't see why not, the whole lot would go into a medium sized van, You'd need to be able to connect the van to mains electricity."

"Let me get this clear. Professor Schultz, suppose that I can get a van and the equipment to examine the manuscripts but who does the actual examination, someone like you?"

"Not necessarily, I can give you instructions telling you what I would do in each case and with a little practice you'll be able to do it yourself."

"Would it be a lot of trouble if I asked you to tell me what equipment to buy and instructions on how to use it?"

"No trouble at all," he smiled at her. "All you need is a copy of the notes that I give my sophomore year."

He went over to a filing cabinet, rummaged about a bit and produced a bound folder "Here they are." He went back to his desk, opened the folder and picked up a red marker pen with which he proceeded to mark paragraphs. When he'd finished he said,

"There you are fraulein Professor, I've marked the equipment you'll need and the important things you should look for. You may be able to hire the equipment, you can here in the United States and I suppose that you can in England. I would volunteer to ask academics who I know at Cambridge to get the instruments for you but they would be slow, they've doubtless got their winter research planned and I'm afraid your thing would just come at the end of the line. If you're in a hurry to complete the investigation, it's best to make your own arrangements."

Kathryn thanked him for his help and walked across the campus to her own quarters where she settled down to read the notes that Professor Schwartz had given her. It didn't appear to be all that difficult. There was a chapter on chemical methods that the professor had crossed through with the caution 'Don't attempt this.' Obviously that was the clever bit or was it simply the last ditch attempt that damaged the specimen?

She discussed it with her parents over dinner. If she were to pursue the search for Pastor Hawkins' origins in England she would have to subject those few scraps of paper to the tests that Professor Shultz had specified and this would have to be done in England.

"The question is, Mummy, I'll have to go over there and buy or hire the instruments to do it, probably buy them. Is it worth-while?"

Her father answered immediately, "Of course it is, my dear, your mother has talked about the Hawkins' ever since we were married and by now even I'd like to know where the fellow came from. It'd be a shame to stop now when you've come so far. If you can spare the time, go back and do it and if you can't sell the equipment afterwards,

The Body in the Churchyard

dump it in the harbour at this place Bournemouth and we'll call it the Bournemouth tea-party."

"Yes baby let's see the thing through," said her mother. "Would you like me to come and help you?"

"I'd love to have you come, Mummy, but we mustn't forget all those three hundred years old bugs and things, must we?"

"No," said her mother, "perhaps you'd better go alone, you're immune to them by now."

"The problem is how to set about it. How to buy or hire the instruments and get them put in a van in England when I'm in Boston. There's no point in going over there to do it and then kicking my heels until they're ready."

"Did you make any friends when you were there who might do it for you?" asked her mother, famous for her work for charity and infamous among her circle for the little tasks she shed on them in the good causes.

"There's Paula, she's a private detective, I wonder if she'd do it? and then I'll have to write to the Hawkridge's for permission to subject their old documents to the further tests."

"Oh I'm sure that they won't mind," said her mother, "they must be as keen to know about Hawkins as we are."

"Mummy, you don't seem to realize, these old manuscripts have been in their house for over three hundred years without them bothering to read them or do anything with them and, anyway, it's only me who thinks that there's a link somewhere between the Hawkins' and the Hawkridge family history."

"I'm sure you're right baby. Won't they be surprised?"

Kathryn grinned at her father. "I have their e-mail addresses, I'll write to them tomorrow."

The following morning Kathryn wrote an explanation of the problem of deciphering the early manuscripts and her wish to have access once more to examine them under different radiation spectra as recommended by Professor Schwartz. She detailed the equipment that the professor had recommended and that it could all be mounted in a van. She then stated her requests, could Southern Enquiries act as her agent in purchasing or hiring the equipment and a van? The second request was to General Sir David Hawkridge for permission to subject the 1600 to 1700 bundle to these further examinations. She sent the same e-mail to both parties with a rider that should Fred and Paula (she used their names) be willing to act for her in this she would forward a banker's draft for a hundred thousand dollars for initial expenditure.

Fred and Paula read the e-mail when they arrived in the office the following day. Fred's first reaction was to ring Tim Hawkridge.

Penny buzzed Timmy and said that Sherlock Holmes was on line two.

"Morning Fred, how can I help you?"

"Have you seen the e-mail from that American girl professor?"

"No, what has she done, accused us of forging old manuscripts?"

"No, she wants to come back and examine the old documents under ultra violet light or something and she's asked us to buy or hire the instruments on her behalf and put them in a van."

"Has she any idea how long it may take to assemble the kit?"

"No, nor have Paula and I," said Fred.

"Do you want the job?"

"Not really. Of course we'd like to help her, she's a nice girl, but organizing a thing like this could be an awful time waster."

"Would you like to leave it with me," said Timmy. "I expect that Bill Lawrence has got all the things she needs in his labs and he could spare them for a week or so."

"That would be fine, will you reply on behalf of both of us?"

Timmy had Penny call up his computer at the Manor House and transfer Kathryn's message to her office machine for him to read.

He told his Research Manager, Bill Lawrence about it that morning and Bill said that they had all that stuff in the labs and could spare a set in a good cause.

He mentioned it to Helene at lunchtime. She reminded him that they had meant to study the old papers themselves to see if they would provide material for a TV documentary and now was their chance, they'd keep Bill's instruments there and read them themselves. Helene guessed that it would take less than four weekends. Timmy said more like forty. She phoned Margaret that afternoon and told her about it.

Margaret's reaction was, "Oh good, I'm pleased about that because I couldn't see how the photographs alone could tell the whole story."

Helene pondered over that when they'd rung off.

Thus it was that Kathryn received an e-mail from Timmy Hawkridge, saying that his organization would provide the equipment that she required at no cost to herself and put it into the Rumpus Room unless she particularly wanted it in a van and that, in a day or so, he would tell her when it would be ready.

She told her parents this good news that evening and her mother said, "I told you so, they're as interested as we are."

Timmy e-mailed Kathryn to say that the instruments would be installed and ready for use, by the following Monday. When could they expect her?

Kathryn replied "Monday, thanks," and sent a separate e-mail to the Tolbrite Arms asking for a room for the week commencing Sunday.

She spent the rest of the week in the library brushing-up on her reading and understanding of the English writing of the late seventeenth century.

Georgio Sabatini was badly rattled. He tackled his wife the moment she got back from the police station. He repeatedly asked, "What did they ask you?" and "What did you say?"

She said that the police had wanted to know where he was on the evening of 23rd May and that she'd said that she couldn't remember. They had also asked her about her car-rug. Why was that? Eventually the time came for her to collect the boys and when she returned her husband wasn't there. Nor was his car. Which was a relief.

The following day the assistant from the shop rang to ask if Mr Sabatini would be coming to the shop, he hadn't brought the day's supply of fresh flowers and other florists were complaining that they hadn't had their early morning deliveries. Mrs Swift took a look in the second bedroom. The bed hadn't been slept in. She took the spare set of keys, drove to the shop and collected the handyman-cum-delivery man and took him and his van to the airport unit to collect the day's supply. He went back to the shop while she loaded the other florists orders in her 4 x 4 and delivered them herself. It took her four runs but she was quietly satisfied, she could still do it and some of them remembered her.

She returned to the shop and answered the assistant's questions as best she could about why the police had come for him the previous day. She confessed that he hadn't been home the previous night, no, he wasn't in police custody, he just hadn't slept at home.

She checked the forward ordering position, told the handyman that she'd see him at the airport unit at half past seven the following morning and went back home. She phoned the police station and told Clare Thornton that her husband hadn't slept at home last night. Clare thanked her and asked her to ring the next day if he hadn't returned.

Georgio Sabatini had arrived at the Palermo Bar the previous evening and told his story to his aunt and cousins, admittedly in a somewhat disjointed and sporadic way as they attended to their duties in the restaurant and bar. When trade fell off after midnight and they were finally able to talk all together, Luigi said,

"You're telling us that the Bournemouth police had you in for questioning about the murder of a girl. What was she to you, were you running her or sleeping with her?"

"I was sleeping with her. I had to get it somewhere, didn't I?"

His aunt snorted, "All you men think about is sex."

Benito said, "Why did you top her?"

"I didn't say I did," said Georgio.

"You wouldn't be here if you hadn't," said Benito.

"I'm here because of the reason I had to."

"What was that?" asked Moma.

"She threatened to tell the police about the guns."

"She what?" thundered Luigi, "How in the name of our Lady did she know about the guns?"

"I must have told her." Seeing his cousins about to burst with anger he hurried on, "It was like this, we were on her bed after, well you know, and she was talking about another girl who'd had her face slashed by a pimp from a rival organization and saying that a friend of her's who'd come down from London to work the Bournemouth beat had told her that the girls in the West End were getting frightened. I must have said something like 'not ours, we've given our minders guns'."

"You bloody idiot," said his aunt. "You never could keep you hands off women or your stupid mouth shut."

"That's not all," said Georgio.

"You mean it's worse, how worse could it be?" said his aunt.

"I think that the police know something about the guns."

By now Luigi and Benito were all attention.

"I don't believe what I'm hearing," said Luigi. "How can they, it's been the best kept secret of all time. The Met still can't figure out how that hood was killed in Soho. How can the Bournemouth police know about our guns?"

"While I was being questioned, the policewoman was rolling one of our sabots on the table. She said it was part of her bike but I recognized it when she rolled it across to me."

"Did you pick it up?"

"Of course I did, how could I tell without looking at it?"

"So you gave them your prints," said Luigi.

"I didn't, I refused to let them have my prints or my DNA."

"So they rolled you a nice shiny surface and you picked it up and put your prints on it."

"How was I to know," said a subdued Georgio, "they must have got it from the girl but she didn't have the gun."

"What gun?" said Benito.

"The one that someone stole from my shed about three weeks ago."

Their mother had started to worry earlier that one or other of her sons would either throttle his cousin or have a heart attack. Now they were incoherent with rage,

"You let one of our guns be stolen and didn't tell us?" spluttered Luigi.

"Well, I didn't want to worry you and it's no good without the special bullets, so I thought the thief would probably throw it off the pier."

"You'd better hope that he did," said Benito.

"So, because you killed your pet whore and left enough clues for the police to have you in for questioning," said his aunt, "you come running straight to us and draw the police's attention to us. Are you completely mad?"

"Well, I had to let you know, didn't I?"

"Where are you planning to go now, back to that stuck-up wife of yours?" said Benito.

"I thought that I might stay here," said Georgio.

"You *are* completely mad," said his aunt. "Go back to Bournemouth and forget that we exist, or shoot yourself," she added.

"I'll look after him," said Luigi looking meaningfully at his mother. "I'll put him up at Blackheath. Come on Georgio, you too, Benito, I'll need help."

Georgio's face brightened, it hadn't been so bad. He'd got away with it.

Inspector Stevens was furious that Superintendent Harding had taken over the Barton murder case, an attitude made worse by the fact that he was using his assistant WDC Thornton, on the case. He'd taught her all that she knew and now the Super was benefiting from it. He'd see the Assistant Chief and put in an official complaint, that's what he'd do. Meanwhile he'd take his temper out on Thornton.

Clare had spent the first ten years of her life learning how to avoid situations in which her beastly father would have an excuse to cane her, and the next seven enduring his bullying of her and her mother. His sulks over imagined defiance or things like when his meals weren't ready to the minute or when someone at work had put him in his place, were legendary. All the relatives and neighbours kept clear of him, his wife and daughter couldn't.

The result was that Inspector Stevens meanness and bullying was met with a cheerful smile and an, "If you say so, Inspector," which only made things worse – as she knew full well it would. After a day or so Superintendent Harding had given him a host of minor cases to deal with while requiring Clare to work on the Barton murder and the classified gun thing that the Special Branch had briefed him about. Clare thought that the Inspector would really go spare if he learned about that.

Following Mrs Swift's telephone call, Clare thought that it wouldn't do any harm to see where George Swift was or had been, so she added the green Jaguar and it's registration number to the list of vehicles who's whereabouts the police would like to know.

Two days later the Kent police reported that a dark green Jaguar car with that registration number had been recovered from the River Thames at Gravesend. The body of a man was in the car. There was no wallet, wrist watch or other identifying papers on the body. A post mortem was being performed.

Clare forwarded a photograph of George Swift, his fingerprints and the best description of the man that she could put together.

In due course the Kent police informed the Dorset police that the evidence was that the man found in the driver's seat of the Jaguar car was George Swift and that he had been dead before the car entered the water.

Forensic tests had shown that the fibres found in Marylyns nose and mouth had come from the Swifts' car-rug and there were traces of the girl's DNA on the rug. Clare's reaction was that when one door closes i.e. the murder of Marylyn Barton, another one opens, i.e. the murder of the murderer, George Swift. The latter wasn't hers to solve but what was hers was to tell the widow that she was, in fact, a widow.

She told the Super of the latest developments and drove to the Swift house. Both she and the widow knew that the worst part of the whole business was that two little boys had lost their Daddy.

Superintendent Harding, who had earlier been briefed by Captain Jackie Fraser that an odd sort of gun had been found, and the suspicion that it had come from George Swift's house, sent for the resident Special Branch man and told him to make certain that Scotland yard knew of this development. The message got to Detective Inspector Tom Burton and, by pillow talk, to Kim Bourne.

Jackie Fraser knew the next morning.

Tom Burton called on Jackie and the girls to talk things over.

He opened with, "It's highly suspicious, the man who we know handled the funny guns is murdered within twenty miles of where we believe he delivered the funny guns to."

"Have you spoken with the Bournemouth police?" asked Jackie

"No, I just had the message from our man down there."

"Well, I have," said Jackie. "They had this George Swift in for questioning and as good as accused him of murdering the girl. During the interview the WDC rather naughtily let him see that we had one of the sabots used to hold the bullet. She got his fingerprints but he saw what it was. Next he turns up dead in the Thames at Gravesend."

"What do you make of that?" said Tom.

"I believe that he lost his nerve and went to the people he delivered the box to."

"The Palermo Bar in Lewisham," said Tom. "It's run by two brothers called Sabatini and their mother. George Swift alias Georgio Sabatini must be related to them."

"On his mother's side," said Sandra.

"Now put yourself in their place," went on Jackie. "Out of the blue the cousin from Bournemouth arrives and says that he's been questioned by the police for murdering a prostitute. Oh, they say, were you followed? You can imagine how the discussion went on from there."

"You think that the Lewisham Sabatinis' might have liquidated him?" asked Tom.

"Well, his continued existence would have been a threat to them. He knew about the funny guns and they knew that it wouldn't take the Met long to work out that the man who was shot in Soho was killed by a bullet fired from a funny gun. All roads lead to Rome or, rather, the Palermo."

"You're building a case on a few facts and a lot of assumptions," said Tom.

"Don't we always?" said Kim.

"Do you have any evidence that would put George Swift at the Palermo Bar or the house in Blackheath that night?" asked Jackie.

"As a matter of fact we do. I asked Inspector Patel to keep an eye on the bar and his people reported that a dark green Jaguar was outside the bar late that night and was driven away sometime after midnight by a man who was following Luigi Sabatini's car."

"Bingo," said Jackie, "that must give you grounds for questioning the owners of the Bar."

Chapter Eighteen

BECAUSE the suspects were thought to be trafficking in guns that might be used by airborne terrorists, Inspector Tom Burton consulted his chief, David Vowles, who agreed that the Lewisham Sabatini brothers be brought in to the local 'nick' for questioning. Early the following morning Inspector Patel and his men had the pleasure of bringing them in, Luigi from Blackheath and Benito from Eltham. They were, of course, put in separate rooms. There had been some debate whether their mother should also be brought in and it was decided that she could wait; stew a bit was how Kim put it. Inspector Patel instructed his sergeant that the old woman was to be kept under constant observation, 24 hours a day.

Local police opinion was that Luigi made all the decisions, so Benito was taken first. He demanded a lawyer and there was a delay until his lawyer, a Mr Pinto arrived. Mr Pinto looked like a screen bandit.

Benito Sabatini and Pinto sat across the table from Inspectors Burton and Patel. Jackie watched from the next room.

After the usual preliminaries, Patel said,
"Where were you on the night of 25th June?"
"In the café, I suppose. I'm there most nights."
"Was that the night that your cousin came?"
"I suppose so. Yes that was the night."
"When did he arrive?"
"Sometime after ten, I think."
"Why did he come?"
"Because we're his cousins, there's no law against visiting your cousins, is there?"
"No Mr Sabatini. What did he talk about?"
"He'd been interviewed by the police about the death of a girl he knew and was upset."
"Was he close to this girl, was she his girlfriend?"
"Yes."
"Did he tell you that he had killed her?"
Benito made the mistake of half looking at his lawyer who immediately said,

"My client declines to answer the question."
"We'll take that as a yes," said Patel. "What time did he leave?"
"I'd say about one a.m."
"Where was his car all this time?"
"I don't know. Outside the bar I suppose, that's where it was when we .." he stopped.
"When we what, Mr Sabatini?"
"When we went to the door to see him off." said Benito, smiling.
"Who is we, Mr Sabatini?"
"My brother, my mother and me."
"Did you see him again?"
"No. Next thing we knew, he was dead."
"Do you think he shot himself because he murdered that girl?" asked Tom.
"He didn't shoot himself."
"How was he killed then?" asked Patel.
"I don't know, do I? It wasn't in the papers."
"What sort of gun did he use?"
Benito's voice changed imperceptibly, "I don't know, do I?"
"Do you think it was one of that new sort that cousin Georgio got for you?"
There was a silence as Benito digested the possible implications of what the policeman had said.
Mr Pinto remarked that his client had already said that he didn't know.
Tom Burton put on the table the gun that the petty thief had stolen from the Swift garden shed and took over the questioning.
"A gun like this, Mr Sabatini, don't tell us that you don't recognize it because cousin Georgio put a box of them in the boot of Luigi's car in Sunbury not so long ago and our witness tailed Luigi and the box of guns all the way to your bar where he left them before driving home to Blackheath."
Benito clasped and unclasped his hands but made no reply.
"Your mother will be a party to the possession of prohibited weapons charge, won't she? That, and being madam to all those call-girls in Mayfair will probably get her fifteen to twenty years. She'll probably die in jail."
Benito was stung into a reply, "You've got no proof."

The Body in the Churchyard

"What about that pimp who was shot by one of these guns up West, did she tell you to do that?" continued Tom Barton.

"No I didn't. You can't pin that on me, I've never fired one."

"Ah, I forgot, you're the expert with the stiletto, aren't you? I expect that the officers who are at this very minute searching your home will find the weapon you killed Georgio with, don't you?"

Mr Pinto remarked that he assumed that they had a search warrant and advised his client not to answer any more questions.

"I won't answer any more questions," said Benito.

"In that case you will be detained pending further examination."

Benito was taken downstairs to the cells.

Luigi was brought in with Mr Pinto talking volubly to him in Italian. Jackie, listening outside, could have kicked herself for not suggesting to Tom that he should have an Italian speaking officer present but consoled herself by the fact that it was all being recorded on her pocket recorder. Mr Pinto must realize that there is always a risk that he may be overheard.

They sat as before and the official recording machine was switched on and told their names.

"Your brother Benito has told us that your cousin Georgio came to the Palermo Bar sometime after ten o'clock on the 25th because he was upset that the Bournemouth police had questioned him in connection with the murder of his girl friend. Is that true?"

"Yes," said Luigi.

"He practically admitted that he'd killed the girl."

"Not in as many words," said Luigi, quickly thinking that it might be wise to damn Georgio in advance.

"But he didn't do it with one of those funny guns he got for you."

Luigi became guarded,

"I don't know what you're talking about."

"Of course you do. Georgio put a box of them in the boot of your car in Sunbury and you drove to Lewisham and took them into the bar."

"You're making this up."

"Oh no we're not, we have a witness who was following Georgio and saw the whole thing. Our witness even followed you to your house in Blackheath afterwards."

"That doesn't prove anything."

"Well, for starters you have, or had, prohibited weapons in your possession and one of them was used to kill that pimp in Mayfair so that's down to you as well. Or to your mother," he added as an afterthought.

"It's got nothing to do with Moma."

"Don't be silly, we know that she's the madam of the girls you run in the West End and we know that the killing was in revenge for the knifing of two of your minders. You decided to show them who's boss by introducing guns that you thought would be untraceable, like this."

Tom put the funny gun on the table.

Luigi looked at it in disbelief.

"The officers who are searching all of your homes and the Palermo Bar will doubtless find the ones you haven't given to your minders and also the stiletto that was used to kill Georgio."

"You've got no proof of any of this."

"But we will have, Mr Sabatini, you mark my words, we'll find minute blood stains in one of your houses and on the clothes that you or your brother were wearing and perhaps the stiletto, because no one likes to throw away their favourite weapon. Then there's your cars, who knows what our forensic experts will find in them?"

Mr Pinto said, "I think that you should stop this questioning now. My client hasn't been allowed to consult with me in private."

"What were you doing when you came in the door, then," said Tom Barton, "wishing each other a good weekend in Italian?"

"I will chose to ignore that remark," said Pinto. "I demand that my clients be charged or released."

"They'll be kept in custody at least until our officers complete their searches," said Inspector Patel.

A woman police constable tapped on the door and beckoned to Inspector Patel. He left the room and returned a minute or so later and said,

"Very well, Mr Sabatini, you will be detained while we continue with our enquiries."

Luigi was taken away and Mr Pinto left the room.

Inspector Patel could hardly contain himself. "My sergeant has arrested old Mrs Sabatini. She came out of the Palermo Bar and got into her car. She drove down to the Thames at Erith with my people following. When she got out of her car carrying a bag my people ran forward and seized the bag. In it were five guns and a stiletto in its sheath. They brought the old lady in and she's downstairs, shall we interview her now?"

"Yes," said Tom Burton, "let's get it over with."

"We'd better ask Mr Pinto to come back."

It took nearly an hour to find Mr Pinto and suggest that he should come back. When he arrived he was full of threats against the police and his intention to go to the highest authority to protest at the treatment that his clients and himself had received at the hands of the police that day.

He was told that Mrs Sabatini had been detained and would be interviewed forthwith.

The arrangement was the same as before with Mrs Sabatini sitting in the seat previously occupied by her sons. While the preliminaries were being gone through, Pinto was explaining in a loud voice that she didn't have to answer any questions.

Inspector Patel opened,

"Mrs Sabatini, you have this morning been intercepted by police officers on the bank of the River Thames at Erith in the act of throwing a bag into the river. In that bag were five guns and a stiletto. What have you to say?"

If Mr Pinto was taken aback it didn't show.

"I have nothing to say," said Mrs Sabatini.

"You will be charged with being in possession of prohibited weapons. It is highly likely that additional and more serious charges will follow. You will certainly be charged with running a call-girl organization in the West End and you may be associated with charges relating to a murder in Mayfair and the killing of your nephew Georgio Sabatini. Is there anything you wish to tell us?"

"Georgio was a fool. I always said that he'd be trouble."

Mr Pinto said that his client had nothing further to say.

She was taken to the cells and her sons were brought up and charged with the murder of their cousin Georgio Sabatini.

Their trial, months later, was something of a cause celebre because of the implied Italian Connection but principally because it isn't often that a mother and her two grown-up sons stand side by side in the dock accused of murdering their own nephew and cousin.

Kathryn's flight from Boston arrived at Heathrow early on Sunday morning. She rented a car and drove leisurely anti-clockwise along a section of the M25 and transferred to the M3. Now was her chance, she'd stop at Winchester for sightseeing and coffee. In fact she stayed in this fascinating cathedral city until well after lunch.

She arrived at the Tolbrite Arms at teatime and was greeted as a valued friend and shown to her room by Mrs Trowbridge who assured her that Gloria and Will would be along later. She washed and repaired her make-up and went down into the bar that she liked so much and sat in a window seat. Mrs Trowbridge brought her tea and a Sunday paper opened at a page with the headline, 'Cemetery Murder Case Closed,' and said, "that's the body you found. Reading between the lines it looks as if they think that florist called Sabatini did it and now somebody's murdered him."

Kathryn grinned at her in a lopsided way and said "And to think that I once thought of England as a model law-abiding country."

"It was," said Mrs Trowbridge, "until they let all these foreigners in. Oh, beg pardon Miss, we don't count Americans as foreigners, nor Australians, Canadians and New Zealanders. Don't let your coffee get cold, now."

Kathryn read the article. The Bournemouth police as good as said that Mr Swift, the well known florist who traded under the name Sabatini, was responsible for the death of Marylyn Barton who's body had been found in the Winterborne Stickland Churchyard by a visiting American professor. Some weeks later, Mr Swift's body had been found in the driver's seat of his Jaguar car in the River Thames at Gravesend. Mrs Swift had said that she hadn't seen her husband since he returned from questioning by the police. Asked by reporters if she had any idea what her husband was doing in Gravesend, Mrs Swift said that he had some cousins in South-East London.

Kathryn wondered what Inspector Clouseau made of having the prime suspect escape justice in that way. She was reminded that Stephen had been the Inspector's first prime suspect. She was getting rather fond of Stephen. She recalled what Mrs Trowbridge had said 'and now somebody's murdered him.' There was nothing in the article about that. When she came to take away the tea things, Kathryn said, "Did you say that the florist was murdered? It doesn't say so in the article you gave me."

The Body in the Churchyard

"Ah" said the landlady, "You don't know our English papers." She took the paper and turned over a few pages and folded it again.

"There, see." She pointed to a four line filler near the bottom of a column. 'Kent police say that the man who's body was found in a Jaguar saloon recovered from the Thames near Gravesend last Wednesday did not drown but was stabbed with a pointed weapon.'

"Fancy that," said Kathryn to Mrs Trowbridge's departing back.

Soon Gloria and Will arrived and the pub stirred into life. She explained why she was back and Will described how Tim's chaps had been at the Manor House on Friday installing the instruments that she'd asked for. All the family were now interested, even the General had been in to have a look. Kathryn could expect family visitors tomorrow.

The next morning she drove to the Manor House and parked next to another car close to the Rumpus Room. She had no sooner stopped than the Sergeant appeared walking towards her with long strides to open the car door, saying,

"Good Morning Professor, it's nice to have you back. Mr Tim's got everything ready for you and her Ladyship will look-in during the morning."

They were walking towards the door that he opened for Kathryn to enter. She saw that there was a young man in the room who stood up and smiled as she approached. Kathryn realized that she'd seen him in the pub dining room the previous night.

"This is Roger Holmes, Mr Tim thought that you might welcome having someone here who knows all about the instruments to get you settled in, so he sent Roger." While she was taking this in, he presented her with the keys, saying,

"Here's the key to this room and the key to the room the documents are kept in. If there's anything that you want, we'll be happy to oblige." Whereupon he did a military about-turn and went back the way he had come.

Kathryn smiled at the young man and said, "This is very kind of you. I know nothing about it except what's in the notes that Professor Schultz gave me and I've practically learnt them by heart."

"Then I'm sure that you would have been alright. Schultz is renowned in this field, miss, er professor."

"Look Roger, I'm Kathryn and you're Roger, OK? Now where shall we start?"

"The Sergeant showed me where the documents are kept and I brought the seventeenth century bundle in."

Kathryn carefully extracted the ones that she'd thought were dated from 1690 onward and Roger placed the first in an instrument that displayed it on a screen. He switched on and traces of written words appeared between those that had been visible to the naked eye. He operated switches and turned knobs and the writing stood out or faded. Kathryn noted down all that appeared.

He put the precious document in another machine and twiddled with the knobs. Different marks, words and letters appeared on the screen. Kathryn noted those down too.

The process continued through four different machines, one of which Roger operated by a push on the end of a long lead after bidding her to stand back.

Lady Hawkridge looked in and said how lovely it was to see Kathryn again and that she hoped that the search for her ancestors would bear fruit. She showed an intelligent interest and was shown how the process was able to reveal words and letters lost to the naked eye. She was followed by her husband who observed that if the process was found to be worth-while he supposed that Tim would want to put all the family documents, all four hundred years worth of them, through it because Helene had spoken of making a TV documentary of them. He explained, "they sell well in America, you know," and was then slightly embarrassed and added, "because you're interested in that sort of thing. All the English seem to want to do these days is watch football." Kathryn thought him rather a dear.

Roger pointed out that the documents from about 1800 onwards didn't need the full treatment; most were legible.

At the end of the morning they had done two documents and by the end of the day they had done five.

Roger decided to stay for another day and see the thing through and they discussed the results thus far over dinner and afterwards Kathryn typed what she had made of the documents into her laptop. Three of the five had nothing to do with the Hawkridge family per se and dealt with estate business but two were an exchange between the Dower House and the Manor House.

They resumed the search the following morning and when they stopped for the night had done a further seven documents of which two appeared to be pay-dirt. Roger left for London after ascertaining that Kathryn felt confident to operate the instruments herself.

Kathryn typed them up that evening and after inserting totally missing words or letters in italics thought that they made sense.

By the end of the third day she decided that she had extracted all that there was from the documents that showed that her forebear was undoubtedly a Hawkridge.

She typed the letters upon which she had concentrated and printed them. Tomorrow she'd show them to Lady Hawkridge.

The letters were;

The Dower House
*Da*vid,
My *maid*servant Jane is *with* child. She *says* that Fr*ancis* is the father *and* that he has *promised* to marry *her*. She is a good *gir*l, she can read and has atten*ded* church regula*rly and she swears* that Francis was the first. I believe her.

The prob*lem is*, what shall we do. I'm *willing to* have her *back after* the baby is born. You *must arrange* what *to do* with the baby.

Your *loving* Mo*ther*

The Manor House
Mother,
I have *spoken* with Francis *and told* him that if this becomes *widely known* he won't be able to be*come* the Bishop's *cleric*. He says that he wants to *marry* your maid*servant*, Jane. He says that he *knows that* he was the first *with Jane* and the baby is his and he wants *to keep* it. *I've said* that I will disin*herit* him but it *seems* to make no difference. Mary takes his side. She *doesn't* see *the shame* of her son *mar*rying *a ser*vant and *destroying h*is futu*re* in the chu*rch*. If he *insists* I will send him *away until* he comes to *his senses*.

Your obedient son

The *Dower* House

David,

Francis rides *over here* every day. I've tried to *keep* Jane in*doors* but they talk through the wind*ows*. He *swears that* if you throw him *out he* will go and live with Jane's *father in* that shepherds hovel. I've said *that he* can come here, we can't *have* a Hawkridge living in a *hovel*. What *do you* intend to do *about* the *baby*.

Your loving Mother

The Manor House

Mother,

On *your own* head be it. You let your *maid*servant *lie* with *your gr*andson until she *is* with *child* and now you con*done* this uns*uita*ble union by letting *him* dwell under your roof. I'll have no *more of* it and I'd be obli*ged* if you *don't* men*t*ion his n*ame* again.

Your ob*edient* son

The Dower Ho*use*

Mary,

Francis marr*ied* his Jane in Speti*s*bury Church on 29th May. In order not to embarr*ass* his father Francis *took* the name Francis Ja*mes* Hawkins. I was his witness. They *will stay* with me *until* the baby is about six *months* old and then *go and* make a new *life* in the colonies. I *will* give *them* a hundred guineas. Trust me, I *know how much* you love *your* youngest child.

Your loving *mother in law*

The final letter of the series was quite different in character, written in bold handwriting on much coarser paper.

It was much more creased as if it had been opened and read many times. Kathryn read it many times as doubtless Lady Elizabeth and his mother, Mary Hawkridge had done, all those years ago, and wondered how much of the script had been washed away by tears.

New Towne

Dear Grand*mother,*
Thanks *to* you, *Jane,* baby James *and I are* safely arrived in the Col*onies* and are building a home across the *river from* Boston town. We have *few* of the comforts of our *previous life but* we have each *other* and our *son.* Who knows what the future *holds for* him. Please *give our* love to mother and *to Jane's* father *and* of course your*self.*

Your *loving* grandson

Kathryn accepted that she'd made some assumptions with words that she hadn't put in italics but the brief letters made sense and told a story, a heart rending story. His father ought to have been horsewhipped. Then she realised that if he hadn't been so stern, she wouldn't have been born a US citizen.

The following morning she told the Sergeant that she'd like to see Lady Hawkridge. She was taken to the small sitting room where Margaret had her sewing basket and a bureau to deal with her correspondence and tended to use as her place of work.

"Come in and sit down, my dear, how is your search progressing?"

"I've extracted all that I can from your family papers," said Kathryn, "and am satisfied beyond doubt that my ancestor, Francis James Hawkins who came to New England in 1693 with his wife and baby son was really Francis James Hawkridge."

"But that's marvelous," said Margaret. "What makes you so sure?"

"You'll recall that what brought me to you was the entry in the church register of the marriage of a Francis James Hawkins to a Jane

Mary Sommers in Spetisbury Church in May 1692. More precisely, what brought me to you was the fact that a Lady Elizabeth Sarah Hawkridge was the bridegroom's witness."

"Yes, I remember," said Margaret. "She was in the Dower House."

"Well, there are six letters in your family documents that, I think, shed light on events at about that time. This is what I think was in those letters. The words and letters in italics are mine."

She gave Margaret a copy of the sheets on which her version of the six letters were printed.

Margaret read slowly through them and her eyes filled with tears.

"Poor young people, what a splendid person Elizabeth Sarah was, she got her priorities exactly right. And they made good in the New World but life couldn't have been easy, could it?"

"But as he wrote in his letter to his grandmother, they had each other and their son," said Kathryn. "Jane Mary Sommers must have been quite a girl."

"Do you know," said Margaret "that's exactly what I was thinking. What do you intend to do now?"

"I don't really know. I rather hoped that you would know."

"Know what?"

"Well, how to make it sort of official that we're related. Is it simply a matter of your husband as head of the family saying, 'I agree' or does it have to go to some College of Heralds?"

"I'll have a word with Timmy," said Margaret. "Meanwhile will you join David and me for lunch?"

When Kathryn had gone back to the Rumpus Room, Margaret faxed a copy of Kathryn's sheets with the six letters to Penny and asked her to make sure that Timmy saw them at lunchtime. Helene phoned back, somewhat earlier, to say that they thought that the American professor had interpreted the old letters correctly and that, as a result, she was the youngest member of the American branch of the Hawkridge family. They sent cousin Kathryn their regards, Francoise still spoke of the American lady she met in the Rumpus Room.

"Do you think that this is sufficient evidence or should we go to the Privvy Council or something?" asked Margaret.

"Timmy says that it's good enough," said Helene. "The son who went to America was a younger son and there's no question of inheriting a title and anyway the Hawkridge baronetcy wasn't bestowed until later. He also says that the Glover family is very rich so there won't be any financial questions and so Timmy says you should welcome our new cousins aboard."

"I haven't told David yet and I suppose that I should tell David two."

"Don't worry Margaret, we think that the evidence is good enough and having an American wife, David two will think that it's splendid."

They discussed the matter over lunch. The General had read the letters and heard what Helene had said and thought the whole thing splendid. In fact he made a touching little speech about the contribution that the United States had made to the maintenance of peace and prosperity in the post-war years, that the mantle of progress was in the western hemisphere and that he was pleased to learn that there were Hawkridge's there and playing their part. Kathryn could have hugged him.

"What will you do now?" asked Margaret.

"If you don't object I'd like to continue working in the Rumpus Room this afternoon and tomorrow and just have a word with Timmy and Helene when they get here in the afternoon. More to say 'thank you' for providing all that equipment and a young man called Roger to see that I learnt how to use it. You have a very thoughtful son, Lady Hawkridge."

"Since we're distant cousins please call me Margaret."

"Also, I want to steal an hour to visit Spetisbury Church to see if there's any memorial to the Lady Elizabeth Sarah Hawkridge who's hundred guineas must have paid my ancestor's fare to America. On Saturday, I intend to go back home to Boston and tell my parents that Mummy is really a Hawkridge. I'm afraid that she'll probably want to come over and visit all the places that I've mentioned," said Kathryn a trifle apologetically.

"Of course she will," said the General. "Only natural, and we'd like to meet her, wouldn't we my dear? She shall come and stay here."

And thus it was.